W9-CMO-110

How to Book a Murder

Also available by Cynthia Kuhn

Lila Maclean Academic Mysteries

The Semester of Our Discontent

The Art of Vanishing

The Spirit in Question

The Subject of Malice

The Study of Secrets

How to Book a Murder

A STARLIT BOOKSHOP MYSTERY

Cynthia Kuhn

NEW YORK

This is a work of fiction. All of the names, characters, organizations, places and events portrayed in this novel are either products of the author's imagination or are used fictitiously. Any resemblance to real or actual events, locales, or persons, living or dead, is entirely coincidental.

Published in the United States by Crooked Lane Books, an imprint of The Quick Brown Fox & Company LLC.

Crooked Lane Books and its logo are trademarks of The Quick Brown Fox & Company LLC.

Library of Congress Catalog-in-Publication data available upon request.

ISBN (hardcover): 978-1-64385-859-3
ISBN (ebook): 978-1-64385-860-9

Cover design by Joe Burleson

Printed in the United States.

www.crookedlanebooks.com

Crooked Lane Books
34 West 27th St., 10th Floor
New York, NY 10001

First Edition: December 2021

10 9 8 7 6 5 4 3 2 1

For my family, near and far.

Chapter One

"To be surrounded by books is an exceptional joy," Lucy said.

Anyone else might have been alarmed by the way my sister was tilting from the ladder that allowed us to retrieve items from the top shelves. Our family had owned Starlit Bookshop for decades, though, and I'd seen her do the same thing a thousand times. When we were young, we had even taken turns pushing each other along the iron track that ran the length of the wall.

I gazed fondly around the store. The famous authors in photos behind the register maintained their watch over the long rows of shelves. Tufted armchairs and benches in jewel tones waited to accommodate readers. A softly ticking station clock, antique mirrors in baroque white frames, and large potted ferns contributed to the serene ambience. I picked up a feather duster to swipe along the book spines, which was a never-ending chore.

Lucy swung back to center and climbed down. "But it's time to face facts. At this point, we need a miracle, or we'll have to close before Halloween."

I caught my breath. That was only a month away. When I'd returned to Silvercrest after graduate school to help her run the store, I'd suspected things were verging on grim financially, but Lucy had studiously avoided discussing the subject all summer. It was worse than I'd imagined.

"Have you told anyone?"

"I can't bear the thought of it." Her dark shoulder-length hair gracefully swept from side to side as she shook her head. My long curls had never, not once, been capable of gracefully doing *anything*, but since we both had black hair and hazel eyes, people often assumed we were twins, even though she was two years older.

"How about expanding our special events?" I charged ahead with much more confidence than I was feeling while administering another halfhearted jab with the feathers. "They used to bring in a lot of customers."

"You're right. I should have been doing them all along, but when I took over, it was too overwhelming. That was the first thing to go after Mom and Dad retired." She plunked down on the stool behind the counter and picked up a pen. "Let's make a list of potential activities."

I happily abandoned the dusting project and dove into planning mode. "Readings, panels, workshops, and launch parties—both national and local writers. Silvercrest is close enough to Denver to pull in business."

Lucy looked doubtful. "That sounds like a lot to juggle."

"I'd be glad to—"

"How *dare* you do this to me! It's already Friday afternoon!" A voice just below shrieking level accosted us as a woman burst through the front door, teetering on high heels. She had a cell phone pressed to one ear and a terrified-looking Yorkshire terrier cradled in the nook of her other arm. Her blonde updo was coming loose, and one end of her scarf trailed behind her. As she staggered toward us, she waved the phone around, then began stabbing at the disconnect button with a talon. The shift in position squeezed the dog, who let out a yip. The woman apologized to the adorable creature—who was apparently named Paisley—with coos and baby talk, then fumbled around until the Yorkie was safely tucked away in an oversized bag slung over her shoulder.

"Hello, Tabitha. May I help you?" Lucy calmly addressed the woman.

I gasped, then tried to cover it up with a demure cough. Not Tabitha Louise Saxton Lyme Harmon Gladstone Baxter? Least-favorite-classmate-slash-mean-girl who'd made school horrible for most of us and went through husbands faster than you could say *wedding vows*? I peered at her. Everything on her face was different—thinner nose, higher cheekbones, longer chin—creating a sort of feral perfection. No wonder I hadn't recognized her at first.

"I need some detective stories *stat*," Tabitha said as she fiddled with Paisley's gold bow, which was the same shade as her silk pantsuit. She reknotted her own scarf into a complex, ultra-chic structure that I admired despite myself, then tapped a few times on her phone and shoved it into my sister's face. "From this guy."

"Edgar Allan Poe? Sure. I'll be right back," Lucy replied, after reading Tabitha's screen. She moved in the direction of the appropriate shelf.

I spun around to go anywhere that Tabitha Louise Saxton Lyme Harmon Gladstone Baxter was not. I'd made it about three steps when Tabitha yoo-hooed. I reluctantly turned back and met her eyes.

Her heavily lipsticked mouth fell open. "Emma Starrs, is that you? I haven't seen you in *ages*."

"Hi, Tabitha," I said, immediately feeling as though we were in school again and she'd cornered me in the cafeteria to make some dig about me having my nose in a book all the time or wearing the hideously wrong shoes or whatever was on her insult agenda for the day.

"Or maybe you're married now—with a new last name?"

"No. I'm single."

She smirked, then slid her lips into a pout. "Well, there's still time. I don't know why you haven't been able to attract a husband, but don't worry. Not everyone has that *special gift*, and there's someone out there for everyone, right? You won't be alone forever."

I didn't know what to do with that, so I said nothing.

"You look exactly the same as you did in high school." Her voice dropped to a whisper. "Though I would've imagined you'd discovered the power of blowouts by now. Girl to girl, they might help you with your man problem."

My sister's return probably saved Tabitha and her *special gift* from something unpleasant happening.

Tabitha was rattling on about how astonishing it was that we still dressed the same way too. That might have been true, in a general sense: Lucy tended toward the romantic end of the scale, choosing flowing dresses and sweaters in pastels embellished with ribbons and lace, whereas I leaned the opposite way, preferring classic, minimalist lines—typically a long jacket over a shirt and pants, often in black. Somehow, though, Tabitha made it seem as though we were stuck in fashion yesteryear, not having evolved sartorially like everyone else. I tried to disconnect from the emotions that she evoked by unobtrusively taking a deep breath and reminding myself that high school had ended over a decade ago.

I was a thirty-year-old grown woman, for goodness' sakes. I didn't need to prove anything to Tabitha flipping Baxter.

Even if it felt like I did.

"Here's your book," Lucy said, setting a thick red hardcover gently on the counter. I noted her pink cardigan set and long floral skirt, which she wore with platform Mary Janes. Adorable as always.

"What is *that*?" Tabitha sniffed.

Lucy gestured toward the cover, where the title was spelled out in letters so large they could have been read from the front sidewalk. "This volume has Poe's collected poems and stories."

"But I only need a few stories—specifically the ones with the detective. And I would prefer a paperback. Don't you have that?" Tabitha patted her hair, multiple diamond rings flashing.

"No, but I could order it for you." Lucy smiled politely.

"There's no time. I'll have to buy this thing." Tabitha rolled her eyes and jabbed a finger at the book. "For some reason, my husband *has* to have Mr. Dooping or whatever his name is—"

"Monsieur Dupin?" I offered. She flapped her hand vaguely in my direction, though it was difficult to know if she was dismissing or acknowledging me, and continued her rant.

"—on the shelf during our murder mystery dinner party. Of course, it probably isn't going to happen now anyway. It's scheduled for tomorrow night, and our party planner quit. What nerve, right?" She blew out an exasperated puff of air, like a fussy dragon. "I mean, *so what* if Jacques has a family emergency? We have a *contract*, don't we? And believe you me, he didn't come cheap!"

As I watched her flutter around, squawking in outrage, something dawned on me. Tabitha—thanks to her money and family, *not* her personality—had always been at the top of Silvercrest's social ladder. She had endless connections who might be willing to become bookstore patrons with a little encouragement. The realization sparked an idea. I weighed the pros and cons while Tabitha paid for her book.

Paisley popped her head up from the folds of the bag and gave me a beseeching look, as if asking me to rescue her.

Tabitha snatched the book from Lucy, who patiently held out the receipt.

I cleared my throat. "I'd be glad to help with your dinner, if you like."

Surely I could handle one party thrown by a lifelong foe.

Tabitha laughed as she turned to face me. "As a *cashier*? We aren't selling books, thank you very much."

"No. I could facilitate the murder mystery dinner part." I removed one of the Starlit Bookshop business cards from the filigree holder on the counter and handed it to her.

Behind Tabitha's back, Lucy's eyes widened.

Tabitha inspected the card, then me, then the card again. "This doesn't say anything about parties."

"I work out of the bookstore," I told Tabitha. "Where we also host literary events, in case you know anyone in the market." I left out the fact that we were only now planning to amp those back up again.

"Why would I ever move a dinner party at my gorgeous mansion here?" she asked incredulously. "I don't see that happening."

"The location is up to you, but it sounds like you need help with a mystery event, and Emma is an expert on both mysteries *and* events," Lucy said. "She's too humble to say that, but she is."

When I started to protest, my sister held up her hand to stop me.

"What experience do you have?" Tabitha asked suspiciously.

I explained that my dissertation had focused on mysteries and that I had organized numerous events, including a murder mystery party, for the school's creative writing program.

"Wait, *you* have a PhD?" That obviously wasn't what she'd expected. "In what?"

"English."

Her nose wrinkled. "My least favorite subject. Books put me to *sleep*. Something about all of those words in a row—ugh. Insta-snore."

She was standing in the middle of our bookstore slamming books? Who does that?

Tabitha raised an eyebrow. "Why aren't you teaching? Isn't that why someone gets a PhD? To become a professor?"

People with doctorates did many different things, but I decided to skip that discussion; she wasn't genuinely interested in the first place.

"Tough market," I said, which was true. For every opening, there were hundreds of applicants.

That pleased her tremendously, I could tell.

"Sorry you couldn't find a teaching job," she said, not sounding in any way sorry.

"I love working here," I said. "Always have."

Tabitha reached for her dog, who shrank back into the depths of the bag, perhaps at the sight of those nails coming toward her face. When Tabitha noticed that Lucy and I were witnesses to her inability to coax Paisley into her arms, she straightened and assumed a haughty position so that she could look down her nose at me. "You honestly believe Starlight Bookshop could step in at this late date?"

"Star*lit*," I clarified. "*Lit* is short for *literature*."

She narrowed her eyes.

"And yes, we could step in."

Tabitha pursed her lips, then declined her head the slightest bit. "The dinner has already been finalized by Jacques, my never-going-to-work-in-this-town-again ex–party planner. He was supposed to manage the murder mystery portion of the evening as well, but he didn't leave any instructions behind and he won't take my calls. All I have is the character descriptions, which went out individually to each guest with the invitation. The rest has to be built from scratch. Do you think you can handle that?"

My nod was far more assured than it had any right to be, given the immediate turnaround.

"And I could use someone to be, you know, at the house, in case anything else is needed." She didn't overtly *say* that someone would be at her personal beck and call, but she implied it nonetheless. "We don't have time for you to work up a formal bid, so here's the deal. Take over the murder mystery party, and I'll pay you what I would have paid Jacques."

Then Tabitha named a sum that almost made me dizzy.

Lucy clasped her hands together behind Tabitha's back in a pleading motion.

I quickly agreed to Tabitha's proposal.

"*Minus* the twenty percent I paid him up front," she added in a rush.

I plastered on a smile as I made a mental note not to say yes to anything in the future until all the details were on the table, then countered with a request of my own. "We would ask that our business cards be prominently displayed at the party and that you recommend Starlit Bookshop to your friends during the event."

"And afterwards," Lucy added cheerfully.

"Fine, whatever," Tabitha said, dangling the card from her fingertips. "I'll send you the particulars."

"Thank you. I'm looking forward to it." I managed to sound halfway sincere.

"Don't let me down, Emma. This dinner has to be perfect. Bring your A game." Tabitha clicked across the floor and out the door.

Regret swelled up the instant she was gone.

"Wow," Lucy said. "That was a surprising turn of events. You booked an event with the least likely client in town."

"Well, we need the money, right?"

"When you suggested expanding before, I thought you meant increasing the number of events we'd do here."

"That *is* what I meant. But I'm willing to work on events both on- and off-site. And if that comes with Tabitha Baxter attached, so be it. I will do whatever I can to help save this bookstore."

Lucy came out from behind the register to hug me. "You are the best sister, you know that?"

She picked up the feather duster, and I took a moment to process the conversation with Tabitha. Sun streamed through the arched side windows, the rays warming the back of our store cat, Anne Shirley, a red tabby who had wandered in through the open front door last summer and adopted the space—and us—as her own. As I stood there, she leapt lightly down from the armchair and walked over. I gave her a gentle scratch between the ears, and she rubbed her head against my arm.

My phone chimed, and when I saw the notification, I laughed. "Here's Tabitha's email already. She must have sent it from her car."

My sister secured the list we'd made to a nearby clipboard, the one we stored on the shelf below the register and reviewed every morning to keep priority activities in sight. It was a system my grandparents had instituted when they'd opened the store years ago that had stuck. "Poor Jacques is never going to work in this town again, if Tabitha has her way. And she pretty much always has her way."

"Can Tabitha actually do that?" I asked. I'd been away at school for so long, I had no idea what additional powers she'd been able to accrue. "I thought she was being dramatic. She's not the boss of everyone."

"She sure acts like it. The members of her insufferable clique and their husbands do run more than a few things around here."

"That doesn't mean—"

Lucy shook her head. "Trust me. Her net of influence is wide. Let me give you one example: last year she pulled a muscle walking down the street. Her personal trainer, who was in Aspen skiing that weekend, had nothing to do with it, but as soon as he returned, she accused him of causing the injury by mistraining her."

"Mistraining? Is that a thing?"

She shrugged. "She sued him on top of ruining his reputation *and* stopped her friends from hiring him. He couldn't make a living here anymore and had to move away. So please, Em, be careful."

I ignored the prickle of apprehension at the back of my neck. "I'll be fine."

Lucy nodded, though I knew she wasn't convinced.

What had I set myself up for?

Chapter Two

Early Saturday morning, I turned on my phone to discover a flood of texts and voice mail messages from Tabitha. Even though it was not yet seven o'clock, she had presumably become tired of waiting for me to check my emails and switched over to a more immediate way to hound me.

No wonder Jacques had quit.

I was an inch away from fabricating a family emergency myself.

Not that Jacques had made it up. But if he *had*, I understood the impulse.

Gritting my teeth, I began to scroll and skim. I only had to make it through a single day, I reminded myself. A single day, after which I might be able to persuade Tabitha to recommend the bookstore to millions of friends so that we could stay open.

Still, I could at least have a cup of coffee first.

I stopped reading, threw off the quilt, put the phone into my bag, and resolved to have a shower before trying to deal with Tabitha and her many, many demands.

* * *

Setting down my mug, I thanked Nora—my aunt preferred to be called by her first name, without familial designation—for breakfast. All three of us were sitting in the sunny kitchen nook of the Victorian bought by my grandparents and handed down to my parents, where I was staying until I sorted out my life. Nora had also moved back in after earning her doctorate when she accepted a tenure-track teaching job at Silvercrest College twenty years ago—it had been a temporary plan when she was thirty-five, but the home had plenty of space for all of us, so she'd never left. Nor had Lucy.

I could understand why they wanted to stay in this old house: I cherished every nook and cranny full of heirlooms, photographs, art pieces, and books as well as the wraparound porch adorned with wind chimes and rocking chairs. Through the back windows was an incredible view of the Silvercrest River that ran between the town and the mountains rising majestically to the west. The whole scene was dotted with pine trees and purple sage, which kept their color well into the fall. In the spring and summer, the wildflowers would return and make the view even more glorious. It was one of my favorite places in the world.

It still seemed as though my parents could walk around the corner at any moment. We'd celebrated their retirement with such joy, after which they'd gone to Europe on the dream trip they'd begun saving for long before we were born. There had been a sudden storm. A boating accident. They never came home. The tragedy had happened two years ago, but the pain had the power to stop us in our tracks.

Their love for the bookstore had been second only to their love for our family; Nora, Lucy, and I were determined to protect their legacy as best we could. That was the reason I'd returned to Silvercrest, even though I had been offered a tenure-track position at an East Coast university after a long and involved interview process. The same day the department chair invited me to join the faculty, Nora had called, worried that my sister was struggling to make ends meet. I'd declined the job offer and come straight home.

I watched a hawk circling lazily over the pines, then pulled out the phone again and read Tabitha's messages. Her complaints could be grouped into three categories: wanting to confirm that I'd be arriving on time; asking whether I had anything "decent" to wear so that I didn't embarrass her in front of the guests, followed by a winky-face emoji perhaps intended to soften the critique; and demanding to know why I wasn't returning her messages.

In other words, nonsense. Nothing about the actual event itself, just a Tabitha-like flurry of power moves. I must have made a sound, because my aunt asked me what I was reading.

"Text from a client," I said.

"A *client*?" She set down her spoon and leaned forward, her blue eyes sparkling. "Do tell, darling."

I provided an overview of the Baxter party. Nora and Lucy exchanged a long look.

"What?" I asked, moving my gaze back and forth between them.

Lucy, still in her favorite pink pajamas, winced. "Don't blame me. I only heard about it before you came down." She pointedly turned her attention to her oatmeal, stirring slowly.

My aunt laughed and smoothed her hair, which was mostly dark except for an appealing white stripe along the front. Her signature style was created by pulling her long curls back into a complicated twist; today she had secured the whole thing with an amethyst-and-ruby pin in the shape of a dragonfly and paired it with matching earrings. "The pain your sister is exhibiting stems from the fact that I will be attending that party myself."

"You will?" Tabitha hadn't mentioned that Nora was on her guest list. I didn't know who any of the guests were, come to think of it—just which characters would be participating. Though I did know Tabitha expected me to wear something "decent." She had her priorities.

"I have no choice but to attend. It might even be fun. They sent us character cards with our backgrounds and costume ideas." She struck an elegant pose. "I'm a duchess."

"I can see that for you," Lucy said.

"Actually feels quite natural," my aunt agreed. "Wait until you see my costume."

"So you're friendly with the Baxters now?" Suddenly in need of additional caffeine, I poured more coffee into the lavender stoneware mug my father had made for my sixteenth birthday. He had been a master of many artistic mediums.

Nora picked up her favorite teacup. The ruby shade in the cascade of flowers on the side matched her duster jacket, which also had a purple dragonfly on the back. After sipping, she took her time setting the cup into the saucer, a sign that she was choosing her words carefully. "We aren't friends per se. Tip Baxter is the Arts and Humanities dean. I'm on a particularly argumentative faculty committee: half of us are proposing that we do something, and the other half are trying to block the thing we're proposing. Tip has invited us all to this dinner with some of his close friends, probably as a way to take the animosity down a notch. Our meetings have been quite heated."

"Interesting strategy." For such a small, intimate event, I wouldn't have invited a group of people who couldn't see eye to eye. Then again, the dean wouldn't be the first person who'd tried to smooth tense negotiations through a social gathering.

"Emma, I do appreciate your efforts. But we're at a sensitive point in the process," Nora continued. "If anything were to go wrong at the party, it could have unfortunate consequences for a number of people."

I stared at her. "But I've already accepted the job."

She picked up her teacup again, cradling it in two hands. "I'm not saying that you shouldn't do it, just . . ."

"Just don't mess it up?" I finished for her.

"Precisely. Thank you, darling." She took a sip and smiled at me. Her dragonfly earrings swung gently to and fro, as if urging me on.

No pressure.

* * *

After breakfast, I gathered the instructions I'd typed up and copied at the store the night before and put them into envelopes for the guests. Then I emailed Tabitha the final script for her husband, Tip, who was playing C. Auguste Dupin, along with an explanation of how the murder mystery would unfold and how the guests would participate.

Tabitha hadn't wanted me to come over until right before the festivities began. If I'd had a choice, I would have been onsite much sooner, but she was in charge. This gave her more of an opportunity to blame me if something went wrong, which I couldn't help but feel was part of her plan. Unfortunately, I had more than a little experience in the highly predictable methodologies and ulterior motives of Tabitha Baxter.

She continued to text every thought that popped into her head, however, and I responded all afternoon. Finally, after I told

Tabitha I was on my way, I felt justified in disregarding the alerts coming from my phone for a few minutes. And once I climbed into my car, the fact that I was driving provided even more reason to ignore them. I turned onto River Street and passed Lucy, who was sweeping the sidewalk in front of the bookstore but paused to give me a wave. I waved back, then smiled at the sight of the Riverside Coffeehouse next door, where the neighborly owner had added a Starlit Latte to the menu after I'd ordered the same skinny caramel drink every day one summer.

River Street was the hub of our town, which was known for its flourishing community of painters, glassblowers, textile artists, sculptors, writers, musicians, and other artistic types. Numerous charming cafés and boutiques drew shoppers from around the metropolitan area in addition to serving students from the local college and other townspeople. The shops and restaurants on the west side of the street, like our bookstore, all featured a back porch with easy access to the paved riverwalk behind the buildings. There was nothing quite as calming as looking at the rushing water, letting your cares momentarily swirl away with it. We had never done much with our own porch, but it occurred to me that adding furniture and accessories would turn the area into a properly cozy space for book-related gatherings.

At the end of the main drag was the gated driveway to Silvercrest Castle, which commanded the river bank facing the town. Towers on either end of the long stone building were topped by flags waving in the wind. The architecture was modeled after a famous castle in England, the story went. One of the town's prominent families had won it in a card game in the 1920s and turned the castle into a hotel. Most of the dances, weddings, and other formal affairs I'd attended in Silvercrest had taken place there.

For the rest of the drive, I was lost in bittersweet memories, the kind that arise only when you revisit the haunts of your childhood.

* * *

A few miles outside of town, I pulled up in front of the oversized double doors at the Baxters' McMansion and gave an appreciative whistle. The size was designed to impress, and it did accomplish that goal, though no one else I knew needed to have *that* many columns. The place bore a vague resemblance to the White House.

"Oh no," Tabitha said, running toward me on her stilettos. Paisley was lodged in the crook of her arm, her bow now in an ivory shade that matched Tabitha's silky floor-length gown and faux-fur stole.

I hoped it was faux, anyway.

When she reached the car, I smiled up at her as politely as I could. One does what one has to when acting in a professional capacity.

"No, no, no." Tabitha patted her marble-sized pearls. "You can't park *here*, Emma." She didn't say *where people can see your tiny embarrassing car*, but the meaning landed. "Go to the back, and I'll meet you by the door."

"Will do." I followed the curving driveway around the house until I saw several other cars—the other worker bees like me, I presumed—lined up in a row.

By the time I'd parked, Tabitha was waving impatiently from the back door, and I hurried over.

"Come with me," she ordered. We moved through a large mudroom down a short hallway to the kitchen, which was probably bigger than the ones used to serve customers in most of the restaurants on River Street. It was bustling with people chopping and stirring things. She introduced me to the caterer, a tall, energetic woman named Vivi Yang, who was waving her arms while issuing directions to her staff like a music conductor. Vivi greeted me with a bright smile and paused to go over the plan for the night—she had kindly agreed to perform the role of the unfortunate victim of the murder mystery.

Tabitha then led me through swinging doors to the dining room, where three geometric chandeliers hung over a long walnut table with clean lines that had been set for sixteen. A pale man with a handlebar moustache was polishing the glasses with a cloth; he nodded at us gravely. As Tabitha sprinted ahead of me, he made a face behind her back.

I returned his nod in solidarity.

For the next several minutes, Tabitha raced me through the hallways and floors of her home. In addition to the usual spaces, there was every kind of room you could think of: library, theater, spa, conservatory, study, basketball court, craft workshop, and gym. All were enormous and shiny but oddly cold, lacking personal touches, as if they had been lifted from a modern-design catalog spread. I'd take our old house full of quirky treasures that had been acquired over time any day of the week.

Tabitha finally coasted to a stop near a round marble table in the grand foyer. The immense vase in the center held a bouquet so high and wide it was like standing below a tree made of flowers. I wasn't sure if her whirlwind tour had been to prepare me for my duties or to show off the magnitude of her possessions.

Maybe both.

She had an expectant look.

"Your home is beautiful," I said.

Tabitha looked around proudly. "I've been working on it since the day Tip and I moved in, right after we got home from *Bali*."

She paused briefly, anticipating a response. I tried to make my smile even wider, but my face was hurting from all the professionalism I'd already mustered up.

"Bali is where we went for our honeymoon. He owns a resort there." She waited for that fact to sink in, then chattered on. "Let's discuss the agenda for tonight. All I know is that the guests have been assigned a character and are expected to dress and behave in a manner that aligns with their persona. What else do you have for me?"

As if I hadn't emailed every single detail to her already. "When they arrive, they'll pick up an envelope with objectives for their detecting efforts from a basket at the bar. The murder will happen sometime during cocktails, after which they'll receive further instructions and chat among themselves to gather more information. At dinner, they'll fill out accusation sheets with their final guesses about whodunit before we get to the reveal."

"And who will be doing the reveal?"

"I sent the script for you to give to Tip—"

"Oh, right. I did. By the way, once we get started, I would prefer that you stay out of sight, though I have set out a little bell, and if I need you, I'll ring it. Be listening for it, mm-kay?"

A bell? Tabitha was clearly enjoying this new dynamic between us.

She went on. "The guests will be here at any moment. I'd like you to keep an eye on things—*unseen*, mind you—and maybe even help out the caterers as needed. You don't have any problem with that, do you?"

I shook my head, even though Tabitha had revised the scope of what she'd hired me to do. It was clear that now she had the murder mystery materials, she mostly just wanted to order me around. But as long as there was the promised paycheck at the end of the night, that was fine with me.

"Right now, do a loop through the dining room, patio bar, and kitchen to make sure that everything is perfect. And Emma"—she stepped close enough that her cloying, musky perfume, which I'd been trying not to breathe in, completely enveloped me—"this is very important for my husband. Do *not* let us down."

"I'll try to stay out of sight, but I may need to—"

"Unseen!" Tabitha repeated, pointing at me.

I nodded to indicate that I had received her request to become invisible. "If there's an issue, do you want me to call you?"

"That's ridiculous. I would never carry my cell phone at a *party*." She reached up and fussed with one of the flowers.

"Then how—"

Tabitha gave me a hard glare. "You're the PhD. Why don't *you* figure it out?"

I had opened my mouth to suggest walkie-talkies out of desperation when she spoke again, her voice rising. "Are we going to have a *problem*?"

"What's all this?" A stocky, handsome man in a black tuxedo and top hat strode up to us. His thick gray brows bristled over dark, intelligent eyes. A sharp whiff of alcohol accompanied his arrival.

"Tip, honey!" Tabitha exclaimed, instantly retracting her claws and softening her expression. "Meet Emma Starrs."

"Starrs? The purveyors of Starlit Bookshop, yes?" he said, brightening. "Wonderful place. And your aunt is my colleague. What a firecracker!"

"Nice to meet you."

"You are attending our dinner? Welcome."

Tabitha laughed a little too hard at that idea. "Oh, honey, no. She's working for us, filling in for that good-for-nothing Jacques. She wrote the script I gave you this morning."

"Sorry, I couldn't quite deduce the role you were playing from your, uh, costume." He indicated my long brocade jacket over a shirt and pants—all black. "Not a very inspiring display of my brain power, I'm afraid. Glad that my performance tonight has been scripted so I'll sound more impressive. And thank you for writing it—I've been busily memorizing all day." He bowed slightly. "C. Auguste Dupin, armchair detective, at your service."

"As you know, he's playing the starring role, and I'm the lady of the manor," Tabitha supplied, unprompted. "Which means that I will take care of the guests while my big brain here solves the mystery through his ratio pronunciation."

"*Ratiocination*," Tip told her. "Reasoning through the evidence."

"That's what I said." She batted her eyelashes at him.

He adjusted a cuff link. "As my wife may have told you, I'm a Dupin superfan."

"Ah." I found myself looking forward to their performances.

"Did you notice that before he quit, Jacques brought in props representing each of the Dupin stories? My favorite is the purloined letter. Take a stroll around the first floor and see if you can find it! Also, my beautiful wife picked out a very handsome volume for my shelves as a special gift after I'd mentioned Dupin in passing. Thank you, Tabby."

She blew him an air kiss. "Only the best for you, honey. I knew you needed that very book as a finishing touch. It was a thoughtful choice, if I do say so myself."

It took everything in my power not to administer a pop quiz to her right then and there. I would have bet Tabitha couldn't name the title of the book she'd bought. It was difficult to watch her act as though she gave one whit about Poe's writing—or any literature, for that matter. Not to mention that she'd balked at having to pay for a hardcover when she lived in a house that was larger than our entire store.

"You both look marvelous," I said instead.

They preened. He was more charming about it.

"Good to meet you, Emma Starrs," he said, tipping his hat. "Please do join us for a cocktail if you get a minute."

Tabitha sputtered.

He ignored her reaction. "See you soon, I hope."

She watched him go, then removed a small black hat with a veil from the table. "To clarify, the staff is *not* invited for drinks. You're staff, in case you forgot."

I had not.

Tabitha applied the hat and secured it with a pin, then picked up long dark gloves. "But I suppose if you *have* to talk to me, you can. Just be discreet. We're working very hard to make this whole thing feel authentic, as though our guests are inside a mystery story. I don't want the magical spell of the moment broken by *you* and *your clogs* showing up."

My clogs? I loved my clogs. I gave them an affectionate look.

Tabitha waited, but I didn't allow her the satisfaction of any other response. Finally, the doorbell rang, breaking our little standoff, and she fluttered her fingers toward the kitchen in dismissal.

I heard Nora's voice in the foyer, however, so I turned around to wave at her. Playing a duchess complete with tiara, she unwound a velvet cape from her shoulders and handed it to Tabitha, who looked horrified at having to touch it. One of the caterers hurried to the foyer, arms outstretched, and Tabitha shoved the cloth at him. After a beat, she activated her lady-of-the-manor persona and waved her guests toward the bar area set up on the stone patio outside with a spectacular view of the mountains. As they followed her orders, I caught sight of Tabitha's closest friends, all clustered together and whispering as usual.

Suddenly the command to remain unseen seemed much more appealing.

There had been three couples in Tabitha's orbit since our school days: Bruce and Melody (Booth) Crenshaw, Clive and Ainsley (Wells) Fowler, and Aston and Felicity (Cromwell) Edwards. They were all perfect smiles and inside jokes, having basically grown up together on the grounds of the Silvercrest Country Club. Tabitha was their queen, regardless of whom she happened to be married to at the time; her husbands were welcomed into the group for as long as she was with them, then quietly ousted.

"Emma!" Nora interrupted my musings. Her floor-length gown shimmered in a dark-gold shade that matched her filigree choker and dangling earrings. "Do come with me and have a drink."

Tabitha would be *most* displeased about yet another such invitation extended to staff-member-me.

"You look amazing, Nora."

"*Merci*, darling." My aunt pointed to the patio. "I can't wait to introduce you to my colleagues. Thanks to retirements and such, we have a batch of new professors since you went off to school. They're excited to meet you."

"That's so kind, but we'll have to wait on that, I'm sorry. Tabitha practically ordered me to hide behind the curtains until she needs me."

"How strange." Nora frowned.

"Agreed. But I'm trying to be careful. I don't want to give Tabitha any reason not to pay me." I had the sneaking suspicion that she was already trying to find such a reason, and I was going to do my best not to deliver it to her outright.

"Lucy told me about the finances," Nora said, sotto voce. "I know that you're doing this on behalf of the store. *Endless* gratitude. Though it must be excruciating to let Tabitha boss you around. After how she's treated you."

"Thank you. I can handle it for one night. But please go have fun out there."

She beamed and swept through the doors, every inch a duchess in carriage.

I followed, then veered over to a row of manicured hedges, away from the guests. The space was filled with the country club clique—whom I intended to avoid—circled up on the left side, with professors from Silvercrest College engaged in animated conversation from various chaise lounges on the right. Costumes fell mainly into two camps: elegant gowns with feathers, pearls, or sparkling gems and suits worn with top hats, fedoras, or caps. Classical music played in the background while servers offered appealing hors d'oeuvres on trays and kept the drinks refreshed. The sun setting over the peaks in the background cast everything in a rosy glow.

When a piercing scream came from somewhere in the house, everyone froze, then hurried inside en masse. Another shriek helpfully led us to the billiards room, where the caterer, Vivi Yang, in a long velvet dressing gown, was lying on the thick carpet with a feather boa wrapped around her throat. She held a rose in one hand and a book in the other and was so still that I caught my breath.

We all stared down at her motionless body.

"That looks *very* uncomfortable," a woman whispered loudly.

Vivi's mouth twitched.

"I wonder if she needs a pillow," the woman whispered again.

"She's a corpse," came a frustrated reply. "Corpses don't need pillows."

"Theoretically, yes, but practically speaking—"

"Will you stop? This is the *murder* and you're *ruining* it."

Vivi pressed her lips together, trying to stifle her laughter, but her shoulders were shaking. To her credit, she never opened her eyes, but chuckles and giggles broke out among the guests. Tabitha, clearly annoyed at having the mood broken, curtly directed the attendees to pick up a second round of envelopes from the bar on the patio and reminded them that it was important to mingle in order to gather clues.

Back outside, everyone pored over the new pages and chatted about the information therein. They had returned to their original corners rather than mingling but still seemed to be having a perfectly splendid time—most of all Tip, who was laughing uproariously at something Bruce, Aston, and Clive were saying. Eventually, he clapped the men on the back one by one and made his way—listing slightly, though he didn't spill his drink—over to the academic side of the gathering. His grin faded several degrees when he reached his Silvercrest College colleagues, but he greeted them politely and asked if they needed anything. While his words were not fully slurred, they were definitely on the cusp of sliding into one another. I wondered if he'd be able to follow his script for the upcoming reveal.

Tabitha cut a swath through the crowd and took his arm briefly. Was she steadying him or displaying affection? He gave her an absent-minded hug with his free arm while taking a long drink from his glass; she looked up at him adoringly.

The smile she gave the professors, however, was tight. "It's time for dinner, and I wanted to remind you that staying in character this evening is essential. We've had our fun talking with friends so far, and that's *fine*"—her tone suggested otherwise—"but this game only works if we play our parts. Do try to gather as much evidence as possible through energetic conversation so that you can make informed choices on your accusation sheet. Don't forget, we have gone to the trouble of arranging prizes. Trust me, when you see them later, you're going to kick yourself if you haven't given it everything you've got."

There were a few mumbled apologies from the chastened professors. She had just ended her rebuke when a ruckus arose on the other side of the patio. Clive and Aston had pulled two tall torchlights from the ground and were using them to joust. Bruce was egging them on, and their wives were cheering. Tabitha spun around, threw her hands in the air, and headed over to deliver another stern reminder of the rules.

The professors leaned forward and whispered among themselves. It was hard to tell whether her little speech had inspired them to increase their efforts or to rebel even more.

Tip finished the rest of the liquid in his glass, then grabbed a refill from a passing server and tossed that down too for good measure.

No one said a word.

It was his party, after all.

* * *

A few hours later, the evening was winding down. The attendees had reviewed all the evidence, filled out their accusation sheets, and appeared to be dazzled by Tip-as-Dupin's brilliant—if slightly jumbled—ratiocinations at dinner. The murderer, a pinstriped professor playing a banker, was identified by the detective, and the guests enjoyed coffee in the great room while prizes were handed out. Judging from the many bursts of laughter and applause, the rest of the night had gone smashingly well.

Tabitha hadn't even rung her bell.

Thank goodness.

"Follow me for the pièce de résistance!" Tabitha led the group through the foyer, and everyone seemed to be in high spirits. The final menu item was a special dessert, which awaited them in the library. Jacques had organized the creation of individual chocolate cakes for each guest, featuring an image of their character made entirely of icing.

I was standing near the stairs in the shadows, trying to be inconspicuous, when my aunt came over, eyes shining and cheeks flushed. Verbal sparring with colleagues always invigorated her.

"Guess who won best dressed?" She held up a small gold trophy for me to admire. "And maybe it was the Scotch talking, but the dean told me that he wanted to meet Monday morning about the committee work. I sense victory on the horizon."

"Congratulations on both fronts—that's wonderful." I smiled at her.

Nora waved her trophy, readjusted her tiara, and followed the group.

After the door to the library had closed, I emerged from the shadows and checked the great room, where I found a number of stray glasses. I took a tray from the kitchen, collected them all, and dropped them off next to the sink. When I complimented Vivi on her dramatic performance, she confided that Tabitha had expressed "extreme disappointment" at her "sabotage of the crucial party moment." I tried to make her feel better by sharing the instructions I had received to become somehow invisible. We commiserated about working for Tabitha, then exchanged business cards. She promised to recommend the bookstore as a site for events; I told her that I'd do likewise for her catering company.

After passing through the dining room to confirm that the table had been fully cleared, I went to perform a final visual sweep of the patio. I pushed open the French doors and stepped outside into the cool night, where the moon shone dully on the concrete and the glittering stars above seemed bright and hard. Something on the farthest chaise lounge caught my eye, and I walked over to gather up whatever had been left behind.

Only when I got closer, I realized that it was a person—who wasn't moving.

Or breathing.

Chapter Three

After I screamed, others rushed out onto the patio, and chaos descended. I helped with CPR efforts, pushing desperately on Tip's chest while the handlebar moustache guy did the mouth-to-mouth. By the time the paramedics arrived and took over, it was too late.

Tip was gone.

Guests milled around, conjecturing. As I made my way through the crowd, looking for Nora, I gathered that the presiding theory assumed a heart-related event. But before I could find my aunt, I was asked to give a statement, then sequestered in the library with a trim man going gray at the temples who introduced himself as Detective Trujillo. I didn't know who had called the police, but I was aware that the appearance of the detective suggested potential foul play.

Maybe it hadn't been Tip's heart at all but something more nefarious.

Or perhaps when you were a Silvercrest VIP—in this case, a college dean—the response was more comprehensive than it might be otherwise. I had no idea how such things were decided. But the detective was here and he wanted to speak to me.

From what I'd observed in the past several minutes, Detective Trujillo was direct with his orders and emanated competence. He showed me his badge, then removed a notepad from the inside pocket of his blue suit. We went through the basics, establishing my identity and other vital information. He reviewed the statement I'd written for the first officer to whom I'd spoken and asked me to reconstruct for him each step leading up to how I'd found Tip. The whole time I felt as though I might faint, but I struggled through somehow.

"How well did you know him?" His voice was calm, but he stared at me with laser focus.

I looked down to better concentrate. My hands were shaking and everything seemed distorted, as if it were unfolding at a slower pace than usual. On top of that, I was nervous sitting in this house, especially if their suspicions about foul play were correct. No one had left, which meant there could be a murderer here.

A fresh wave of dizziness hit me.

"Get her something with sugar," Trujillo said to one of the officers outside the door. He ran a hand impatiently through his dark hair as he gave the directive.

"No," I protested. "I'm . . ."

"In shock," he said decisively. "Low-level, perhaps, but let's err on the side of caution, shall we? Take some deep breaths."

I took some deep breaths—I honestly couldn't tell if it was helping or hurting—until the officer returned with one of those juice boxes for kids. Feeling slightly ridiculous, I peeled off the straw and poked it through the top of the package. Then I took a long drink, which resulted in a loud gurgle when I hit the bottom, having misjudged the liquid capacity of the container.

So that happened.

The juice did seem to steady me, though.

"Now," the detective said. "Back to the question of how well you knew Tip Baxter."

"I met him tonight." I set the juice on the coffee table between us. The box was now bent and looked out of place on the polished wood glowing softly in the lamplight, the way that any scrap of debris would mar the effect of a well-tended garden. It captured the way I felt in this house: crumpled and unwanted.

He wrote something down on the notepad. "Tell me about your conversation."

"Tip seemed excited for the party. Happy that he was playing Monsieur Dupin. Oh, and he invited me to join the guests for a drink, but I didn't because I was working."

"In what capacity?"

"Tabitha's party planner quit, so I stepped in at the last minute to keep an eye on things."

He made another note. "Are you an event planner by trade?"

"I am," I said confidently.

"How long have you been doing that in Silvercrest?"

"A little while," I said, slightly less confidently.

"And how long is a little while?"

"Since . . . tonight."

The detective squinted at me.

"Technically, I'm a bookseller, but we're expanding the event component of our work," I explained.

He made a much longer note. That didn't seem like a good sign.

"*There* you are. Emma, I need you to go take care of everything out there." Tabitha flounced right into the room. The officers outside the door must have left their post.

Detective Trujillo held up a hand, palm out, without looking at her. "I'll release Ms. Starrs when we're done talking."

Tabitha sighed dramatically. "I'll be in the dining room waiting for you, Emma. Come find me." The sound of her heels clicking angrily across the foyer eventually grew fainter.

Detective Trujillo shifted position but didn't break eye contact with me. "And how long have you known Ms. Baxter?"

"Years and years."

"Specify, please."

"We went to school together, from kindergarten forward."

"So she hired you, as her friend, to work this event, even though you have no experience with party planning."

That didn't sound like a theory that would end well for me. I hastened to assure him otherwise. "No, we are *not* friends."

Something crossed his face—a flash of intrigue, perhaps. "Enemies, then?"

That wasn't a direction I wanted him to go in either.

He waited.

"Enemy is a strong word," I said slowly.

He leaned back and crossed one of his legs over the other. "Go on."

"She came into the bookstore yesterday complaining about how her party planner had quit. I've organized this type of event before, so I offered to help."

"You offered to help your *enemy*." His tone was flat. He wasn't letting go of that angle without some convincing. Unfortunately, I didn't have the energy to do much persuading at the moment.

I shrugged. "I needed the money."

When I heard that out loud, even *I* thought it sounded suspicious.

"People do a lot of things for money," he said softly. "How much was she paying you?"

When I stated the sum, he wrote it down and underlined the number twice.

"You can see why I accepted her offer." I smiled.

He didn't smile back. "What were the duties she wanted you to perform, specifically?"

"Make sure that the murder went off without a hitch."

His eyebrows shot up. "The murder?"

"Mystery. Murder *mystery*," I said quickly.

"Well . . ." His pause demonstrated the belief that I'd failed in that regard.

"Maybe I should reword that. I was hired to write the script and to organize the progression of the murder mystery *party* events. And technically, that phase of the evening had already ended before Tip . . . you know."

He studied my face. "Ms. Baxter didn't propose anything else to you?"

"Like what?"

"Like something with her husband, perhaps?"

He was really circling here. "No, and I would *not* have agreed to participate in anything illegal if she had," I said firmly.

The detective tapped the notepad against his knee. "I'm still having trouble understanding why you would work for Ms. Baxter if you don't like her. Enlighten me."

I leaned forward. "I have experience planning events. There was money to be made. It's true that I'm not Tabitha's biggest fan, but that's not a crime, right? To dislike the way someone behaves?"

"I hear you," he said, after a minute. He removed a business card that had been tucked into the notepad and handed it to me. "Call me if you think of anything that might be useful to this investigation."

I stood to leave.

"And I may be calling you too," he added. "Down the road."

I picked up the juice box. "I'll take care of this."

"Thank you." He dipped his chin. "Please send in Ms. Baxter."

When I passed through the door, someone clutched my bicep.

"I'm not *your* biggest fan either," Tabitha hissed. I'd heard her walk away from the room. She must have sneaked back to listen outside the door. I didn't know why I hadn't expected that. "And if you ever slander me again in front of the police, you'll find out what I'm *really* capable of."

"I answered the questions honestly."

"How about don't talk about me at all, Emma?" She leaned right into my face. "Ever again. Or *else*."

"Or else? Are you threatening me?" I said loudly, hoping the detective would overhear, as I wrenched my arm away from her.

Tabitha continued looking daggers at me. At least until the detective poked his head out of the library. Then she transformed, her whole body softening and her expression going carefully blank. After a second, she curved up her lips and greeted the detective. It was eerie how quickly she could visibly shift gears.

"Please come in," he said sternly.

I approved of his tone.

As Tabitha strode into the library, he asked if I was okay.

Good. He had heard what she'd said, or at least he'd surmised what was going down.

I nodded and left him to it.

* * *

"What a horrible night." Nora stared glumly at her teacup. "A horrible, horrible night."

We were sitting at our kitchen table Sunday morning, exchanging stories about having been interviewed by the police. She'd spoken with the detective after Tabitha did, while I'd been helping the caterers pack up. By the time I came home, she had already gone to bed.

I passed the blueberry scones around the table. It had been a bumpy night with much tossing and turning, so I'd risen early and baked to take my mind off poor Tip. It hadn't worked as well as I'd hoped—I couldn't stop thinking about him—but at least now we had scones.

"He didn't deserve it," my aunt said, as she took one and passed the plate to my sister.

I agreed.

"I heard he was smothered by a pillow," Lucy said, while cutting her scone in half.

"*That* was the murder weapon?" When we were trying to revive Tip, I had glimpsed a red embroidered pillow, feathers spilling out of a hole in the seam, lying on the stone patio next to the chaise lounge.

"Someone must have been strong, because he would have fought like the dickens, and he was a sturdy guy," Lucy continued.

"You heard about that already today?" I'd forgotten how quickly news circulated around our small town.

"My book club had a whole email discussion this morning." She added that Allison Colt, who ran the group, was married to the chief of police.

That seemed odd. "Is she allowed to tell your club—"

"We have a circle of trust," Lucy said gravely.

"But you just told *us*, darling," Nora pointed out.

"Yes, but"—she smiled—"you're family."

"So family members can be part of the book club circle of trust?" my aunt inquired.

"Well, not part of it, exactly," Lucy said, tilting her head as she thought. "But we have our own circle which *overlaps* the other circle, if that makes sense."

"So it's more of a Venn diagram of trust." Nora smiled at her.

"Precisely."

"Before we chart any additional configurations of trust, could we please go back to what happened to Tip?" I stirred cream into my coffee. "How could someone hold him down and smother him with a pillow?"

"Well, he did have a great deal to drink." My aunt glanced at me. "Did you hear him slurring at dinner?"

"I noticed beforehand."

Lucy spread some butter on her scone. "Although we all know Tabitha is beastly, I do feel for her. She must be distraught. Did she say anything to you, Emma?"

"She sort of hissed at me after I spoke to the detective."

"What do you mean *hissed*?" My sister's alarm was palpable.

"She grabbed my arm and warned me not to say anything negative about her to the police. Or to anyone. Then she literally said 'or else.' "

Nora's mouth fell open.

"Or *else*?" Lucy repeated.

"Don't worry. I didn't take it that she'd actually be coming after me."

"Maybe you *should* have taken it that way." Lucy sliced the knife through the air for emphasis.

"You should be careful, darling," Nora said. "There's a reason that the police look at the spouse in such matters. In this case, she's not a very kind person to begin with, so I hope they do pay close attention to the possibilities. Not to be gruesome, but Tabitha didn't even seem upset. I didn't see her cry, did you?"

"I did not. She seemed more concerned about wrapping up the party."

"Wouldn't you expect a little bit of emotion? If anything happened to my family, I'd be *weeping*," my aunt said. "Despondent. Full-on keening. Pounding my chest. Inconsolable."

"They say that everyone grieves differently—" I began.

"That's true," Nora said. "But *still*."

For the next few minutes, we ate our scones in comfortable silence.

When we were finished, I tried a new tack. "Do you have any theories about who might have been upset with Tip? Any of the other committee members who were there?"

"*All* of them are upset with Tip," my aunt said. "The ones who want change are frustrated that he hasn't approved the project yet, and the ones who don't want change are frustrated that he's even listening to us in the first place."

"Who are the other committee members?" I reached over to the nearby counter to pick up a notepad and pen that I'd been using to jot down ideas for events while baking.

"Dodd Stimson," she began. "Who is a churlish son of a—"

"Nora!" Lucy exclaimed, but she was laughing as she objected.

"He is," my aunt said to me. "He's *very* opinionated."

"Unlike you," Lucy teased her.

"The difference is that *my* opinions are correct, darling." Nora smiled. "In any case, Dodd and I never seem to be on the same page about anything. Then there's Bethany Manzano, Katrina Andrews, and Farley Jennings. They're very dedicated to the cause. Able Holley, however, is on the other side."

Lucy made a face. "I don't know what he's saying half the time—"

"No one does," Nora said. "He's a genuinely confusing person."

I took notes as fast as I could. "How do you know the professors, Lucy?"

"I only know the ones who have come into the store."

"Well, there *was* that faculty party I hosted here back in the nineties," Nora said.

"We were babies then!" Lucy protested. "We don't remember that."

My aunt laughed. "Touché."

"I barely remember who taught the classes I took during college," Lucy admitted. "So many of them were in lecture halls that I never really got to know the professors."

"Same," I said. "And I've taken so many classes since then that they all kind of blur together, with the exception of the last program I was in."

"I understand," said Nora.

"Anyone else to add to the list?" I asked her.

She nodded. "Sorry. Prescott and Cornelia Abernathy are married. You'll never find two people less alike. I have no idea how they got together. Or how they stay together."

"Let's consider them one at a time," I suggested. "What do you think of her?"

"Cornelia's fine. A little woo-woo but gets the job done. Once she tried to institute a mandatory meditation session at the beginning of every department meeting."

"That might be relaxing," Lucy mused. "Maybe, at the bookstore, we could—"

"The professors did *not* go for that idea," Nora replied briskly. "And Prescott is wound tighter than a spinning top. Always asking for more data. Data, data, data. You know the type."

I finished adding the names and affiliations. "You mentioned that the committee was split. How did the division break down?"

"Able, Dodd, Prescott, and Tip were on the other side; Bethany, Katrina, and Farley were with me."

"How about Cornelia?"

"She was a swing voter. You never knew where she would land." My aunt poured more tea.

"Which makes her, in some ways, the most interesting," Lucy said.

"And the most important," Nora conceded.

"Were they all there last night?" I asked.

"Yes." She added some milk and stirred slowly.

"And what exactly were you arguing about? On the committee, I mean?"

The phone on the wall rang, and we jumped. You don't see many landlines anymore, but my parents had insisted on keeping one here and one at the bookstore. They had accepted the ubiquity of cell phones but weren't ready to give up the ones that had reliably connected them to the world for so long. The ringer had been set on high so that my father could hear it over the records he always played. The result was a knock-you-sideways volume that startled whoever was in the house no matter how many times we heard it.

We all clutched our chests, then Lucy jumped up to answer.

"We should really turn that volume down, Nora," I said, wondering why we had never addressed the issue before. Perhaps because it reminded us of our parents.

"The dial broke years ago. Not that Austen or Nina would let me adjust it anyway. I did try several times." She sipped her tea.

"We could always buy a new phone," I suggested. There were a million other ways we could—and did—honor my parents' memory without being jolted out of our skin every time it rang.

She snapped her fingers. "Now that's an excellent idea. Or maybe we don't need to continue to pay for the phone service here anymore, especially since we're trying to put every available penny toward the store these days. I'll look into options."

As my sister dealt with whoever was on the other end of the line, my aunt summarized the committee project for me. It seemed that she, along with the other professors in agreement, had proposed that the English department take over the currently empty top floor of the Arts and Humanities building.

It had originally been intended to serve administrators, but then a surprise donation to the college from an alum funded a new structure overlooking the river, and people threw tantrums—"There's really no other word for it," Nora clarified—until they were granted permission to move into the shiny construction with a better view.

The upper floor in the Arts and Humanities building was admittedly nicer than the rest, but English had long been crammed into the ground level, which had never been big enough to serve their needs in the first place. They had the highest number of instructors and nowhere to house them. So the department had made a plea for residence in the unexpectedly available suite of offices. The president agreed, and moving plans were under way, but when other departments had caught wind of it, they'd begun pitching the reasons why *they* should be allowed to move there, even though everyone knew the real reason was perceived status, not space requirements. The president became weary of the arguments and ultimately dealt with the problem by decreeing that no one would be allowed to move there.

For ten years, it had stood empty.

Nora and her colleagues had brought this to the attention of Tip Baxter several semesters ago, highlighting the absurdity of not utilizing the space, yet the more they talked about it, the more that strange things happened to the English department—budgets dried up inexplicably, hiring lines disappeared, and courses were scheduled in random locations across campus rather than in the usual classrooms.

"It genuinely feels as though we're being punished. I had to teach a studio in the gymnasium during the basketball team's practice hours," she said. "Can you imagine?"

"Wow. That must have been difficult."

"The students were good sports about it, no pun intended, and I suppose it could be argued that writing can be taught anywhere, but it wasn't the *best* situation, I'll admit. It was a bit loud."

"I can see why you'd . . ." I trailed off at the sight of Lucy's face when she returned. She had gone three shades paler and was visibly fighting back tears.

"We have to go downtown," my sister said. "The police want to speak to you again right away, Nora."

"What? Why?"

"Someone told them that you were the most likely suspect."

Chapter Four

I dropped my aunt off at the police station. Nora didn't want me to come in, saying that she didn't know how long she'd be there and would prefer to handle things herself. I'd just wished her good luck when I received a text from Tabitha asking me to swing by. Since she hadn't paid me last night, I was willing to do so, but there wasn't much else in the world that would convince me to enter her sphere of influence.

When I pulled up in front of her house, I left my car there. I didn't care if she came barreling out screaming bloody heck—I was *not* driving around to the back this time.

Tabitha opened the doors shortly after I pressed the button and stepped aside to let me in. I was shocked at her appearance—not because she was disheveled but quite the opposite: she was impeccably put together in a taupe sheath dress with matching headband. Not a hair was out of place. She looked as though she'd recently left the salon. Even her long nails had been repainted since last night in a new shade that matched her outfit. Was there anyone else who would go for a spa day the morning after her husband passed?

I chided myself. Maybe she was still in shock. Or denial. But I couldn't help but acknowledge how much I wanted her to display any shred of human emotion. Tip deserved to be mourned, didn't he?

"Thank you, but I don't need to come in, Tabitha. I know you have a lot going on. I'll just take the check and go. And I didn't have a chance to say this last night, but I'm very sorry for your loss—"

"Come *in*, Emma." She handed me an envelope that I tucked away in my pocket.

I stepped into the foyer and froze when I caught sight of several women in the library.

"Would you like to join us for tea?" Tabitha said, almost sweetly.

I scanned the room and recognized her closest friends clutching martini glasses.

That didn't look like tea.

I'd managed to stay away from them at the party, but there was nowhere to hide now. I straightened my shoulders and stepped into the library.

"As I live and breathe, is that Emma Starrs?" I'd have recognized that throaty laugh and drawl anywhere. Melody Crenshaw, who had always been a Tabitha wannabe, waved gaily at me from the center of the sleek leather sofa, in the precise spot where I'd sat when Detective Trujillo was going over my statement and not believing anything I said. Her expression hovered somewhere between a smile and a sneer, which brought back so many unwanted memories that my hands clenched at the sight of it. Flanking her were Ainsley Fowler and Felicity Edwards. The three women were artfully blonded the same shade and dressed exactly like Tabitha—simple but elegant dresses with matching headbands, though in varying hues. Melody wore a rich chocolate, Ainsley a muted yellow, and Felicity dark green.

They looked for all the world like Tabitha's backup singers.

"It's us! From school! Come sit!" Felicity, who had always been the kindest of the four, said in her breathless, high voice. Her large blue eyes and pink bow mouth reminded me of those old-fashioned dolls whose eyelids would close when you tilted them. Cute but vaguely unsettling. When I was little, someone had left that kind of doll behind at the bookstore. It had been in the lost-and-found box for almost a year when Lucy and I begged our parents to donate it because every time we went into the box, it scared us. The doll disappeared the next day, but for a long time afterward, I still expected to come upon it lying on the bottom of the box, staring up at me. It had imprinted itself deeply upon my imagination.

"Care for a drink?" Melody waved her cocktail around, interrupting my memories. It was a neon-pink concoction with a sword sticking out of it that held three cherries. "They're called Scarlet Bridesmaids and they're a bit lethal, but we wanted to help Tabitha get through her"—she lowered her voice—"*difficult time*."

"We invented them," Felicity squeaked, "when we were bridesmaids for Tabitha. We *didn't* wear scarlet dresses, though, so it's *funny*." She giggled, covering her mouth with her non-drinking hand, upon which were numerous rings that sparkled in the sunlight.

I declined politely. Tabitha shoved a glass into my hand anyway.

"Come *in*, Emma," she repeated. She took a seat on the sofa opposite Melody and patted the cushion next to her.

"Yes, *do*," Ainsley said, though it was clear she meant the opposite. She checked her diamond-studded watch so that I would know how much of her time I was wasting and rolled her eyes, which were a deep purple in homage to her favorite movie star, Elizabeth Taylor. I didn't even know what her actual eye color was, since she'd been wearing purple contacts forever. Not that I could ask her. Ainsley was the kind of person who didn't exactly have conversations with others—she sat back and inserted comments intended to unsettle.

I didn't want to join them, but I didn't want to be rude. My traitorous feet carried me forward, and I sat gingerly on the edge of the sofa, my brain attempting to plot a rapid escape.

"Tabitha tells us you're a party planner now. I didn't even see you last night. How fascinating. How long have you been doing that?" Behind her long artificial lashes, Melody's brown eyes had a calculating cast. She had always reminded me of a beautiful queen in a fairy tale, the way she carried herself. Her face was flawless—all four of them had that in common—and she held her chin slightly higher than everyone else. I could imagine her consulting with her mirror every morning, asking who in Silvercrest was the prettiest of them all.

I had the sense that I was being set up for something, but I didn't know what. To stall a response, I took a mouthful of the drink, then regretted it. Straining the ice-cold puddle of pure alcohol and sugar slowly through my teeth, which immediately began to ache, I swallowed carefully and set the glass onto the coffee table.

"I've been organizing events for the past few years," I said, which was true if you counted the work at school.

I counted it.

"Tell us *everything*." Melody performed one of her patented once-overs, starting with the top of my head and ending at my feet. Her eyes widened in horror at the sight of my clogs.

What *was* it with this group and clogs?

"Everything?" I ignored her judgmental scan and smiled pleasantly.

"You know, your work and your love life."

"Helping my sister run Starlit Bookshop. Not dating. How about all of you?"

They launched into their own updates: Melody, mother of twins, was married to Bruce, the CEO of Flashtown Digital, and did "gobs" of charity work; Ainsley was married to Clive, the manager of Silvercrest National Bank, and sold organic soap on Etsy; Felicity, mother of one, was married to Aston, senior partner at his family law firm, and volunteered for a pet rescue.

They must not have remembered that I knew their spouses—who had once been their high school boyfriends—because they all reported their statuses formally, in the same order: number of children if applicable, name and position of husband, then additional redeeming work.

Very Stepford, on the whole.

Maybe it was high-society protocol.

Not that I had anything against high society. Or even against the rest of the socialites in Silvercrest. It was pretty much just this group, with their history of unkindness to others, including people I loved.

After their reports, I was congratulating them on their lives when I felt a tap on my wrist. It was so light and quick that by the time I realized Tabitha had touched me, her hands were back in her lap.

"I have something to say," she said. "About last night."

"I'm very sorry for your loss," I told her again.

Tabitha maintained her glare without acknowledging that I had spoken.

I went on. "If there's anything I can do—"

"Us too! It's devastating," Felicity interjected. "We loved him *so* much!"

The other women followed suit with similar commentary, and Tip was lauded in various ways for the next few minutes. Tabitha pulled a handkerchief out from behind the pillow next to her and touched her eyes gently, even though there weren't any tears in them that I could see. Like a row of attentive birds, the other women began to flutter their hands and chirp comforting sounds in her direction.

"Obviously, you can't do anything about Tip. But I do think you owe me an apology, Emma." Tabitha was still dabbing away at her heavily made-up eyes, but she lowered the cloth in order to enunciate what came next. "For your behavior."

"What behavior?"

She went on as if I hadn't said anything. "You gave me such a hard time about the bell that I was *afraid* to ring it. That's standard practice here when we have parties, you know. And let's not forget that you were awful to me in the bookstore!"

"You mean when I offered to *help* you?"

"No, when you were being all condescending about books."

What? The way I remembered it, Tabitha had been standing in the middle of our family's bookstore denigrating books. But, I reminded myself, she was grieving. Maybe she was focusing on this because she couldn't deal with the reality of her situation.

"Obviously," she said, "you think you're *smarter* than I am."

"No, I don't, Tabitha."

"I would have let the bookstore go, but then you came *here*, to my own house, and acted all superior again. Why would you treat me that way? All I do is try to help people." Her voice grew louder and louder. "I mean, I'm *an incredibly nice* person! Everyone else *loves* me!"

I was fairly certain that her perception was not accurate.

The other three women burst out in a cacophony of support, their comments characterizing Tabitha as a very stylish saint. After getting her fill of that, she faced me. "Well, Emma?"

I didn't know what she wanted.

"Would you like to say that you're sorry?"

Not even a little bit.

Tabitha's expression was victorious. She knew she'd backed me into a corner in front of her friends. "I think you owe me that, at least. What is it they say, that the client is always right?"

Time to be at my most professional. Although I felt a flurry of counterarguments rising up, I squashed them down and apologized.

Quickly. Firmly. Like I was pulling off a bandage.

The others launched themselves off the couch and surrounded her to provide consolation—which they alternated with sending dirty looks in my direction. I stood and slipped out of the room.

Tabitha's voice followed me, sounding much stronger now. "By the way, Emma, I told the detective he should look closely at your aunt. I don't know what she had against Tip, but she's been *bothering* him for months. And I have my suspicions about *you* too."

I ignored the gasps that this pronouncement provoked and kept on walking.

* * *

"It was dreadful," I said to Lucy the next day at the bookstore. "I wanted to crawl under the coffee table. The only reason I apologized was in the vague hope that maybe Tabitha would still be willing to recommend Starlit Bookshop—and Starlit Events—to her contacts. But now I'm both humiliated *and* convinced that she won't be doing that anytime soon."

"I'm sorry, Em," my sister said, as she threaded a new roll of register tape. "Try not to worry about it. She needed to put on a show for her friends. Prove that she still has power."

"How is it possible that their disdain carries as much potency as it did back in the day? I'd forgotten how quickly they can get under my skin."

"I understand. Whenever I've run into them around town, I've felt exactly the same way. But we don't have to care about what they think anymore."

"We never *did* have to care," I said slowly. "Not ever."

"True, though not caring is easier said than done," she said. "But let's make a concerted effort to ignore them from now on."

"Deal."

Nora burst through the doorway that led to the office, arms full of paper. Her vintage tapestry bag was slung over one shoulder. It had a wide mouth when opened and was so large that one time I'd seen her pack a new teapot for her office, a slew of graded papers, and a fringed pillow—and she still had room to add her lunch. Mary Poppins had nothing on her.

"Hello, darling nieces." She set down a stack of papers on the counter and began sorting them. "Need to organize these copies—you don't mind if I spread out, do you?"

"Not at all. No one else is here. So you can tell us what happened. We're *dying* to know how everything went." Lucy flinched. "Sorry. Not the best choice of words, obviously."

"Oh, at the police station? Fine. I repeated myself ad infinitum." She rolled up the sleeves of her sapphire kimono jacket and shuffled pages. Once she had organized them to her liking, she began stapling the corners. "On my way home, I ran into Delilah and we decided to see the movie you recommended last week. You were right—loved the twist at the end."

We were both familiar with Nora's spontaneity—she often started out going in one direction and ended up in the opposite. Although we lived in the same house, we all came and went as we pleased. It wasn't like when my parents had been home, insisting that we eat dinner together every night. Sometimes we did, sometimes we didn't. And Delilah Stoneham, my aunt's best friend and agent, was always up to something interesting. Once, Nora had run into her on the street unexpectedly, and the two of them had flown to New York City for a week to binge on Broadway shows. Other times it had been a spa in California, a film festival in France, and a cruise in the Caribbean. Long story short: Delilah loved to spend her late husband's money.

"Did the police bring up anything new?" I asked.

"They did confirm the smothering theory, so your source was correct on that, Lucy." She stapled several packets, then made a single grouping and tapped the bottom of the pages against the counter to align the pile. "They wanted to know where I was after dinner."

"Is that when they think . . . it . . ." I couldn't bring myself to say the words defining Tip's passing. They were so final.

"The murder happened? Yes," Nora said. "They've narrowed it down to the window between finishing dinner and having dessert in the library. Remember how there was about twenty minutes during which we had coffee in the great room? Before I saw you in the hallway, people were coming and going. Some went to the powder room. Some went in search of a fresh drink. Some went out on the patio with Tip—" She stopped abruptly.

"Do you remember who?" I was practically tapping my foot. Maybe we could solve this crime right now.

Nora tucked a few flyaway strands of hair behind her ears as she thought. "No. I sensed people moving around, but I was having a spirited argument with Able and wasn't paying attention to anything other than refuting his absurd points."

"What were you fighting about?"

"The importance of moving to the top floor in our building," she said, picking up the papers and putting them into her bag. "Which feels like all I ever talk about anymore. In fact, I'm on my way right now to meet the committee members to discuss next steps."

"May I come with you?" I wanted a chance to talk to the other dinner party attendees. Now that the police had signaled interest in Nora, I felt compelled to do everything I could to protect her.

She snapped her bag closed and latched it. "We're going for drinks, so it's not like you would be crashing a meeting on campus. And if you become bored—the chances of which are very high—please feel free to wander away. Lucy, would you like to join us too?"

"No, thank you. I need to stay here. Max and Bella are coming in for a meeting." Our part-time booksellers were Silvercrest College students. Max Melendez was tall, dark, and quiet, while Bella Perkins was petite, blonde, and bubbly. Although they brought completely different energies to the store, they were both reliable and trustworthy. We had been lucky to have them on staff for the past two years.

"Everything okay?" Nora asked gently.

Lucy hung her head. "I feel like I should let them know that they might want to start looking for other jobs soon, if things don't turn around."

"Oh, darling, I'm sorry," my aunt murmured.

"Wait, though," I said. "What about Tabitha's big check? I deposited it this morning."

"Even with that, we may need to streamline. But thanks so much, Emma. It has bought us more time." Lucy's voice was calm, but she was wringing her hands.

"I'll try to drum up more business," I assured her. "There are so many writing organizations in Colorado—what if we reached out to their leadership about hosting more book launches and events here at the store? They could share the possibility with their members. And if you know of any book clubs—in addition to yours—you could invite them to meet here too. Perhaps we could offer a small discount in exchange to sweeten the deal."

She brightened. "I'll start working on that immediately."

"What can I do to contribute?" Nora asked.

My sister shook her head. "In addition to working in the store when you're not teaching or writing, you've provided financial support for years. And I *will* find a way to pay you back somehow. We would have closed long ago if you hadn't taken over the mortgage."

"No need," my aunt said. "This is a family business, darling, and I'm happy to give as much as I can. Unfortunately, it's not as much as you need to cover everything."

"I'm sorry," Lucy said quietly. "I can't seem to make the numbers work."

"Whatever happens, thank you both for all you're doing to keep this place alive." Nora gazed around, her expression softening. "It is *so* special here."

"It is. And thank *you*, Lucy," I said to my sister, "for picking up the reins after Mom and Dad retired. You're amazing."

Lucy's eyes glistened. "That's it. You two should go now. I'm about to start bawling, and it's not going to be pretty."

Chapter Five

Nora and I strolled several blocks to Bluestone, a restaurant just down the riverwalk. She led me by the dining room full of patrons at candlelit tables and past the long wooden bar, where there was not one available seat. The patio was also crowded. It was a cold night, but tall silver heaters kept the chill at bay. I followed Nora to a table, where two women and a man greeted her enthusiastically.

"Hello, all. Emma, these are my colleagues. All, this is my niece, Dr. Emma Starrs," she said.

"Congratulations on your PhD—did you find a tenure-track job?" the woman closest to me asked. Her auburn hair, a strong contrast to her pale complexion, was clipped short on the side while her bangs were angled over one eye. She had a textured cardigan over a beaded tank and wore thin silver bands in varying shapes on most of her fingers. Shimmering metallic earrings completed the look.

"No," I replied. I hadn't told Nora or Lucy about the one I'd turned down. They would have felt guilty, and that was the last thing I'd ever want. "I'm working at our bookstore right now."

"Right, the Starlit. *Love* that place. I'm Bethany Manzano, by the way, and I teach contemporary literature." She smiled at me. "Sorry about the job hunt. It's rough out there."

The African American woman sitting next to her waved enthusiastically. "Hi, Emma! I'm Katrina Andrews. Victorian lit." Katrina had long dark curls and wore a stunning teal brocade jacket over a silk blouse and diamond-and-pearl gold lavaliere. "Please order drinks! We're already on our third round."

"Farley Jennings, film," said the man across from her, giving me a jaunty wave. His blond hair was gelled into sharp points that resembled stalagmites over his deeply suntanned face, and he wore squarish black-rimmed glasses. His bow tie and perfectly fitted jacket suggested a more-than-casual interest in fashion.

"Nice to meet you, everyone," I said, sliding into an empty seat beside Nora, who had chosen a spot next to Farley.

Katrina turned to me. "Have we met? You look so familiar."

"I was at the Baxters' dinner party on Saturday," I said.

Katrina snapped her fingers. "Yes! Thank you."

"You didn't eat with us, did you?" Bethany asked. "I would have remembered."

"No. Tabitha hired me as an event planner. I was supposed to remain in the background. It's a new thing," I confessed. "Not sure that I have much of a future in it."

"Why not? That was a wonderful party," Bethany said, smiling at me. "Very elegant and delightful . . . well, until the end."

"Fabulous line of work," Farley said after a beat, skimming over the uncomfortable silence her last words had created. "*And* there's no grading."

The professors laughed, relieved at his attempt to keep the tone light.

I smiled at Farley. "Tabitha did bring me in for the murder mystery part, but Jacques planned the dinner proper, so kudos go to him."

He held up his glass and toasted the absent Jacques.

"If you don't mind my asking, what classes have you taught?" Katrina asked.

"Writing—both composition and creative—and various literature classes."

Farley adjusted his glasses. "What was your focus in graduate school?"

"Fiction, especially crime fiction."

All of them, except my aunt, murmured some kind of response. I couldn't distinguish what they were saying enough to know whether it was in approval or disapproval. People had always produced varying reactions to my professed interest in mysteries. A number of academics had proffered their opinion that the genre wasn't literary enough—a claim with which I wholeheartedly disagreed.

"Like your aunt," Katrina said cheerfully.

"What was the subject of your dissertation?" Bethany asked.

"We had the option of doing sustained creative work, so I wrote a novel—a traditional mystery—with a critical preface that analyzed patterns of conventions among women writers of the Golden Age as historical precedents."

Katrina nodded. "Fascinating."

"How ironic," Bethany said. "I mean you *wrote* a murder mystery, then you hosted a mystery dinner where someone *actually* was murdered."

We all stared at her.

"I'm so sorry. No idea why I said that." She pushed away her wineglass. "I should probably switch to water before the others arrive."

"It *is* an unfortunate coincidence," I said to her. "And who are the others?"

"The rest of the committee." Farley straightened his bow tie. "We came early to do some strategizing. And to stock up on some liquid courage."

"Oh, I've taken up too much of your time. Please strategize—I'll be quiet now. Or do you want me to leave? I can walk home."

They assured me that I was welcome to stay, then launched into a fast and furious discussion about pushing forward now that Tip wasn't blocking them, which basically involved going directly to the provost and president before the other side thought of it.

"Good evening," a voice boomed from the end of the table.

A tall woman with long salt-and-pepper hair and thick, uneven bangs was staring at me. She had layers of black clothes with a clump of crystal necklaces on top. Kohl rimmed her eyes, contrasting the powder that fashioned a rather ghostly pallor, and her lips were painted an unsettling dark shade that added a hint of vampire chic.

I felt unable to move, pinned in her powerful gaze.

Everyone around the table began to eagerly welcome her. She sat down in the empty seat across from me and folded her hands in front of her, armfuls of bracelets on both sides clattering. Like Bethany, she had rings on many fingers, but hers had a spider-and-skull theme.

"I am Calliope Nightfall, English professor and writer. And who are *you*?" Her voice somehow made me think of bats and moonlight.

Nora introduced me.

"Emma Starrs, the one who was working at the dinner where Tip Baxter died? I've been *wanting* to meet you. The universe has brought us to the same place for a reason this evening. I believe we are destined to work together."

"We are?"

"Because of the party."

I steeled myself for another mention of Tip's demise.

"It had an Edgar Allan Poe theme, I'm told. Poe's work has had a profound impact on my own writing," she said, pressing her palms together and shaking them skyward, as if thanking him. "Not straightforwardly—goddess forbid—but in my efforts to talk back to him. In fact, my latest collection of stories had their genesis in the enduring presence of Annabel Lee. You're familiar with the poem by that title?"

I nodded.

"The eponymous character haunted the speaker of the poem, and she haunts me. I don't mean Poe's wife, of course, or whoever Annabel Lee may be based upon, if anyone, which is arguable, as you know. I mean the *imaginary*—though no less potent for being in that state—Annabel Lee constructed within the world of the poem itself, if you follow me. *Divorced* from any potential biographical roots. I dreamed about her every night for a year—or I should say that I *sensed* her within my dreams, feeling around the edges of them, trying to get in. Eventually she took shape, was embodied, was born within my dream realm."

The waiter came up to take Calliope's order, and she waved him away. "I began writing stories at the speed of light. Faster than I've ever experienced before. They were simply *pouring* out of me. I wrote hundreds of them: long, short, and everything in between. All writing *against* the idea that 'the death, then, of a beautiful woman is, unquestionably, the most poetical topic in the world,' as Poe famously claimed. Annabel Lee and I *were* questioning, and we questioned until I was creatively spent!" She put her head down on the table. After a full minute of silence during which the other professors exchanged knowing smiles, she raised it again, victoriously. "But then I selected a collection of the very best of those tales and will soon share them with the world!"

I found myself applauding. After a moment, the Silvercrest faculty members joined in. The people at tables around us looked over curiously.

"Thank you for honoring my story." Calliope closed her eyes and took a deep breath, then regarded each of us in turn. When she got to me, she lowered her chin slightly. "It is—and I say this with all gratitude to the universe—my finest work. I have utterly *transcended* the author I used to be."

"Are all of the stories you wrote about Annabel Lee?" I asked.

She seemed perplexed. "No. Why would you think *that*?"

"Because you just said all of that—"

Calliope shook her head as if I were speaking gibberish.

"—about Annabel Lee."

"No, dear Raven."

Now it was my turn to be confused.

She pointed at my hair. "It's dark as a raven's wing. I have decided to call you Raven. My gift to you. You're welcome."

"Oh," I said. "Thank you?"

She had already begun speaking again. "Annabel Lee was my muse. Once I started writing—or perhaps I should say that once *she and I* started writing—the subjects that emerged were extraordinarily varied and vivid, though all of them obviously contested patriarchal limitations. Then again, many of the best stories were about her, so the collection as a whole *did* ultimately focus upon Annabel Lee herself."

"Ah."

She arched an eyebrow.

"Thank you." I concentrated very hard on not letting my tone go up at the end this time.

"My pleasure. And now I need you, Raven, to create a party—a lift-off, if you will—that properly celebrates this advanced level of work and sends it out into the world. Not just anyone can put together the appropriate tribute to my powerful act of literary resistance. Will you accept?"

"Do you have space in your schedule, Emma?" Nora asked. She used an encouraging tone, but I appreciated the way she was offering an out if I wanted to take it. She always had my back.

"Calliope, I should tell you that it was Jacques, the previous party planner, who made most of the arrangements for the last party." Seemed important to give credit where credit was due if she was hiring me based on the Poe flourishes.

"But you oversaw the execution. And you are *qualified*, if what I've heard about your educational background from Nora is true. Particularly your advanced studies and attention to mysteries. *Is* it true?"

"It is," Nora said to her, then turned to me. "I do talk about you and Lucy all the time, darling. I'm so proud of you both."

Heat rose to my cheeks, and I thanked her, then smiled at Calliope. "What sort of party are you thinking about?"

Calliope folded her hands in front of her again. "I have long been a fan of Starlit Bookshop. I believe that location would be appropriate. Would you be willing to host me there?"

"Yes, we'd be delighted." I knew Lucy would be thrilled to have a crowd attend an event and hopefully purchase many books.

"I'd like to invigorate my appearance though various aspects of decor. To illuminate familiar icons, then subvert them with my acts of resistance. To sever meaning through *my* new words written—or spoken—on top of his imagery. Would you be willing to imagine the necessary adornment into being?"

"Yes." I would untangle exactly what she meant by that later. "What date are you thinking?"

"Halloween, of course."

I should have guessed.

"My publisher and I believe that there is extra potency on that date."

"I'll double-check our calendar and come up with some ideas for your approval." I pulled a Starlit Bookshop business card out of my bag and offered it to her.

She took the card, which disappeared immediately into some hidden pocket among her many layers. "I *do* know that I'll require, at the very least, a flock of ravens and a heartbeat under the floor."

Not your standard party elements, but I could figure something out.

I hoped.

Chapter Six

After Calliope left, the others addressed the business they had come here to discuss. I listened to them finalize their plan, but more of my attention was on the deliciousness of the Cabernet Sauvignon that had been set at my elbow, thanks to Nora, while we'd been conferring about the party. The sounds of the flowing river water in the background worked some magic as well, and my shoulders started to loosen. But they tensed up again when I heard a familiar voice call my name. I considered not turning around.

Legally speaking, there was nothing impelling me to acknowledge someone, was there?

"Good evening, all," Tabitha said, coming up from behind me. She looked around the table at everyone else and smiled. The professors extended their condolences about Tip, and she accepted them gracefully.

"What are *you* doing here?" she asked me, with exaggerated surprise. "I didn't know you taught at Silvercrest. Or that you were on this particular committee."

"I'm not." That was as much as I was going to explain. I was allowed to have a drink with whomever I chose. "Are you on the committee?"

"I'm here to represent Tip's interests," she said. "Dodd invited me."

She stared at me in a *so there* kind of way, then moved down to the other end of the table, where she took an empty seat. A white-haired man in a baseball cap and sneakers incongruously paired with a baggy blue suit padded after her.

Nora shifted in her seat. I could tell that Tabitha being here to represent Tip was news to her. I could also tell that she wasn't pleased about it.

Another man in a brown suit topped off with a wide plaid necktie was next in line. He gave a brisk wave to the group and sat down without saying anything. Tall, with an ill-fitting toupee and exceedingly long sideburns, he had a used-car-salesman vibe.

A third man followed him, also in a suit—though his was dark gray and tailored. He had a short, pointy white beard and hair standing up every which way, as if he ran his hand through it constantly. He held his head at a strange angle—peering forward—like when your windshield is fogged up. His round wireless glasses were indeed thoroughly smudged, but he didn't make any effort to clean them.

Nora introduced me yet again. Over the next few minutes, I learned that Baseball Cap was Dodd Stimson, who specialized in Neoclassical literature; Plaid Tie was Able Holley, who taught Renaissance; and Pointy Beard was Prescott Abernathy, who was an expert in Modernism.

"And here's my beautiful Cornelia," the latter said.

A woman with long wispy brown hair joined us. She wore a loose floral dress with a crocheted shawl over her slim shoulders. "I teach Romantic literature. Hello, Emma."

I greeted them warmly. Although I knew that these were the members of the opposing team in this situation, I didn't want to make any waves during the discussion. I wasn't involved in the matter in the first place, but also I hoped one day to interview for a position at Silvercrest College. My aunt had started her career there the year I turned ten. I'd grown up hearing about—and admiring—her professorial work, day in and day out. The campus was right down the street from our house, and Lucy and I had spent many an hour frolicking around the grounds in our youth. Later, we'd attended the college as undergraduates. It had always been my dream to teach there, but there hadn't been any openings since I became qualified. Now that I was close enough to stroll on the green quad every day, it almost hurt even more.

My goal was to do whatever I could to help Nora but also to keep from crossing swords with any faculty members who might one day preside over a hiring interview.

Tabitha cleared her throat to draw the attention back to her. "Where are we with the committee work?" She was acting like she was in charge. I wondered why no one called her out on it. "How about a quick summary of the activities to date?"

"Gladly," Nora said. "A few semesters back, I raised the issue that the top floor of the Arts and Humanities building remained empty. English needs more space. This committee was convened last year to explore the possibilities. It seems like a logical idea to move us there—"

Prescott interrupted her. "We don't have *any* data to support that it is the best use of the space, however."

"What kind of data could you possibly need to show that it *is* or *isn't*?" Bethany asked him.

Prescott pursed his lips and ran his hand through his hair. "Well, there could be, you know, a location compatibility survey. A budget analysis. Things along those lines."

Bethany glared at him. "With all due respect, Prescott, we've been meeting regularly for a year, and you bring that up at every meeting. Why haven't you *done* any of those things, if you truly need such data? I'll tell you why: because you don't *really* care about it. You're using it as a way to stall progress."

"I beg your pardon," Prescott said, jutting out his chin.

"I think what my esteemed colleague is trying to say"—Dodd repositioned his baseball cap—"has to do with the viability of the move. It will cost money. We'll have expenses."

"In the short term, perhaps. But afterwards we'll have room for all of our professors and instructors," Nora said. "Who deserve it. And *we* have gathered some information that may be useful." She passed out the stapled packets, adding that the moving costs were actually minimal, as the budget analysis chart showed.

Farley turned to Prescott. "Your data, sir."

His comment carried the weight of a checkmate.

Prescott scowled as he flipped rapidly through the pages along with the others around the table.

"I still don't know why we need to change anything at all," Able said finally, scratching a patchy sideburn. "There are enough offices for full-time faculty members already."

"But there should be offices for *all* faculty members," Nora said. "Everyone who teaches requires space to meet with students, to prepare for classes, and to do intellectual work."

"Perhaps you don't want to give up your office," Farley suggested to Able. "I can understand that. You've been there for a long time and you're happy there. But perhaps on the top floor, your office will be better. You might be happier."

Able snorted.

"I can't even imagine packing up *my* bookshelf," Dodd said. "It's overflowing with tomes and has been precisely calibrated for maximum usage."

"I understand that too," Farley assured him. "But it doesn't seem like a strong enough reason to—"

"English has always been on the first floor," Able grumbled, crossing his arms over his chest.

"Why does that matter?" Katrina asked.

"It's *tradition*," he insisted. Dodd bobbed his head up and down vigorously, and Prescott jabbed his finger at Able as if he'd nailed the heart of the matter.

Katrina sighed. "Can you tell us, once and for all, why it wouldn't be better for the department to have more space? Specifically and one at a time, please."

Able clamped his mouth shut.

Prescott's eyes were unreadable behind the smudged glasses.

Dodd looked at the ceiling.

After a long silence, Katrina threw up her hands. "See? Can we get over the self-interest and do what's best for the department as a whole?"

All three men bristled at that.

"I'm sorry," she said. "But it's true. Someone had to say it."

Cornelia raised her hand. All faces turned to her. "Do we know why Tip was against the move? He never really said, but he did consistently vote against it."

Tabitha straightened up and gave us an unnaturally wide smile. "As Tip's wife, partner, and confidante, I know how he felt. For him, it didn't have anything to do with whether or not the space was necessary. It had to do with keeping the peace within the school of Arts and Humanities. Any department who moved to the top floor would necessarily be setting themselves up as targets of jealousy. It would have created long-lasting bitterness."

"So what?" Bethany asked. "There already *is* long-lasting bitterness on multiple levels. An empty floor is actually perpetuating the problem. It's been a decade. Everyone would get over it in time."

"*Would* they, though?" Tabitha asked, still smiling woodenly.

"Yes," Bethany said. "They would."

"Let's try looking at this from another perspective. What good does it do to leave the space open?" Nora pressed her. "The first floor could be converted to classrooms, and we always need more of those."

"The top floor could be converted into classrooms too," Able said smugly.

"But the first floor is *closer* to the other classrooms, which allows students better access," Bethany pointed out. "They don't have a lot of time to move from place to place between classes, as you know. And the top floor is set up perfectly for our needs already, so there doesn't need to be any renovation, which would save the school money."

"But the moving," Dodd whined. "I *hate* moving."

"It would be over within days," Bethany snapped at him. "And if it would make you feel better, I will volunteer right now to pack up your office *for* you. You don't even have to lift a finger. All of your possessions will magically appear in your new location."

Able snorted again. "Will you pack up mine too?"

"If that's what it takes," Bethany retorted, brushing her bangs out of her eyes. "And I'm not joking. I'll do it."

"What do you think, Cornelia?" Nora asked.

The department chair appeared highly alarmed at being put on the spot. Her face turned blotchy, and she put her hand to her throat as she replied. "I can see both sides."

"You always say that," Farley muttered.

"Come on, Cornelia," Bethany said. "Please consider how much better it would be for all of us. Plus, we could disband this committee and get back to our regular workload, which is already overwhelming."

Cornelia steepled her fingers. "Well, it's not like an affirmative vote will end this process. We still need approval from the new dean . . . whoever that will be."

"But," Nora said, "we will have completed the work of *this* committee, which was tasked by the department to determine whether or not to submit an official request. Anyone who doesn't want to be involved in the logistics of the move itself will be finished as of now. Let's call a vote. And please, no abstentions this time."

"I don't think that's appropriate unless we give Tip's vote to Tabitha," Able said craftily.

"What? She doesn't even *work* at Silvercrest!" Bethany exclaimed.

"She's here as Tip's representative," Able insisted.

"But she's *not* Tip," Katrina replied. "He may have been persuaded to see the benefit of the idea."

"At the dinner party, in fact, he invited me to meet with him privately," Nora said. "I had the feeling that he may have been changing his mind."

"Did he say *explicitly* that he'd changed his mind?" Prescott demanded.

"No," my aunt admitted.

"Then we should wait until we have a new dean in place," Dodd said smoothly.

"Why?" Farley stared him down. "So that you can keep blocking us? I'm over that maneuver. In fact, if you don't allow us to vote, I'm going to the president to complain. This committee has been stalled since the beginning. It's taken up a year of our time with no discernible progress."

"I dare you," Dodd said out of the corner of his mouth.

"You got it," Farley replied, matching his tone.

"Calling the vote." Katrina held her palms up. "Officially."

"Second," Bethany said quickly.

Katrina smiled at her. "All in favor of moving the English department to the top floor—"

Tabitha interrupted Katrina, fluttering her hands around. "I may not be able to vote, but I can deliver some important information before you do. Tip had a deep and abiding respect for all of you."

Her gaze fell on me. "Well, *not* Emma, since she wasn't on the committee."

Thanks for clarifying that.

"And *not* you, Nora. I doubt very much that your interpretation of why he wanted to meet was correct. In fact, he was exhausted by your obsession with this issue."

Nora began to speak, but Tabitha shushed her.

Big mistake.

My aunt fell silent, but I could sense her fury.

"It's very hard for me to see you sitting there like nothing happened," Tabitha said, pointing somewhere between the two of us. "I heard you and Tip arguing at the party, Nora. And it's not the first time—you've been pestering him for over a year now."

My aunt stood up and faced her. "Nonsense. We were discussing this very proposal. Not arguing. There was no pestering. Stop blaming me—"

Tabitha stood too, her chair rocketing backward. "I am going to *prove* what you did. Wait and see."

"That's enough, Tabitha," I said sharply, rising to my feet. "She—we—didn't do anything."

A circle of waiters had formed around our table and were staring openmouthed at the exchange.

"I think you'd better go, Tabitha," Nora said calmly. "You're not a member of this committee."

Tabitha sputtered. "Neither is Emma. Why does she get to—"

"That's not your concern." My aunt's voice was steely. "Good-bye, Tabitha."

"But . . ." Tabitha looked around the table for assistance, but none of the professors would meet her eyes. They might not have agreed with Nora, but Tabitha was not their colleague. Realizing that she had no support, she threw her napkin down on top of her plate and strode off.

She'd rolled in here sure of herself and her plan, but she'd just been schooled on the inadvisability of overestimating the solidity of her faculty faction. In academia, you never knew who—if anyone—was going to stand up for you when the going got tough. It wasn't necessarily the nature of the people as much as the corruption of a system that rewarded *winning* over doing the more difficult thing, time and time again.

Farley, Bethany, and Katrina made supportive sounds in my aunt's direction. I didn't know if Tabitha's accusations had landed—she hadn't overtly said "murder," but I had no doubt that she had been leading up to it.

"Let's take that vote," Nora said with authority. "Committee members only."

Nora, Bethany, Katrina, and Farley voted yes while Dodd, Able, and Prescott voted no. Cornelia didn't move when either option was called.

"No abstentions," Nora reminded her. "We need a vote, please."

Cornelia closed her eyes and thought for an extended period of time. It was so long that I was able to pay one of the servers standing near the table and still have a few minutes to wait in suspense with everyone else.

"C'mon, honey." Prescott nudged her arm with his elbow.

"No vote tampering!" Bethany exclaimed.

Cornelia's eyes flew open, and she said something.

"What was that?" Prescott put his ear closer to her face.

She spoke more loudly. "I vote yes."

Reactions from Dodd, Able, and Prescott ranged from moans to curses.

"I'm sorry, Pres," she said to her husband. "But it's the right thing to do for the whole department, and we need to move on from this committee work."

His mouth tightened.

The others didn't high-five or anything, but a sense of relief washed over the table at large.

"Anyone who would like to be involved in the logistics of the actual move, if the administration gives us permission, please email me," Nora said.

"I haven't forgotten your offer," Able sneered at Bethany. "Be sure to set up my office nice and neat, would ya?"

"With pleasure," she said, not blinking in the face of his contempt.

Dodd, Able, and Prescott gathered their things and left without another word, not even a good-bye. Cordelia gave us a little nod before she hurried after them.

"Are you really going to move his office for him?" Farley asked Bethany.

"I am. I can't promise that he'll be able to *find* anything in the usual places when I'm done, but his possessions will indeed be transported from one location to another."

They laughed.

Nora beckoned to me from the riverwalk. I hadn't even seen her leave.

Bethany whispered something that I couldn't quite catch but then made the phone sign with her pinkie and thumb and cut her eyes at my aunt. I grabbed my bag and followed Nora out to the riverwalk. "Bethany's going to call you. Or maybe she wants you to call her. In any case, she is interested in a phone call."

My aunt didn't respond.

I kept going. "Congratulations on the vote, but are you okay? I can't even *believe* Tabitha—"

"Nor can I," she said. "But could we please discuss it later, darling? I need to think."

"Of course."

We moved quickly and silently, and before long, I was appreciating the opportunity to release some of the intensity of the evening, sensing it dissipate like the small puffs of our breath busily curling up into the cold October air.

Chapter Seven

"Wow. Can't believe I missed *that*," Lucy said after I filled her in on what had transpired with the committee members the night before. Since no one was in the store, we were unpacking new stock. Anne Shirley had claimed the smallest box as her own and was purring contentedly as she supervised our movements.

"Oh, and I forgot—I have a new client! Please tell me that we can host something here on Halloween." I crossed my fingers.

"Yes. For whom? One of the professors?"

As soon as she heard the name Calliope Nightfall, Lucy clasped her hands together. "Are you serious? I love her stories. So unique."

"So is she, from what I could gather."

Lucy picked up the scissors and cut the packing tape on the last box. "I'm thrilled that you're doing these events, Em. I'd never be able to handle her myself. Whenever she comes into the store, I start fangirling, and it doesn't end well. The last time I wanted to tell her how much I had loved her latest collection, but somehow I ended up trying to sell her one of my favorite romance novels instead because I panicked."

"Did she buy it?" I pulled open the cardboard flaps and reached inside for a cluster of books, which I stacked on the counter so that Lucy could check them into our inventory system.

"No. She thought I meant the one I was holding in my hand, which was incredibly battered because I've read it a million times. I couldn't get the words out to explain that I didn't mean that *exact* copy, with the cover all ripped and falling off."

I laughed.

"But she did say I'd given her an idea for a character." She twirled the scissors around one finger, then popped them into the small ceramic crock we used to hold pens and utensils. "Though that may not be a good thing."

"I'm sure if you did inspire a character, it's a delightful one, Luce."

She shook her head. "It's probably someone who tries to sell a secondhand book to a famous author and ends up—considering that it's Calliope we're talking about—getting cursed, then has to travel the world trying to sell that book to anyone who crosses her path forevermore."

"That would make for an interesting tale, actually," I said, removing another bunch of books.

"Sure," Lucy said, then snapped her fingers. "Wait, I think I drew her." Lucy retrieved her sketch pad from a shelf under the register and flipped the pages over the spiral coil until she found what she was looking for, then handed it to me.

Calliope was standing in what looked like a clearing, her arms raised as if she were conjuring something. The moon was large, taking up half the background. All around her were fluttering bats.

I stared at Lucy.

"What? You're making me nervous, Em."

I tapped the drawing. "This is so eerie. I *swear*, when I met her yesterday, her voice made me think of bats and moonlight."

"Pretty spooky," Lucy agreed. "Though that is a *very* weird description of someone's voice."

"True," I said. "I didn't plan it or anything. My brain did it."

I set the pad down on top of the tallest stack and was admiring the image when the door opened and the woman herself walked in. Once again, she was clad in airy layers—a jacket over a vest over a tunic over a skirt—only this time, they were in murky gray tones.

My sister and I said hello.

"Greetings, Raven," she called out in her gravelly voice.

I shook my head slightly at Lucy as a warning not to ask.

"And greetings to you as well," she said to my sister. "It's your lucky day. I'm gifting you the name Romance based on our last encounter, which served as a catalyst for some *extremely* inspired writing afterwards."

Lucy blushed and thanked her. I detected a faint question mark at the end of her reaction too.

Calliope moved farther into the store. Eventually she was standing at the center, looking at the second-level mezzanine, which was a ring-shaped area open to the floor below. Bookshelves lined the walls on three sides, mirroring the downstairs. The front was all glass on both levels, with a wide strip in bright colors featuring a star design serving as a divider between floors. A spiral staircase in the back corner provided entry to the space, as did a small elevator tucked behind a wall that extended halfway across the room.

Calliope gestured upstairs. "Could we have skeletons along the railings there, all the way around? Perhaps in different positions?"

"We could. Or do you want to mix it up?"

She looked sharply at me. "Mix it up? How?"

"With other monsters, I mean. Like vampires—"

"You *do* understand that we're doing a Poe-specific party, not an everything-in-the-world-related-to-Halloween party, right?" Calliope stiffened. "Skeletons, to my mind, are often *implied* in Poe, if not actually seen, and I suppose you *could* argue for a certain level of vampirism, though that's more commonly associated with authors like Bram Stoker, and I don't want guests thinking about anyone *except* Poe."

"I see," I said.

"I'm not sure you do, Raven. Let me be clear. I want elements that are quickly recognizable to all, not only to those who have studied the entire Poe canon. Items must be selected precisely. The signaling of Poe at a glance—the immediate and unmistakable perception of him—is necessary to establish his presence, in order for me to accomplish his undoing. Without explanation."

"Understood," I said, though that may have been a teensy exaggeration. "Sorry about that. Poe it is."

Calliope dipped her head to indicate that she'd accepted my apology and drifted toward the back of the store, which was filled with rectangular tables and black parson chairs that could be moved into various configurations for larger groups or divided up, as they were now, for shoppers to use individually. She pointed at the wooden tables. "These will be piled high with my books at my launch party, correct?"

Anne Shirley went trotting past us, then nimbly leapt onto the closest table, where she settled down in the center to remind us that she was the true star of this group, the bookstore, and the whole world.

Lucy glanced at me. "We were planning to use some of them to set up a signing area."

I retrieved the composition notebook I used as a catchall from behind the register and hurried over to Calliope, inviting her to sit down at one of the tables. If she wanted to do a spontaneous planning session, I needed to jot things down.

Calliope chose the table occupied by Anne Shirley and made a kissing sound in her direction. She reached out a hand to pet her. Anne Shirley twitched her tail but maintained the same expression, which conveyed acceptance of the affection offered her but a disinclination to respond. "Perhaps we should discuss up front how much this will be costing me."

"What's your budget?" I asked, caught off guard and not wanting to make any financial promises before I knew all the details. Tabitha had taught me the importance of that, at least.

Calliope whirled to face me. I could almost see bats swooping around her head. "Raven, don't ask me what I *can* spend, tell me what you are *asking* me to spend."

"If I know what you are comfortable paying, I can tailor everything to keep the price within those needs. But if you prefer, we can talk about everything you'd like included, then I can research costs and provide you with a written bid before we go any further. A more specific approach might be better for both of us."

Calliope nodded briskly. "I'd prefer the latter."

Lucy said she wanted to finish unpacking books and, as she was heading to the back, glanced over her shoulder at me and performed an extravagant shiver.

I agreed with her assessment: Calliope was formidable.

"Let's talk more about the decor," I said.

Ignoring me, Calliope raised her arm so that her spider rings were all facing the center front spot of the upper level. "I will be reading *there*. I presume you have a spotlight?"

"We'll figure something out." Maybe someone could hold a flashlight above their head?

"And perhaps some dry ice. I know it can be tricky to handle safely, but fog would be properly atmospheric."

"I'll look into it." By which I meant *I'll tell you at a future time that it's not going to happen*. Hardly seemed like an ideal environment for the books.

I needed to steer us toward things that we *could* do for her. I opened my notebook to a fresh page, wrote her name at the top, then began a new list with the word *Skeleton*.

She peered over my shoulder and *tsk*ed. "Skeleton*s*, plural. A *dancing* ring of skeletons."

"Wait, you want them to be dancing?"

"No," she said flatly.

"No?"

"*No*. I was being *poetic*." Calliope seemed disappointed with my obtuseness.

"Thank you for clarifying. Could we please back up for a moment? I want to be sure that I understand everything you asked for when we spoke yesterday."

"Yes." She tilted her head graciously.

"Are you sure that you want ravens *plural*?"

She shrugged. "Why wouldn't I? They'll be magnificent."

I wrote down *Conspiracy of ravens*.

"Very good," she said approvingly. "You know your collective nouns. Did you know that you could also call them an *unkindness of ravens*?" Before I had a chance to answer, she sprang into a lengthy comparison of the two, finally coasting to a stop with the pronouncement that it didn't matter because ultimately *a murder of crows* was her favorite anyway.

I wondered why she wanted a group of birds in the first place, since there was only one in Poe's famous poem "The Raven." But since she'd nearly bitten my head off when I mentioned vampires, I moved on instead to the heartbeat-under-the-floorboards idea, about which she said only that I should use my ingenuity, so that was less than helpful.

Then she added that the refreshments would need to be thematically connected to Poe's writing as well.

I told her that I'd put something together by the end of the week and email her. She said that would suit her.

"I'm glad to be working with you," I added, which was true, even if it had been a tad bit bumpy finding our way so far.

"Likewise, Raven," she said, much more calmly. "And I thank you for listening carefully and honoring my vision. This event is extremely important to me."

"Of course," I said. "We'll be sure that it is special for you."

We were walking to the front of the store when she stopped abruptly next to the register. I realized that she had caught sight of Lucy's sketch.

Over by the display window, Lucy had the same realization. She reached her arm out, but she was too far away to accomplish anything.

Calliope studied the image closely. She tilted her head this way and that, squinted her eyes, and made a sound deep in her throat.

My sister and I waited.

"Who drew this? Is it supposed to be *me*?" Her voice had gone up several notches in volume.

Lucy swallowed hard and raised her hand.

Well, so much for hosting the launch party. I'd have to rustle up another job.

My sister went pale and swayed slightly.

Calliope touched the page. "May I have this?"

Lucy darted forward and carefully ripped the sketch off of the pad.

"Sign your name, please, in the lower right," Calliope instructed her. "I like to have the artist's signatures visible when I frame them."

My sister, dazed, slowly did what she was told.

"How much do I owe you?" Calliope asked.

"Nothing. It's a gift," Lucy whispered, holding out the paper.

"The universe smiles upon gift exchanges," Calliope announced as she took the sketch. "And I have already fulfilled my end of the bargain with your new name, haven't I? That works out nicely. So I'll just say *thank* you, Romance." She turned to me. "And I look forward to hearing from you, Raven."

We didn't dare utter another word until the door closed behind her.

"I like *your* new name better," Lucy said.

* * *

The next few days went by in a flash. I secured prices for an army of skeleton figures and a group of plush ravens that could be hung from the ceiling among the large star pendant lights that normally illuminated the space. Calliope hadn't specified *live* birds, though I was afraid that might be what she was thinking. Aside from the fact that there might be health or safety issues related to a live flock, we didn't want them around books that we were trying to sell, so it would be stuffed animals or nothing. Yes, it would rachet up the cuteness factor—more than, say, a taxidermy version—but they would be high in the air, so perhaps the overall effect, with the right lighting, could work.

Lucy recruited her friend Ryan Mahoney, who owned a theater in town and had worked every aspect of the business, including lighting. According to Lucy, he'd said that he would take care of the spotlight problem at the very least. It would be far better than my flashlight idea, though any rays in your face while you're trying to read from a book must be adjusted with precision.

That left the disembodied heartbeat-under-the-floor sound to tackle. A quick internet search yielded multiple sound files, so I downloaded and ran a few experiments with low speaker positions until I was satisfied that Calliope would approve. It was chilling, which I thought was what she was going for.

I reached out to Vivi Yang at Silver Blossom Catering and did my best to articulate Calliope's concept of incorporating Poe stories. After a great deal of brainstorming, we came up with a dessert-and-drink buffet menu, including House of Usher Madeleines, Rue Morgue Rum Cake, and Tell-Tale Tiramisu to be served alongside Black Cat Bellinis and Maelstrom Melon Martinis. Vivi's catering company was already booked that night for a full-service party, but she promised that she could deliver the food to the bookstore in the afternoon and even provide a few bartenders who could do double duty in a pinch, if there happened to be any dessert-related emergencies. I was impressed by her enthusiastic, can-do attitude and thanked her about a hundred times.

By Thursday afternoon, I had compiled the details in an official proposal. It looked pretty snazzy, I had to admit, especially after I'd added the store's shooting-star logo to the header. When Calliope agreed, I would formalize the orders and make some calls to ensure that her books arrived on time. We would order through the usual channels and follow up with her publisher in case they wanted to send along any marketing materials. Once during graduate school, an author had showed up for his reading with several life-sized cutouts of himself because he hadn't wanted to pose for pictures after the event. He'd left them behind for audience members to use for selfies and gone out for drinks with some of the faculty. You never knew what might happen.

I stared at the computer screen, wondering if Calliope would be happy with what we'd done.

"Just do it," Lucy advised, as she walked past the open office door. I hadn't said a word aloud, but no one knew me as well as my sister.

I took a deep breath and hit the button that would send the proposal hurtling through the ether to the unpredictable Calliope.

* * *

An hour later, Lucy came through the doorway. I was still sitting at the computer, updating the website to foreground the types of events we could offer to readers and writers.

"You know that ad you put online at the *Silvercrest Sentinel*? Well, someone saw it and called to say that he wanted to host his critique group here. He invited me to join, but obviously *I'm* not going to, since I'm not a writer. But you have that novel you wrote for your dissertation, right? All summer you talked about revising and sending it out. Perhaps this is the universe saying it's time."

Her words reached me through a fog as I tried to fix a spacing issue.

"Emma, did you hear me?"

I looked up. "Sorry. What did you say? The universe called?"

Lucy giggled. "Sort of." She repeated what she'd said.

"What was the person's name?"

"Oh, I forgot to ask. But the group is called West Side Writers, and they'll be here tomorrow night at six. You should join them . . . unless you have a hot date." She laughed as she walked away.

I didn't think the idea was *that* funny.

Chapter Eight

At six PM on Friday, I was seated at a table with Tevo Akina, a man in a purple fleece and matching beanie pulled down to his brown eyes, and Alyssa Clarkston, a red-cheeked brunette in yellow running gear. They both looked as though they'd come directly from vigorous activities and had a general air of outdoorsiness, which was pretty common in Colorado. We introduced ourselves as we waited for the group's founder and organizer. They'd moved here to go to college—Tevo was from Hawaii and Alyssa from California—and both ended up staying in town. They told me that they'd been working on their novels for over a year and were in the heavy-duty-revision phase. Another member had gotten a book deal and immediately disappeared; they'd never heard from her again. I detected a bit of sadness mixed with frustration in their account of her abandonment. The founder of the group, on the other hand, had already published two thrillers and he'd encouraged them, provided feedback, and helped them prepare to submit their work. Clearly, they adored him.

"Here I am, everyone. Sorry I'm late," said a deep voice behind me. I turned around to say hello and froze. The tall man with short, spiky brown hair and high cheekbones also stopped short when he caught sight of me. The dazzling smile he'd been displaying slowly slid away. Like Tevo, he wore a fleece jacket, jeans, and hiking boots.

"Starrs." His tone was cool.

"Hollister," I said frostily.

"What are you doing here?"

"My family owns this bookstore, as you may remember."

He grinned. "Yes, but I heard you were off somewhere getting yet another degree."

"Done with that."

"So you're visiting Silvercrest?"

I folded my arms across my chest. "No, I'm back now."

"I'd always thought you'd end up on the East Coast. Didn't you want to live there? You talked about it all the time in high school, if I remember correctly."

I was getting tired of having to explain to everyone why I was in my own hometown, so I turned around instead, only to realize that Tevo and Alyssa were watching us with great interest. They appeared to be confused about how their fearless leader and the newbie could have a history.

Join the club. Jake Hollister had always thrown me for a loop too.

"Glad you could make it." He took the empty seat next to mine and unzipped his black jacket, then pulled several manuscripts out of his backpack and set a pen down next to them. "Who's going first tonight?"

"Maybe we should explain our process to Emma," Alyssa said.

I threw her a grateful look.

Jake explained, without looking at me, that they swapped pages over email, printed them out in order to read and comment on them, then spent their meeting time discussing the work.

I was beginning to get the distinct impression that I made him uncomfortable. Which, in all honesty, didn't bother me one bit.

He had been a thorn in my side all through school. We both were serious about writing, and we never seemed to go very long without competing with each other in one way or another. Sometimes he won, sometimes I did. But the whole time, he exuded a level of seemingly unshakable self-assurance that somehow got under my skin. It, among other things, had prevented us from ever becoming friends, despite what we had in common.

He slid some pages over. "In case you want to read while we're talking."

I scanned them quickly. Tevo's chapter was from the point of view of a bear who had some strong feelings about the people who were renting a cottage for the summer. It was charming and strange and raised thought-provoking questions about the interactions between humans and nature. In addition, it had some definite Kafka-esque qualities that I was interested in hearing more about. As Jake asked Tevo about the metaphors, a guitar riff interrupted us.

The entire group twisted their heads around to identify where the jarring noise was coming from. It sounded as though we had been invaded by a rock band—and the sound kept escalating in volume.

I glanced over at the register, where Lucy stood with her hands over her ears. We made eye contact and I pointed toward the street. The music grew incomprehensibly louder still.

I raced out the front to the next store, which had been empty since June when the Candy Emporium moved down the street, and yanked angrily on the glass door. As I hurried inside, I was surprised to note that Jake was following me. No idea why.

Plastic sheeting hung from exposed beams, ghostlike in the dim light, and I could barely make out metal tracks on the ceiling. The volume of the music still playing was overwhelming. As the singer screamed out lyrics that had something to do with rage, I hurried across the room to the figure standing near the back wall, illuminated by a single bulb dangling from the ceiling. The broad-shouldered man watched me arrive.

"Could you turn that down, please?" I shouted.

He put his hand next to his ear to indicate that he couldn't hear what I was saying.

"Exactly," I said, then yelled the request again, miming the action of turning a knob.

He did something on his cell phone and it stopped.

The silence was so sweet I could almost taste it.

He tapped his screen a second time, and all the lights came on.

"*Thank* you," I said. "We have a bookstore next door, where we aim to provide a peaceful oasis for readers—"

"I know. Nice place. A bit sleepy for my tastes, but to each their own."

He looked vaguely familiar, but I couldn't place him.

"What are you doing here?" Jake asked from behind me.

"I'm turning it into a bar," the man said.

Yikes.

"Actually more of a live-music venue. Though of course on the other nights, we'll have a deejay."

Double yikes.

Jake introduced himself. After a pause, he added my name as well.

"Ian Gladstone," the man said.

Now I recognized him. Ian was one of Tabitha's exes. The most attractive of the bunch, if that sort of thing mattered to you. A longtime model with hair down to the middle of his back and a face like one of the heroes on the covers of romance novels. For all I knew, he'd actually *been* the model for half the books we carried.

I shook my head.

Focus, Emma.

"Let me show you around," he said excitedly. "I have the best designer, who came up with this industrial-loft vibe. We'll be able to configure this space however we want with movable walls. See them over there?" He indicated a collection of huge white slabs waiting to be suspended from the ceiling.

So that's what the track system was for.

"The bar is going to float too, depending on how we set things up. But we're going to put the stage here," he said, pointing at the wall next to our bookstore. I cringed. Our building was a standalone, but already we weren't far away enough to avoid the level of noise he was producing. "Or along there, maybe. Still working it out." He redirected his point toward a lone filing cabinet in the center of the back wall.

"Please use the latter," I said. "As I mentioned, our bookshop offers a quiet haven for readers. The wall facing our store will bleed far more sound into our space."

He stared at me. "Hadn't thought about that."

"Please, please *do* think about that."

"Emma, they'll add soundproofing," Jake spoke up. "So it won't be as loud as it was tonight."

"But that was on his phone—"

"And a speaker," Ian said. "Top of the line. Only the best for Hatchet."

"Hatchet?" I repeated.

"That's the name of my bar."

My spirits sank lower with every detail. I could just imagine us cheerily telling people that *yes, we're the bookstore right next door to Hatchet*.

I fought to keep my voice steady. "It will be ten times louder with instruments and amplifiers."

"It *will*," Ian said, clapping his hands. "It's gonna be *epic*!"

"Again, though," Jake said, "soundproofing will help. When will you be installing that?"

Ian didn't say anything. He looked happily back and forth between us.

Jake repeated his question.

Ian scratched his chin. "When we bought the place, we were told that it was already up to code and everything in that regard. So, y'know, we're good to go, far as I can tell."

I stared at him in dismay. "It may have been up to code to mask the sounds of *candy bars being purchased* at the last store, but it's *not* up to snuff for rock bands and bar fights!"

"Bar fights?" Ian's eyes began to sparkle at the thought. "That will be a legit milestone."

I couldn't believe what he was excited about. "How did you ever get the permits with such a repurposing of the space?"

He shrugged. "My business people take care of that. I'm the visionary and the guy who will run the operation."

I tried again. "Could we please be sure to find a way to keep the volume contained to your own space?"

"I think we're good," he said to me calmly.

"I am positive that we're *not* good." I didn't sound anywhere near as calm as Ian.

"Agree to disagree?" Ian added one of his trademark killer smiles.

Starlit Bookshop was definitely in another kind of trouble.

Chapter Nine

On Sunday afternoon, we approached the campus chapel, a somber trio in black. Nora and I had selected simple suits, and Lucy wore her usual long skirt and cardigan—though this time it was plain instead of her favored floral pattern. The area outside was dotted with groups of people speaking quietly. When the bells rang four times to mark the hour, everyone moved inside.

The stone chapel had a high, peaked ceiling. The wall behind the pulpit featured an exquisite stained-glass window with a flowering garden beneath a large sun. Smaller windows along the sides contained selected blossoms in close-up. Nora had mentioned as we walked over that the original windows with more traditional iconography had been vandalized since we'd been there for our parents' memorial. Administrators had replaced them with nature images in an attempt to make the space useful for as many faiths as possible. The result was striking.

All of the wooden pews were full, so we stood in the back for the whole service, during which Tip was lauded by his colleagues and family members. As I listened to their words, the sadness of his passing washed over me again. Although I'd met him only once, he'd seemed to be a kind soul, and his untimely passing brought on a powerful melancholy.

The organ played a final song, the notes echoing off the rafters. We waited for the ushers to help the family outside, where they would receive condolences, then followed the other mourners in forming a line, which began to move very slowly.

After a good long while, I suggested that we leave. Coming face-to-face with Tabitha was something I'd always tried to avoid, given her propensity for nasty commentary, but now that she'd voiced her suspicions about Nora and me, those feelings were compounded. I had no idea what she would say to my aunt.

"We're almost there," Nora said. "I have to pay my respects. He was my colleague."

"It's the right thing to do," Lucy agreed.

I stood there, fidgeting, until the people in front of us had spoken with the family and we moved forward.

I greeted Tip's family members, all of whom had spoken at the service, and followed my aunt and sister in expressing our condolences.

Then there was Tabitha.

The wind picked up as we moved toward her, and while everyone exclaimed something and clutched at their hats or coats, Tabitha just stood there, like she was a model at a photo shoot and her long blonde hair was being blown around on purpose. Like the forces of nature were there for her own personal benefit.

Nora spoke to Tabitha, who acknowledged her—barely—with a cool nod. It was the same with Lucy.

But when I went up, she took both of my hands. I hid my surprise at her gesture the best I could.

"Tabitha, I am so sorry—"

"Don't say another word to me, Emma Starrs. Not *one* single word." She squeezed until I yelped in pain and snatched my hands away. "I don't want your family here. Take your fake sympathy elsewhere."

She stared me down. Stunned, I didn't move. It wasn't until she cut her eyes to the next person in line that I was able to stumble away. It was as though she'd cast a temporary spell on me.

"What did she say?" my sister asked, when I caught up to them.

"She said she didn't want us here and that we should take our fake sympathy somewhere else."

"It may be the grief talking," Nora said.

"More likely the mean talking," Lucy countered.

"In any case, let's go." I wanted to get as far away from her as possible.

Just then, I heard my name being called in a perky kind of way. When I turned, Felicity was waving at us. My aunt and sister accompanied me over to where she was standing with Melody, Ainsley, and their husbands. The women had identical black sheaths and the men wore black suits. They were in a U shape, so we closed the circle when we approached.

I was wary but undeniably curious. Last time I'd seen them, they'd been shooting me death glares from Tabitha's couch.

"Are you going to the wake at the Baxter house?" Felicity said, smiling brightly. She and Aston were holding hands. Brown-haired with horn-rimmed glasses, he looked every bit the lawyer that he was.

"I don't think so," I said.

"It's being catered," she replied, as if that made a difference. "I'm sure Tabitha would love for you to come."

Only to humiliate us, I was sure, but I didn't know if Felicity meant that.

"Thank you, but we have plans," Nora said.

They didn't need to know that our plans were basically to do *anything* else.

Beside me, I could hear Bruce and Melody talking.

He was an ex–football player with sandy blond hair and nearly translucent blue eyes who still looked as though he could take the field at any moment, an impression helped along by the championship ring that he wore. He had his arm around Melody, whose eyes were brimming below her impossibly long lashes. "I can't believe he's gone," she said, sniffling.

"It's a genuine loss," he agreed. "Tip was a great guy."

"Change of subject," Clive barked. "Can we talk about the proposal?" A dark-haired, loud, and jittery person, he was on our right. He was not comforting Ainsley, who didn't appear to need comforting. She was surveying something over Melody's shoulder with a bored expression.

If Tabitha was icy, Ainsley was glacial.

"Proposal?" I asked, confused.

"Clive's bank is helping Bruce's company fund some project," Melody said. "Nothing exciting."

"Hey now," Bruce said. "It's exciting to *me*. Matter of fact, we have a lot of exciting things going on right now."

"What's your company?" I asked.

"Flashtown Digital. You've heard of us, I'm sure."

Before I could confirm or deny, he launched into a long list of corporate clients in alphabetical order by company name. When he switched to primary opportunities and strategies, my attention wandered. He didn't seem to notice, however, dispensing more information than I'd ever be able to absorb about data-driven solutions, boldly executed deliverables, and optimization of metrics. He bragged about making multimillion-dollar deals, expanding branches internationally, and donating money for a training institute that would prepare students for what he called the endlessly lucrative world of digital media. After waxing poetic on harnessing the vast potential of intentional synergies, whatever that meant, Bruce wrapped up his impromptu presentation by asking me which one of his company's projects intrigued me the most. I told him that they all sounded interesting and added some overly enthusiastic nods to make up for my lack of specificity.

When it became clear that no further praise was forthcoming, his eyes flicked away and he began talking animatedly to Clive. Aston threw us an apologetic smile, then stepped over and joined them. One of them mumbled what sounded like "tornado power," which prompted some kind of chant. It reminded me of walking past a fraternity house and catching a random thread of some inexplicable ritual through an open window.

Melody threw up her hands. "Well, we've lost them. How does Tabitha seem to everyone? I'd say—"

"Sad," Felicity said.

"Angry," Melody continued.

Ainsley yawned.

"What do you mean by *angry*?" Felicity asked her friend.

"Why wouldn't she be? Her husband's dead. She doesn't know who killed him. Though she does have her suspicions." Melody tilted her head toward us.

"We didn't kill Tip," I said. "You know that."

Ainsley rolled her eyes.

"*I* believe you," Felicity said. "But you understand that we have to be supportive of our friend, especially in her time of need."

"*Felicity!*" Melody exclaimed, sounding shocked. "Tabitha is *not* going to like that."

"Don't tell her then," Felicity said lightly, then her smile disappeared in the face of Melody's obvious disapproval. "I was only kidding anyway. I believe *whatever* Tabitha believes, I promise."

The other two women turned and walked away, and Felicity followed them, her tone growing increasingly desperate. "I'm super sorry! Please don't tell her. Ladies? Don't tell her, okay?"

We watched them go.

"Wow," my aunt said under her breath.

"Tabitha really has them all under her thumb," Lucy observed.

"I don't know why she has so much power over them." I watched Felicity scampering after them.

"Old habits," my sister suggested.

"Dynamics like that can be hard to change," Nora agreed.

"Why wouldn't they stand up to her?" Lucy asked. "Real friends tolerate different points of view."

"Not toxic friends," I said.

We walked across campus and turned onto River Street. Businesses along the main drag had decked themselves out for Halloween, as we'd done at Starlit Bookshop. There were witches, monsters, and ghosts on window clings, in store displays, and hanging from rafters. The town council had approved festive touches like black garlands wound around the old-fashioned streetlamps, twinkle lights in the potted trees, and huge planters full of orange chrysanthemums at regular intervals.

The wind picked up again and sent the leaves skittering past us. The smell of kettle corn hit us in full force as we reached the Candy Emporium, a store that had been our next-door neighbor for years but had recently moved into a larger location when it became available.

"Let's stop in and see Phoebe," Lucy said.

We walked into the sweet shop, the bells hanging on the door announcing our presence. It was overwhelmingly cute inside: the walls were painted a cheery yellow and depicted happy unicorns with rainbow manes and tails who, apparently, loved to eat. There were unicorns eating ice cream, unicorns eating popcorn, and of course, unicorns eating candy. The shelves themselves were bursting with treats.

A woman wearing a polka-dotted apron set down the glitter she'd been sprinkling into a gift basket. I'd forgotten how much Phoebe Hansen resembled popular depictions of Mrs. Claus—she was round, white-haired, and beaming. Nora said hello, then wandered over to a display of teapots spun out of sugar.

"Hello, girls," Phoebe said. She always called us that, as if we were still in pigtails coming in to blow our allowance on candy.

"How are you?" Lucy asked her. "I haven't seen you since the grand opening. Things going well?"

"It's been terrific. The only thing I miss is seeing you every day." She smiled sweetly.

"Aw," Lucy said. "Same."

"How's the new neighbor?"

"Ugh," I said.

Phoebe tilted her head, an unspoken question.

"Sorry. I shouldn't have blurted that out. But I had a run-in with him yesterday, and I'm still seething."

"What happened?" She slid a sheet of rainbow-tinted cellophane beneath the basket and pulled it up on all sides so that the gift was fully wrapped.

"Do you know the new owner?"

"I only dealt with the leasing office, so I'm not sure who took over."

"Does the name Ian Gladstone ring a bell? He used to be married to—"

"Tabitha Baxter," Phoebe said as she tied a ribbon. "Yes. I know who he is. Good-looking fellow."

"Guess what he's doing with your old store space?"

"Opening a salon?" We must have looked confused, because she went on to clarify. "He appears to spend a fair amount of time working on his hair. I thought he might have some expertise in that area."

"I wish," I said. "He's transforming the space into a live-music venue. And he's naming it Hatchet."

She gasped. "Oh no. How ghastly."

"Exactly," Lucy said.

"I suppose, with a name like Hatchet," she mused, "it won't be classical music we're talking about."

"It will not." I sighed. "There hasn't been a single band there yet, but he's been blasting music during construction, and it's already so loud that we can't think straight."

"Is that what your confrontation was about?" she asked me, tucking a delicate plastic blossom into the bow as a finishing touch.

"Yes. It's a serious problem. I don't know what we're going to do."

"Perhaps there are zoning restrictions for noise. You could look into that."

"He assured me that his permissions were in order."

"Well, I don't like to be a gossip"—she leaned forward, her eyes dancing—"but there *have* been numerous rumors about Ian Gladstone and his business dealings before. Nothing I know for sure. Nothing I could prove. Yet rumors exist."

I leaned forward too. "About what?"

"Choices he's made. That's all I can say."

"C'mon, Phoebe. Tell us," my sister begged. "You know more about what goes on in this town than anyone else."

"That's certainly not true." Phoebe winked at her.

"I'm pretty sure it is," Lucy said, winking back.

"Anyway, what can I interest you in today?" Phoebe opened both arms to indicate the delights awaiting us. "Remember that Halloween is around the corner. Have you stocked up for the approaching legions of adorable trick-or-treaters ahead?"

"Excellent point." I picked up one of her signature bags, which had always reminded me of peppermints with their red stripes on the white background.

She returned to her basket preparation while we strolled down the holiday aisle, where she had set up plastic cauldrons full of candy corn packets, miniature chocolate bars, and other goodies. We added items to our bags until they were overflowing.

When Phoebe was ringing up our purchases, my sister gushed over her sales skills. "I stopped by to say hello, and look at all of this that we're leaving with! How do you do it?"

"The kettle corn aroma is a powerful lure," I said. "Made me want to come straight inside."

"Oh, did you want some kettle corn too?" Phoebe asked.

"Yes, please," I said.

My sister laughed. "See? You just did it again. You should offer lessons. What's your secret?"

"Power of suggestion," Phoebe said, adding the popcorn to my pile. "By the way, Ian goes to the Business Owners Organization meetings. There's one tomorrow night, in case you wanted to see him in action for yourself."

Chapter Ten

"Hurry," Lucy said, quickening her pace. "I don't want to walk in late."

I sped up, and we made it into the community center before the man standing at the podium up front slammed down his gavel. As the sound ricocheted around the room, my sister slid into the last row, where only two chairs remained, and pulled a pen and notepad out of the yellow purse that matched the flowers on her dress. I sat down next to her.

"Welcome to the quarterly meeting of the Business Owners Organization," intoned the gavel-wielding man, who sported slicked-back waves of jarring neon-orange hair. "It is now time to begin. Please note in the minutes that it's Monday, October eleventh. As you know, I'm Davin Mulligan, BOO president and owner of Mulligan's Department Store."

"BOO?" I whispered to Lucy. "Now that's funny. Especially in October."

She frowned and put her finger to her lips. My sister wasn't one for making snarky remarks during events—something I was all *for*, officially. Perhaps she was remembering that once we'd laughed so hard while watching a play here at the community center that we'd been escorted out by Ms. Brill, our elementary school principal, who had taken it upon herself to ensure that her pupils always behaved, no matter if they were in school at the time or not. Lucy had never forgotten the horror of being marched out in front of the whole town, especially since Ms. Brill had decided to steer us by grabbing one of our ears.

I had never attended a BOO meeting before, but it only made sense that we'd take up the practice for Starlit Bookshop. Lucy had not been very keen on joining, which would add meetings to her already busy schedule, but after the nudge from Phoebe, she'd agreed to let me fill out the paperwork for membership online this morning. Networking was always a good idea, especially now that I was trying to get the event planning off the ground. And Phoebe's suggestion to see Ian in action was intriguing.

Davin droned on for a while, approving the minutes from the last meeting, which apparently was controversial because it continued for about a half hour while different people moved to amend this or that. Either the BOO members were engaged in something political to make a point that we didn't know enough about to recognize or they really needed to find a new person to produce the minutes; from what I could gather, practically every item had been recorded incorrectly. The secretary kept rubbing his eyes after he scribbled down each change, as if he couldn't believe what he was being forced to do.

As they battled over grammar and contrasting recollections of what had been discussed last time, I contemplated the familiar room. The meeting space was big enough to comfortably hold the entire group of about a hundred people and could have handled many more times that, if the partitions had been opened—they were usually closed, since the community center ran an ambitious schedule of workshops and programs that needed housing. Large silver fans hanging from the high ceiling churned the air slowly. Through the tall windows in the front and across the street, the river was barely visible. Someone was fly-fishing, and I watched the way the rod moved back and forth, dancing through the air, until I was almost mesmerized.

Finally, there was a motion to vote again for approval, and the minutes passed.

"Maybe they should *record* the meetings and transcribe them," I said to Lucy. "Should we suggest that?"

She gave me a horrified look. Through gritted teeth, she whispered, "Do *not* make a scene."

I'd never thought of myself as someone who made scenes. It was true that I'd sometimes found myself in the middle of one, but it was never intentional. Filing her comment away for future examination, I made the gesture for locking my mouth and throwing away the key.

Her shoulders relaxed.

"On to new business," Davin said. "I'd like to welcome our new members. Please stand when I identify you." He rattled off a list of names, and one by one, the individuals stood and received applause. When he recognized Lucy and me, we rose as well. The entire room of people swiveled in their seats and stared at us, clapping hard.

We awkwardly bobbed our heads in gratitude. And then my eyes met those of Tabitha Louise Saxton Lyme Harmon Gladstone Baxter. Her eyes locked onto mine with the concentration of an animal watching its prey, and the smirk slowly spreading across her face did not bode well. Melody, Ainsley, and Felicity were next to her in the front row, and it only increased my concern to note that all three had expressions of gleeful anticipation.

Tabitha lifted her arm, and I watched, helplessly, as she extended it in our direction and pointed. "Emma Starrs should not be here! Does this group really want a *murderer* in their ranks?"

Lucy exhaled hard, like her breath had been knocked out of her.

Everything went into slow motion—the faces that had been beaming sunshine at us a second ago turned to stones. The buzz of audible reactions grew more menacing, like a swarm of bees approaching.

Davin banged the gavel until the room was quieter, though I could still hear whispers. To my dismay, Tabitha stood and began moving down the aisle toward us. Heads turned in concert with her slow creep. Davin called out for her to sit down, but nothing could have stopped her: she'd been training for this moment for years. All of her digs, snide comments, and sabotages were nothing compared to what was about to happen. I knew it in my bones.

My heart beat faster, and I began to scramble up, but Lucy's grip on my forearm kept me where I was. As Tabitha narrowed the space between us, her eyes shone triumphantly. When she was about halfway down the aisle—in the exact center of the room—she raised both hands. Davin even stopped banging the gavel, probably as curious as the rest of us to hear what she would say next.

"I'm so sorry to interrupt, everyone. But as you all know, my beloved husband Tip was recently killed." She bowed her head, and sympathetic murmurs flowed. Eventually, Tabitha lifted her head and aimed a sad smile around the room. "What you don't know is that Emma Starrs and her aunt Nora are *primary suspects*."

This time, I did rise and stepped out into the aisle. "Stop—"

Tabitha whirled around and addressed the people near the front, attempting to ensure participation from every direction. "You are aware that Nora Haven is a famous *author*, aren't you?"

The crowd began to nod. Of course they knew. Nora had written thirty mysteries. In Silvercrest, she was treated like the rest of us—she'd lived here long before her books came out, after all—but whenever we went somewhere else, there was a good chance she would be approached by fans asking for autographs and pictures. She had achieved a certain level of celebrity.

"Well, I'm sure many of you have read *A Refined Taste for Murder*? In that book, a wealthy man is smothered to death during a dinner party. Exactly like my Tip."

There were audible gasps. An icy sensation crawled up my spine. I hadn't even *made* that connection.

"What's more, Emma Starrs here invited herself to take over the dinner supervision after my precious Jacques had to bow out due to a family emergency."

Precious Jacques? What happened to never-going-to-work-in-this-town-again Jacques?

"She pretended to be a party planner and wheedled her way into my home *just* in time for the dinner . . . which her aunt Nora was *also* attending! Now if that isn't suspicious, I don't know what is!"

There were even louder gasps this time.

"What do you have to say for yourself, Emma?" She put both hands on her hips and glared at me.

"*None* of that is true. Not *one* word. Except that I am a planner focusing on literary events . . ." I trailed off, alarmed by the way my defense was starting to sound as though I were squeezing in an advertisement.

Lucy came over to stand next to me. "Hi, everyone. This is a big misunderstanding. No one in my family is a murderer. I think Tabitha is looking for answers—"

"I *have* answers!" Tabitha said. "I just gave them to you!"

Lucy ignored her and continued speaking calmly to the crowd. "I'm sure the truth will come out soon. But in the meantime, please remember that you *know* us. You know my family. We're your friends, and we would never—"

"You're not *my* friends," Tabitha said. Her tone seemed more off-putting than usual, an assessment that was confirmed when BOO members began to smile at Lucy instead.

Sensing defeat, Tabitha pulled out all the stops and covered her eyes. Her shoulders began jerking as if a puppet master were pulling strings. Not very convincing, but Melody, Ainsley, and Felicity scurried down the aisle from the front and led her back to her seat, cooing over her.

Lucy tugged me toward the door. "I begged you not to make a scene," she said, her lips trembling.

"Blame Tabitha for that one."

"That was the *last* thing I wanted to happen, Emma."

"I'm sorry—it was awful, and I know that was upsetting. But why was Tabitha there, anyway? She doesn't have a job, right?"

She sniffled. "Not as far as I know. She does charity work. Maybe it overlaps."

"Maybe. And she did show up at the committee meeting at Bluestone, supposedly to stand in for Tip. Perhaps she's taking over something else for him. Did he own another business on the side in addition to being the Silvercrest College dean? Here, I mean, in town. Tabitha already mentioned that he owned a resort in Bali."

Lucy thought about this. "I haven't heard anything about that, but Nora might know."

"Speaking of Nora, she's not going to like Tabitha using her book as evidence."

"Do we have to tell her about the accusation? She'll be so upset."

"Yes, we do. But Luce, I have to say, Tabitha bringing that up in front of everyone may not have delivered the knockout punch that she thinks it does."

"Why not?"

"Because it proves that *she herself* was familiar with the method in the book. The same method that was used on her husband."

Chapter Eleven

"Why don't I talk to Nora?" Lucy said at Starlit Bookshop later that night. "It's almost closing time. If you and Max can take care of the cleanup, I'll call her right now."

I agreed. Max, ever the studious sort, shut the book he was reading behind the register, then picked up the broom and dustpan from the closet. He came toward me with a shy smile, and I pointed at the second level.

"Could you please start up there? I dusted all the shelves earlier today."

"Got it, boss," he said. His thermal shirt had a grizzly bear on it; the fierce image was a direct contrast to Max's quiet, gentle nature.

"*Emma* is fine," I suggested for the millionth time. He seemed to like calling us *boss*, but I wanted him to know that he didn't have to, so we often repeated this exchange, even though neither of us changed anything.

Once he had been dispatched, I picked up supplies and headed over to the display case. We had selected a monster theme for the upcoming holiday, with books ranging from Mary Shelley's *Frankenstein* to Stephen King's *It*, as well as a plethora of picture books with friendlier specimens on the cover. I dusted the books and repositioned a few of the smiling zombies, ghosts, vampires, werewolves, and the like to make space for the easel, upon which I propped a sign announcing Calliope Nightfall's book launch party.

She had agreed to the proposal and signed the standard contract that my parents had used for readings, adapted to include costs for the decorations and food. I'd been so relieved to find their contract with its careful boilerplate language already in the computer. They'd covered things I hadn't even considered, like what happened in the case of cancellation. Thank goodness.

I went outside and examined the display from the street. Everything looked fine, and I felt a small lifting of spirits. If this went well, perhaps we could draw in more authors. Calliope's publicity person, Mavis, was spreading the news far and wide, she said, which would help raise our profile in the writing community too. So far, so good, though Calliope peppered me with new ideas daily. The latest had me searching far and wide for a "life-sized replica of a pit and a pendulum."

Deep in thought, I was startled when someone said my name and was even more surprised to see that it was Jake standing in front of me. Instead of the fleece-and-jeans combo he favored, he was wearing a dark suit and tie.

"Are you going to a banquet or something?"

"What?"

I gestured to his formal wear.

He looked down. "No, it's for work."

"I thought you were a novelist."

"I am."

"But I heard that wearing pajamas to work was one of the perks."

Jake laughed and gave the store a once-over. "You know, I'd forgotten how impressive this building is. Love the gray stone. And I have always meant to ask—who did the window?"

I followed his gaze above the display window to the strip of colored glass that ran the length of the building. The whimsical design featured a row of stars in an elaborately scrolled frame and included all the colors of the rainbow in one way or another. It paired well with the shooting-star logo carved on the front door.

"My father created it," I said. "During his stained-glass phase."

"I had no idea. There are so many artists in Silvercrest. I figured that your family had it commissioned."

"They did, in a way. They commissioned my dad."

Jake laughed. "The artist they knew best."

"He didn't take any money for it, of course. But he always said it was his favorite piece because there are seven stars, one for each family member who worked in the store. Lucy and I were kids when he made it, but we were already doing what we could to help out. Sometimes they'd ask us to draw pictures, which our parents proudly hung all over the store. We took most of those down once we were teenagers, though now I wish we hadn't. Oh well. Live and learn."

"You said there were seven of you?"

"Yes." I held up fingers as I counted. "My grandparents, parents, sister, aunt, and me."

Jake gave the window another appreciative look. "He was very talented. And Emma, I'm sorry about your parents. I know it happened a while ago, but I never had the chance to tell you. They are very much missed—people talk about them all the time around here."

My throat seemed to close up. I couldn't even get the words out to thank him. It never failed to surprise me how grief could take over so suddenly and completely sometimes, even in situations you'd handled many times before.

I nodded instead.

Jake asked if we could go inside.

"We close in a few minutes," I told him. My powers of speech had returned, along with a sense of bewilderment that I was opening up on any level to Jake Hollister in the first place.

"I'll make it short." He pulled open the door and waited for me to go in first.

I glanced down the sidewalk before I moved and caught sight of Tabitha walking into the building next door. She was immersed in whatever was on her phone screen and didn't look up, so I scurried quickly inside.

Hopefully she hadn't seen me.

Jake followed. "What was that about?"

"Suffice it to say that Tabitha is not my favorite person."

"Still up to her old tricks? That's unfortunate."

"Always."

After a beat, he asked if we could sit down at one of the tables in back. I sighed and walked down the aisle, but I couldn't imagine what the two of us might have to talk about.

He chose the same seat he'd been in when we'd met the critique group, and I sat down across from him.

"What's going on, Jake?"

He rubbed his chin. "I need to ask you some questions."

"About what?"

He shifted in his seat. "First of all, are you joining West Side Writers?"

"I don't know if I have time to write."

Which was a lie. I knew very well that you had to *make* time to write, but I wasn't sure I wanted to sign up for any further intentional interactions with him.

"Well, you're welcome to do so. It's a good group. Tevo and Alyssa liked you and asked me to convey that you were invited to become a permanent member. We've auditioned a bunch of people."

"That was an audition?"

He grinned. "It's hard to find the right blend of personalities, and they thought yours would work well."

"That's very kind; thank you. I'll think about it. So if that's all, I need to get back to—"

He reached into his pocket and removed a rectangular black notepad and a pen and set them on the table.

"That looks like—"

Then he pulled out a badge that had been hanging around his neck but was hidden beneath his tie. "Detective Hollister, at your service."

I stared at him. "*Detective*?"

"Newly promoted," he said with a grin.

"But I thought you were a novelist."

"I'm both," he said simply.

Something clicked inside me, that old competitive spark that Jake always ignited. If he could write thrillers while working full-time as a detective, I could revise my novel while working at the bookstore. A sense of resolve emerged from whatever space within my psyche where it had been hiding. I *was* going to revise my novel and submit it, no matter what. Plus, I knew Nora could help me figure out the next steps and would be glad to do so. She'd been offering since the very first time I'd told her I wanted to be a writer too.

I sat up a little straighter.

"What's going on over there, Starrs? You look like you just won a prize." He chuckled.

I rolled my eyes.

When I didn't explain, he shrugged and flipped open the notepad. "I'm actually here on official business."

"*Official* business? As opposed to the business in which we are engaged right now?"

"Seriously, Starrs, I have to ask you some questions." His tone was solemn.

"Go for it," I said warily.

"We received a lot of phone calls after the Business Owners Organization meeting. Can you help me understand what transpired there?"

"What transpired was that Tabitha Baxter accused Nora and me of killing her husband. She got up during a meeting, walked to the middle of the room, and blamed us in front of everyone." I crossed my arms over my chest, then uncrossed them, as I knew it signaled defensiveness. While I did feel defensive, it wouldn't be beneficial to show that right now.

He made some notes. I wondered what kinds of observations detectives were always making in those little pads. Maybe someday I'd ask him to show me for research purposes. I could see how being on the force gave him an edge as far as details went in his thrillers. Now that I knew he juggled both things, I was eager to hear more about how he balanced the writing life with the working life. It couldn't be easy.

He tapped his pen on the table. "When you say *blamed* us, what do you mean, exactly?"

"I mean that Tabitha brought up my aunt's book and claimed that just because the murder in there was performed in the same manner as Tip's, it meant we were the killers. She also maintains that I somehow wormed my way into her house by pretending to be a party planner, which is ludicrous."

"How long have you been doing events in Silvercrest?"

Why did everyone keep asking me that? I wished I could evoke a need-to-know-basis requirement.

"Not long," I said.

He lifted his shoulders. "Ballpark it."

"That was my first gig."

Not surprisingly, he scribbled away.

"But it's really just an expansion of my work at the bookstore. I do have years of experience planning events in grad school, and it only came about because Tabitha came into our store and went on and on about her party planner quitting. I offered to help at that moment. But I didn't seek her out. I didn't put on party planner clothes and ring her doorbell to peddle my services, which was how she made it sound."

He unsuccessfully attempted to hide a smile. "And what are party planner clothes?"

"I meant something with, like, a logo on it."

Come to think of it, we *should* sell more things with the store logo on them. I filed that away to bring up later with Lucy.

He tapped his pen again. "Let's move on. Don't you think it's unusual that Mr. Baxter's demise follows the same pattern as the one in Nora's book?"

"It's a coincidence, Jake."

"Or not."

"Maybe someone's trying to frame Nora. Or me, I guess. Or both of us."

He grimaced. "It does look bad."

"But Tabitha's accusation also shows she knew that murder method was in the book—so doesn't it also point a finger at her?" I sat back triumphantly.

"It could," he said. "But she was in full view of the rest of the guests throughout the whole party. We can't find a single instant of time that she wasn't."

My shoulders slumped, then I thought of another possibility. "Perhaps she's working with someone else. Then she could have been playing lady of the manor all night long in plain sight while the murderer took care of business. Have you thought about that?"

"Yes," Jake said. "There's also the issue of fingerprints. Your aunt's fingerprints were found on the chaise lounge along with the body. Not Tabitha's."

"But the guests were on the patio before dinner. She could have been sitting in that very chair earlier. The professors were clustered on the same side as where Tip was . . . found."

"That's what Nora said too. You can see, though, that there is more than one reason your aunt has not been cleared yet. Things seem to keep turning up."

"Someone *may* be trying to make it look like she did this, but there's no way. She is not a murderer." I met his eyes. The green shade had always reminded me of the ocean before a storm: lighter than expected and illuminated by some mysterious confluence of sky and sea. I'd never seen that color on anyone else.

"Which brings us back to you, Starrs."

"I'm not a killer, and you know that."

"Great. We'll cross you off the list, then," he said.

"Really?"

"No."

I sighed. "Are we done?"

"For now. Let me know what you decide about the critique group."

I was surprised that he still wanted me to join them, given that he evidently suspected me of murder.

Chapter Twelve

The next day, Nora and I sat at one of the tables in the back of the store, scanning forthcoming releases as Lucy had requested. She wanted to know if she'd missed any books that we thought she should order. My aunt and I had a laptop open between us and were debating a particular choice when Jake Hollister came through the front door and moved efficiently down the aisle toward us.

"Would it be possible to speak with you alone, Professor Haven? I have some questions." He lifted his badge to indicate that it was in a professional capacity.

"Have a seat," Nora said cheerily.

"I can give you some privacy." I started to push my chair back, but my aunt's hand fell like a stone upon mine.

"Emma stays. And please call me Nora." She removed her reading glasses and set them down.

Jake settled himself at the table across from us. Once he'd pulled out his trusty notepad, he began speaking softly. "As you may or may not be aware, at the Business Owners Organization meeting, Tabitha Baxter made a statement—"

"More of an accusation," Nora corrected him. "And a defamation."

"So you've heard?"

"Yes. She said, in front of everyone there, that because a character smothered someone at a dinner party in my book, I must have done the same thing."

"Correct," he said.

Nora sighed. "It's not true. And we've already talked about fingerprints on the chair where I sat before dinner. We've already accounted for my every movement at the Baxters' house that night. What else could you possibly have to ask me?" Her hands were folded in front of her and her voice was calm, but she somehow exuded the energy of a crouched lioness who was watching someone get too close and could spring at any moment.

Jake flipped back and forth through some pages without saying anything. Clearly, she'd rattled him. "Could you please tell me about the book with that scene?"

"It's called *A Refined Taste for Murder*. And yes, in it, the owner of the mansion is smothered."

"At a dinner party." Jake looked up and made eye contact with Nora.

"Yes."

"A *murder mystery* dinner party."

"Yes." My aunt's face began to look mottled, as if the effort to remain composed was too much for her skin to contain.

He sat back in his chair. "That seems fairly odd, wouldn't you say? The exact thing that appears in your book happens in real life?"

"But Jake," I jumped in, "we know Tabitha read the book. She referenced it. So *she* could have planned this out ahead of time."

"You mentioned that theory, yes."

I went on. "It makes perfect sense. She is the one who chose the murder mystery theme and could have invited my aunt for the *express purpose* of framing her. She already stated that she felt that Nora was bothering Tip somehow and she wanted her to stop. It's all there. Why aren't you focusing your spotlight on Tabitha?"

"We have done so. She was in full view of guests the entire time," Jake replied quickly. "As I said last night."

"It's possible that she hired someone else to do the actual, uh, deed." As I made the same arguments I'd offered before, I began to feel increasingly helpless. I was putting forth a coherent and logical argument. Why wasn't he listening to me?

He tapped his pen on the desk, then shifted positions and looked directly at Nora again. "Why didn't you point out, when you were talking to the police earlier, that one of your novels depicted a murder in the same manner?"

Nora shook her head slightly. "It honestly didn't even enter my mind."

"Or mine," I said, "and I've read all of her books too. Multiple times."

He wrote something down. I realized that anyone who had read *A Refined Taste for Murder* now had a connection to the method that had been used by the killer.

"I've written thirty mysteries," Nora said. "That was my earliest. When I'm finished with one book, I immediately turn my attention to the next. Since that first book, I've created so many different stories."

"It didn't pop up in your mind *at all*?"

"No," she said. "I'm sorry, I don't know what to say. I wrote it over two decades ago."

"Still," he said. "No recognition of the action as having any kind of parallel?"

"No."

"How can that be?"

"Think about when you have a dream," she said. "It can be incredibly vivid when you first wake up, then the pieces start to drift away over time, and eventually, you may not remember it at all."

He leaned forward and made what seemed like a lengthy note. "Can you tell me more, now that your memory has been refreshed?"

"Like what?"

"Like what gave you the idea for that scene the first time around?"

"Heavens, I can't remember. Let me think." She rested her chin on one hand and looked down the empty aisle behind him.

"What does this have to do with anything, Hollister?" I asked.

"*Detective* Hollister," he said, rather smugly. "And please, let me do my job without second-guessing every little thing, Starrs."

"*Dr.* Starrs," I said, in retaliation for his title grab.

In that moment, it seemed worth all the years of hard work and study to see the expression on Jake's face.

My aunt was smiling as she watched the exchange.

"Anyway," he said, turning back to Nora, "what was the genesis?"

"It came to me one day," she replied.

"It came to you." His flat repetition was pointedly doubtful.

She waved her hands around. "Well, you're a writer, Jake. You know that things can come from somewhere inexplicable."

"Doesn't happen to me that way." He set down the notepad and crossed his arms.

"Really? You know everything you're going to say before you say it?"

"Pretty much. I'm a heavy-duty outliner. And I don't write until I have the scene imagined thoroughly, down to every last detail."

"That must be comforting," my aunt replied. "Typically, I have *no* idea what's going to come out next until I'm already there at my computer writing."

They were silent for a bit, then both lifted their shoulders at each other, having reached the eternal impasse between writers who are firmly on opposite ends of the plotting versus writing-by-the-seat-of-one's-pants spectrum.

I was more in the middle; I always made a plan but inevitably wandered away from it, exactly for the reason my aunt had said—sometimes when you're writing, things come to you.

Not that anyone was asking me.

Jake cleared his throat. "I'd like to know about the other methods of murder in your books in order to keep an eye out for potential parallels."

"Then I suppose," Nora said sweetly, "you'll have to read them all."

"We do have those in stock," I said, matching her tone.

"I would be happy to sign them for you," she added.

Jake looked back and forth between us. "Well played. I guess I have some books to buy."

* * *

When Jake had gone, a full bag of books in either hand, I returned to the table where Nora was still sitting.

"Are you doing okay?" I asked.

She closed the laptop. "Yes, and Lucy will be delighted with that sale. Did he buy every single one?"

"Yes, and he bought a copy of your writing textbook too, for good measure."

Nora laughed. "He won't find any motive, means, and opportunity there unless he's on the hunt for better revision techniques."

"The way that Tabitha keeps pointing at you as a suspect is itself highly suspect."

"Pointing at *us*," she reminded me. "Though hasn't she always been a pointer, so to speak?"

"Indeed. Tabitha loves to blame everyone else for her problems. But I do think the police should be looking at *her* more closely. I wonder if they're interviewing her with the same kind of intensity."

"I'm sure they're considering all the options, darling. Though it's not likely that they'd reveal their hand to us in casual conversation. Especially since they haven't cleared us yet. They don't tend to update suspects."

I slid into the seat next to her. "Maybe we should do some digging of our own. Do you mind if we pause on the order research for the time being?"

"Not at all. I think we have a good list already. Let me send this to Lucy." She wrote a quick email and attached the information we'd put together for my sister, then signed out and angled the laptop toward me. "All yours."

I typed Tabitha's name into the browser search bar and hit return.

There were many people with the same name, but Silvercrest Tabitha took up the first ten pages of hits, most of which were stories about her social activities. We scanned page after page of mentions of Tabitha at charity balls or galas or heading up committees. I clicked around and found her social media streams, which were peppered with pictures of Tabitha, Melody, Ainsley, and Felicity posing like a hashtag-blessed super-happy BFF squad in their matching clothes and matching smiles.

"What are we looking for exactly?" my aunt asked, her eyebrows drawn together.

"I don't know," I said. "We're just looking."

We did the same thing for each member of the group. No one else had their profile settings on public, but we did spend some time contemplating their business ventures. Ainsley's soap store on Etsy was highly rated and appealing; I almost ordered some lavender and lemon organic soap before I caught myself. Felicity was listed as a lead volunteer at the pet rescue she had mentioned, and there were pictures of her holding numerous adorable kittens and puppies. It didn't say much about either of them personally, so we moved on to the men's bios at Flashtown Digital, Silvercrest Bank, and Edwards Law Offices. Each one listed accomplishments galore from prep schools, first-tier universities, and graduate programs. Descriptions of their work achievements were similarly stuffed with superlatives. They had lived privileged lives indeed.

"Now do Tip," Nora suggested.

His Silvercrest College profile offered the academic edition of the same kinds of triumphs the other husbands had accrued. There were even more of them, as his career had been longer, though there was no mention of his owning a resort in Bali or anywhere. Maybe he'd chosen to focus only on his higher education credentials here, but it wouldn't have surprised me to learn that he had assets in a variety of businesses.

"Pretty impressive," I admitted.

"But not helpful," Nora said.

"You never know. But at least we can check that off our list. We've searched."

"And now we can eat, right?" Her eyes were filled with hope.

"Now we can eat."

As we gathered up our things, though, I couldn't help feeling that we were missing something right in front of us.

I stopped and went back to Tabitha's photos.

"What are you doing?" Nora asked.

"Checking something." I pulled up the pictures she had posted of her wedding to Ian. They'd married on a beach in Hawaii. Blue skies, sandy beaches, and blossoms everywhere—in a word, paradise. Melody and Bruce, Ainsley and Clive, and Felicity and Aston were there too, holding up fruit-laden cocktails in pictures at the pool bar and more formally arranged on the beach at sunset.

I moved from that date forward, through multiple gatherings with the group of friends who seemed to do everything together. All the pictures were magazine worthy; Tabitha had carefully curated a dream stream of her life events. I scrolled quickly through those, then came upon her wedding to Tip. The same people who had served as bridesmaids and groomsmen in her wedding to Ian were at the next wedding, which had taken place in Aspen. The poses were so reminiscent of those in Hawaii that it was as if they had simply switched in Tip for Ian, and mountain for island, then continued with business as usual.

However, in many of the pictures that followed, Ian was back. He was at fundraisers, cookouts, and bars. On golf courses, ski trips, and cruises. Smiling in every case as though he didn't have a care in the world, his arms thrown around the other members of the group.

"Do you think it's strange that Tabitha's ex-husband never stopped hanging around with her friends?" I asked.

Nora put her glasses back on and leaned forward to study the photos closely. "Good question. It seems a little unusual, though if the split was not acrimonious, perhaps it's not so strange that friendships continue."

"What about these?" I pointed out a few that caught Ian regarding Tabitha with an air of longing. "How would you describe his expression?"

"Like he was looking at the only woman in the world that he'd ever loved."

"Exactly."

We stared at each other.

"Do you think they were having an affair?" I asked. "Maybe she only married Tip for his money but never stopped seeing Ian."

Nora took off her glasses. "It's a possibility. It's not like that very thing hasn't been done before."

"Did you ever see any evidence of that over the years?"

She shook her head. "She seemed very devoted to Tip."

"Seemed, you say?"

Nora sighed. "Tabitha has always been good at performing, as you know. At some of the events we've both attended, I have found myself admiring the way she handles herself. Then I remember how awful she was to you in school and have to rein in my respect."

"You know," I said slowly, "Ian was the only member of the group that didn't attend the dinner party."

"And?"

"So everyone else's movements were accounted for that night, but since he wasn't a guest, he could have sneaked in and attacked Tip on the porch."

"You're right," she said.

"Should we tell the police?"

"We don't have any evidence," my aunt said. "Plus, have they listened to *anything* you've told them yet? One single thing?"

I reflected on the way Jake had dismissed my theories out of hand already.

Twice.

Nora sighed. "I don't know about you, but I am extremely tired of officers asking me questions every time I turn around, then not wanting to hear the answers we're offering. Don't you want to take a breath for a minute?"

"Yes," I said.

"And don't you have enough on your plate with Calliope's launch party?"

I did. I definitely did.

Chapter Thirteen

The rest of the week flew by as I continued planning the upcoming event. As soon as one item was crossed off, another was there waiting. It felt as though I'd never reach the end of the list. On Saturday morning, I resolved to turn the short journey from our house to the store into a brief respite. Autumn was my favorite season—she of the brilliant colors and invigorating breezes—and I asked my sister to walk as slowly as possible so we could admire the aspens and maples. Their crimsons and golds were in full display along the riverwalk. Anne Shirley, at the end of her leash, was pouncing on various fallen leaves and having a generally wonderful time.

The scenery worked its magic, but when we arrived at the back of the store, Lucy clutched my arm. A crowd of people was standing on our back porch.

"What's going on?" I asked, stepping instinctively in front of my sister to protect her. She tried to step in front of me at the same time, so we ended up crashing into each other, which led to some flailing, much to the amusement of the observers.

Once we'd untangled ourselves, she gestured for me to go first.

Anne Shirley sat facing the crowd at the end of her leash, licking her paw and pretending not to be associated with us. Couldn't blame her.

I tried to regain some dignity during my walk up to the individuals, who appeared to be college students. The fact that they were, without exception, dressed in Silvercrest College gear supported the premise. I scanned the sea of red and silver sweatshirts and hats, many of which sported the school mascot—a cougar—but I didn't recognize anyone.

Then the crowd parted and there was Tabitha, standing at the back, hands on hips in a power pose. Surprise, surprise.

"How can we help you?" I asked in their general direction.

"We're boycotting your store," Tabitha answered smugly.

"Why?" Lucy asked, coming to stand next to me.

"Show them the sign." Tabitha muttered to a ponytailed woman next to her, who turned around a piece of cardboard that had the words *Starlit Bookshop = Dead* in puffy paint letters floating in a sea of multicolored flowers.

"That doesn't make any sense," Lucy said, perplexed. "Our bookstore kills people? Or our bookstore has been killed? What does it even mean?"

Ponytail huffed and whispered angrily to the woman next to her, who made a face.

"And may I ask about the flowers?" my sister continued. "It doesn't seem to match the tone of—"

Ponytail's friend interrupted her. "We *always* put flowers on our signs."

"We do that for *rush parties*," Ponytail said, rolling her eyes. "Not protests."

"Hey, don't blame us. You just said to make a sign," her friend said sulkily.

"Forget that one. Show them another," Tabitha commanded.

Heads turned quickly back and forth, but no other slogan was produced.

"I'm sorry," Ponytail said to Tabitha. "The sisters only had time to make this one, I guess. We were mostly focused on the game today."

I addressed the crowd. "Could we please back up here? Who are all of you and what are you upset about?"

"They're from my sorority," Tabitha said proudly. "I'm an alum member now, but I've stayed in close contact with my chapter. I was the president, you know."

Everyone knew that Tabitha had been the president of her sorority. She made sure that everyone knew.

"It's true. She totally helps us out all the time," Ponytail said, smiling at her.

"And I'm here to support my girl," a stocky, dark-haired man said loudly, putting an arm around Ponytail. He had the swollen face of someone for whom beer was considered a primary food group.

A bunch of the guys surrounding him whooped and whistled.

"Thanks, Kirk," Ponytail murmured, looking up through her eyelashes at him. After a beat, she slid her eyes back to me. "We're taking the opportunity to let the *world* know *not* to shop here. For our philanthropy points."

"I don't think that's what philanthropy—" I began.

"Whatever," she said impatiently. "We're here because of Dean Baxter. He and Ms. Baxter came to dinner at the house all the time. They were our *mentors*."

Tabitha acting as a mentor was a horrifying idea; I couldn't imagine what she was taking it upon herself to teach them.

"Thank you so much for that, Amber." Tabitha's beautifully manicured hand fell upon the student's shoulder. For a millisecond, it sounded as though she was actually choked up; then she expelled a delicate cough, and it went away. "We all miss him."

"And Ms. Baxter said that the person who murdered him works at this store. That's so wrong on so many levels. Is it you? Are you the murderer?"

"No," I said with a sigh.

"Are *you*?" she asked Lucy.

My sister's whole body stiffened. "Absolutely not."

"Well, *whoever* it is should *totally* be in jail," Amber continued.

"And we're going to protest right here, right now," Kirk said, drawing a circle with his finger around the area where we were standing.

"Here in the back?" I asked. "You're going to protest *behind* our store?"

"Yep. This is where the best rays are." He pulled his sunglasses down and flexed both arms. "All about the tan, man!"

Tabitha's smile faltered.

"With just the one sign?" I pressed.

"Yeah!" said Kirk, loudly.

"Well, have at it," I said.

Lucy stared at me. "*What*?"

Kirk pulled out a flask and held it aloft, yelling, "Protest on!"

The crowd cheered and streamed past us to take up positions along the riverwalk, where they milled around excitedly.

Kirk shouted something unintelligible as I told Lucy to follow me. We slipped around the side of the store to the front entrance. I wasn't about to open the back door with all of them standing there. The sounds of the Silvercrest College fight song filled the air.

"What are you doing?" Lucy sounded panicky. "You're going to *leave* them there?"

I put the key into the door and unlocked it. "Yes. They'll be gone soon."

"What makes you so confident?"

"One, they have a single sign. Two, I don't hear any chanting. Together, those things suggest that they haven't done much planning at all for this thing. But even more compelling is number three, the fact that the football game at Silvercrest College starts in an hour. It's homecoming weekend, and there's no way that crowd is going to stick around very long."

"I don't know," she said doubtfully. "Maybe we should call the police?"

"Let's wait a bit and see if we need to do that." I unbuckled the cat's harness, and she bounded away to do her morning rounds.

"You're the professor," she said.

"Hardly." I turned on the lights.

"Do you miss teaching?" she asked quietly. "You always sounded so enthusiastic about it."

"Very much."

"We haven't talked about that in a while. Are you thinking about giving it another try?"

Fall was application season, since initial interviews for tenure-track jobs in my discipline were held at one huge conference over holiday break. I was willing to go through the emotional turmoil again—you could count on being rejected, as there were hundreds of candidates for any given position—but I wasn't yet sure what was happening with the bookstore. Unless it was clear that the business could move forward successfully or, to the contrary, had closed, I didn't feel free to leave. Plus, I genuinely loved working at Starlit, and I was finding it harder and harder, as time went on, to imagine being far away from my sister and aunt.

"Sorry, Em. You don't have to say anything. I'm being nosy."

"It's fine. It's just that in order to land a teaching job, I'd have to move. And now that I'm home, I don't know if I want to leave again."

"Hearing that makes me so happy, I can't even tell you how much." Lucy started to hum as she set up the register drawer.

I thought about all the time, money, and energy I'd put into getting the terminal degree. Then I picked up a stack of books and got to work.

* * *

About an hour later, I looked out the back window. The students were gone, but Tabitha was sitting on a metal bench across the street, facing the river. Perhaps she was licking her wounds at having put together the least effective protest in the history of protests.

Or perhaps she was plotting out her next evil plan.

In any case, the students had left, and we were back on track for a normal Saturday.

A *thunk* behind me redirected my attention away from the window. I turned to see my sister with a tower of books in her arms.

"Oops," Lucy said. "Hit the shelf. I may have pulled too many for today." Story time was the one type of event Lucy had kept going when she took over the store. She had always adored being around children and especially loved introducing them to new books and authors.

"There's no such thing as too many books, as they say."

She laughed as she set the books carefully down on a nearby table and checked her watch. "Hey, I'll be ready early for once. Everyone seems to be late today."

I glanced at the large clock on the wall. "Only by a few minutes. It may be the traffic for homecoming. Things are probably at a crawl."

"Good point."

A woman with red hair in a messy bun came partway through the front door, struggling to get her stroller inside. I ran over to help her. She smiled at me gratefully.

"Welcome to Starlit Bookshop," I said. "How can we help you today?"

"I'm here for story hour," she said softly. Her eyes were busily skimming the interior space. "Wait, am I the only one?"

"You're the first one to arrive," Lucy said. She introduced herself, then asked the baby's name.

"Finn," said the woman. "And I'm Claire."

"Hi, Claire. He's beautiful," Lucy breathed. "How old?"

They embarked on a discussion about young Finn as Claire unbuckled his seat belt. I couldn't follow all the details about growth charts, sleep sacks, and organic baby food, so I zoned out, wondering what the best way to approach Tabitha might be. Obviously, we couldn't go on like this, with her calling Nora and me killers all over town. The protest had ended today, but what if they returned tomorrow with a larger group of people who were more organized?

Or what if they did something worse? Who knew what was coming next?

"Oh!" Lucy exclaimed. "She did *what*?"

Refocusing on the conversation, I was surprised at Claire's reaction. Her whole face had gone red, and her blue eyes were welling with tears.

"What happened?" I asked.

Claire held up a hand. "I'm sorry to be the one to tell you, and I'm sorry to be emotional right now. I'm not sleeping, and I barely even know what day it is."

"Please don't worry," Lucy said. "Can you come in and sit down for a few minutes?"

Claire wiped away the tears. "This is so embarrassing."

"Not at all." Lucy led her away, making soothing comments. I stowed the stroller behind the register and gave them some space. Before long, Claire was sitting in an armchair with a steaming cup of tea, and Lucy was opposite her in the matching chair with Finn on her lap. He was chomping contentedly on a band of teething beads.

"You're good with babies," Claire observed. "And this tea is divine. I haven't felt this human in weeks."

"Anytime you want to take a break, I do some babysitting on the side," Lucy said.

"That would be amazing. Finn and I have recently arrived to Silvercrest. We're originally from western Colorado. Glenwood Springs, to be precise. First Ryan moved to Silvercrest, then my parents followed last year."

"Not Ryan Mahoney?"

"The very same."

They launched into a long conversation about Ryan, the friend who had offered to help us with the spotlight for Calliope. Wanting her son to grow up near his family had prompted

Claire to move here too. She'd joined some parent groups in the area, which was how she'd heard about a boycott of our store.

"So no one else is coming?" Lucy asked sadly.

"No. Word went out this morning. Someone in my mommy group emailed, warning us not to come to story time. When I pushed her for more information, she said Tabitha had asked her to let us know out of concern for everyone's safety, considering what had happened to her husband."

"Tabitha was *concerned*?" I said. "Doesn't sound like her."

"No," Lucy agreed. "And now she's expanding the narrative to say that it's not only Nora and you but the whole bookstore that's dangerous."

"Dangerous?" Claire repeated faintly.

"It's a hundred percent untrue," Lucy told her. "It is not dangerous. We are not dangerous. Tabitha just hates us and always has."

"I don't know her," Claire said. "The explanation did seem odd to me, though, like a piece of logic was missing."

"Why did you come here, then?" I asked her gently. "Though we're glad you did."

"I didn't think anyone else would take her warning seriously. And Ryan has mentioned you before, Lucy. He's a good judge of character. Also, I had to get out of the house, frankly. I was going stir-crazy." She glanced fondly at her baby, who was laughing as he bent his knees and pushed himself upright again and again.

"Well, thank you for coming. Do you want me to read some books to Finn?" Lucy asked.

"I'd love that," Claire said. She set down the teacup on the small side table and held out her arms to take her son.

Lucy opened a book, turned it around so that Finn could see the pictures, and began to read.

* * *

"So we're actually being boycotted," Lucy said, after Claire had left with a big bag of books that she'd bought. "That's a first. I told you Tabitha had a long reach."

"I can't believe it," I said. "But maybe story hour will be the worst of it, though I'm sorry because I know how much you love it."

"I hope there are more people like Claire out there," she said. "Or else we'll be closing even sooner than I thought we would."

Chapter Fourteen

"May I say that my students are wonderful?" Nora asked Monday night as she hung up her coat on the rack in the office. "They have been sending me emails of support, and in class today, they said they'd do everything they could to counter the rumors of my supposed heinousness."

"Aw," said Lucy. "That warms my heart. Max and Bella both emailed me this morning with similar sentiments. My book club is also doing everything they can to defend your honor. You have quite the fan club across campus and around town."

"I don't know about that," Nora said, blushing. "But it's good to hear that there are some people who know I would never do anything like what Tabitha is accusing me of."

"She's accusing you *and* Emma of . . ." Lucy paused as she searched for the word. "What is it? Cahooting?"

Nora laughed. "Do you mean they're accusing us of being in cahoots?"

"Yes, that's it." Lucy added more books to the cart she was preparing for shelving. "But the point is that you both are on her list. And Emma, people want to defend you too, I should add. You both have fans."

Nora took a deep breath. "Who cares what Tabitha says? We didn't do anything wrong."

"I care," I protested.

"You cannot live your life paying attention to what other people think, Emma. It will make you miserable." She spread her arms wide. "You must be your authentic self, try to do good in the world, aim for your dreams, and let the chips fall where they may."

Nora had been telling us that our whole lives. She was very comfortable with not worrying about public opinion, but Lucy and I weren't quite there yet. For one thing, the fate of the bookstore was at stake.

The door opened and in swept Delilah, Nora's agent, a tall, thin woman with sharp features and a glossy blonde chin-length bob. The lenses of her signature large round glasses transitioned from dark to light the closer she moved toward us. She pulled off her brown gloves and threw back one side of a matching wool cloak over a green sweater dress.

"Hi, all," she said, waving. She picked her way carefully through the store, her stiletto boots hardly making a sound on the polished wooden floors. Nora went to meet her in front of the register counter, where they delivered air kisses on either side of each other's faces.

We all said hello, and Lucy offered her something to drink. Delilah thought for a moment, then chose an herbal tea. "Surprise me with whatever flavor you like. Having a little mystery in one's day keeps one young. Don't you think?"

"I'd love some too, darling, if you don't mind," Nora said.

Lucy smiled and did a little curtsy before rushing into the office to pick out a tea. She had always been somewhat intimidated by Delilah, a powerhouse New York agent who had moved to Silvercrest ten years ago, seeking a calmer pace of life after her husband passed away. Nora had been her client for over a decade already at that point, but the proximity had helped their relationship turn into a deeper friendship.

Nora and Delilah went over to the tables in the back and settled in. I returned to the office to resume my work on the computer, where I was following up on some details for Calliope's party.

"Will you take the tea out?" Lucy whispered loudly from behind me. "I need to get to the shelving—the cart is overflowing."

"Sure." I closed the browser window and stood up.

My sister thanked me and hurried away before I could change my mind. The kettle whistled soon afterward, and I unplugged it and poured the steaming water into stoneware mugs next to the tea bags, spoons, napkins, milk, and honey on the tray Lucy had already set out. Then I added a few almond biscotti to a small floral plate and surveyed the results. Very cozy, on the whole.

I carried the tray out to where my aunt and her agent were sitting and gently set it on the table.

"Thank you, my dear," Delilah said, busying herself with the tea making. "And I adore hibiscus tea. Perfect choice."

"You should join us," Nora said. "Delilah was just telling me something very interesting."

I slid into the empty seat next to her and turned my attention to Delilah.

"How far back?" she asked my aunt.

"From the beginning," Nora advised her.

"So. I'd heard about Tabitha's accusations—"

"How, if I may ask?" Nora interjected.

"Hmm. Let me think." Delilah readjusted her glasses as she thought, then held one finger up. "I was at the market, waiting at the deli while they sliced me some cheddar. I like my cheese extremely thin, as you know," she said to Nora, who smiled. "They were taking a long time because one of the blades had been removed for washing or sharpening—I don't remember which—and when they tried to replace it, there was some sort of prong that had broken off—"

Nora cleared her throat quietly.

"I'm going on and on, aren't I? Sorry. Cut to: they've fixed the machine, they're slicing away, and a voice behind me starts talking about the Business Owners Organization meeting, describing it in such horrifying detail that the hair on the back of my neck stood up. I'm getting goose bumps all over again." Delilah held out her arm so that we could see them. "To imagine you having to stand there facing those women as they tried to denigrate your reputation, it nearly brought me to tears. I'm very sorry."

"Oh, it's fine," I said. "I mean, the experience itself was not, but I'm fine." I gestured to my aunt. "We're fine."

"Even though everyone in town is talking about you?" Delilah took a sip of tea as she waited for my response.

"I don't love that so much," I admitted.

"Let them talk," Nora said. "Honestly, who gives a hoot?"

"Well, you might give a hoot if they arrest you," Delilah said. "I'm worried about you."

"They're not going to arrest us," Nora insisted. "We didn't do anything."

"Sometimes the wrong people are arrested, though; you know that." Delilah reached across the table and grabbed both of my aunt's hands. "I don't know what I would do without you. Don't get arrested, Nora!"

"I'm trying not to," she replied calmly. "And they don't have any evidence other than fingerprints."

"Dear heart, that *counts* as evidence," Delilah said.

"I meant fingerprints on the chair where I sat surrounded by colleagues who can all vouch to that effect."

"Well, it also happens to be the chair where they found Tip," Delilah reminded her.

"True. But it's not against the law to sit on a chair."

"Right, though they can't be sure your fingerprints are *only* from the faculty chat. You could have returned later. So it's impossible to prove that your fingerprints are unequivocally crime-free, as it were."

"Whose side are you on, anyway?" Nora asked, with a laugh.

"Yours, of course." Delilah squeezed her hands and let them go.

"I was never by myself. All night long, I was with someone from start to finish."

"As long as people step up and tell them that," I murmured.

"What do you mean?" Nora turned to face me.

"I mean . . . as long as no one lies."

She stared at me.

"The murderer might lie to protect themselves," I clarified.

"I hadn't even thought of that. The killer was right there with you the whole time!" Delilah shivered and showed us the goose bumps on her arm again.

"Maybe not. Maybe they ran onto the back porch, committed the crime, then ran away again," I suggested.

"That probably wouldn't play as well," Delilah mused.

"Play as well?" Nora asked.

"Ooh, I forgot to tell you that I have more news. Let me back up. Do you know Slayton Sands, the screenwriter-slash-director-slash-indie-darling?" She reeled off a list of critically acclaimed films. "There I was, about to dive into a superb beet salad, and the phone rang, and I almost didn't pick up because, you know, deliciousness awaited, and also I didn't recognize the number— "

Nora gently closed her eyes for a moment.

Delilah rolled her own. "Sorry, I'm getting distracted. Here's the big news: Slayton Sands wants to make a film about your first book."

Nora put her hand to her heart. The book had been optioned multiple times, but the movie had not yet been made. Her fans had clamored for years, but so far it had remained a dream.

Delilah smiled at her. "The publisher has also agreed to do a new edition of the book with a huge marketing push behind it to tie in with the film release."

My aunt appeared to be dazed.

"He wants to do a whole meta thing, where the original story is interwoven with a true-crime version of Tip's—"

"No," Nora said decisively.

"What?" Her agent blinked rapidly. "But it's *Slayton Sands.*"

"I will not exploit the death of my colleague for any reason."

"No, no, no. I explained it wrong. Slayton doesn't want to exploit anything. He wants to use the current events for context."

"Which would sensationalize it."

Delilah studied her face. "I hear what you're saying. You don't need to make any decisions right away."

Nora shook her head. "If you can get them to make an adaptation of the book that follows it closely *without* crossing over into Tip Baxter's death, then we will have something to talk about. But I do not want any hint of true crime near my story. I could not bear that."

Delilah's shoulders sagged, but she nodded briskly. "Understood, though technically, the publisher may have the right to create an edition that brings in context through an introduction or afterword without your permission. They have been very gracious so far about letting us weigh in, but if they really want to . . ."

"Don't let them," Nora pleaded. "Please."

"I'll call them the instant that we're done here."

"Do you think the publisher might want to bring out a new edition anyway?" I asked. "Without any true-crime or film connection? It could still be a twentieth-anniversary edition."

"I'll talk to them," Delilah acknowledged. "Though we only have a few months left until we're into year twenty-one, and that's probably not enough time to make it happen. And to be honest, without the film connection, I don't think they will feel compelled to do anything like that. Sorry, Norry. Just saying."

"I know," my aunt said.

Delilah pulled out her cell phone and set it on the table. "Unfortunately, the very thing that you *don't* want them to emphasize is what carries the weight of the buzz . . . you know what they say about there being no bad publicity."

"I'm not sure that's true," I offered. "And I understand Nora's point."

My aunt gave me a smile. "Thank you, Emma."

"I understand too, believe me," Delilah said. "But it's my job to bring you offers and possibilities. Speaking of which, you didn't even ask me about the money."

"And I don't want to know," Nora replied. "But thank you all the same."

"You don't want to know about the money," Delilah repeated, looking stunned. "Even if it's the biggest offer yet?"

"Not everything is about money," my aunt said firmly. "Or at least it shouldn't be. I'd prefer to keep my story as far away from Tip's tragic demise as possible."

"Then someone should do something about Tabitha," Delilah said.

"On it," I heard myself say.

Wait, what?

"Any other possibilities?" my aunt asked.

Delilah scrolled through her emails on her phone. "I have been asked if you'd be interested in licensing your main character's look for a costume line."

"Tell me more," Nora said, leaning forward.

I left to go figure out what I had just promised to deliver.

Chapter Fifteen

The whole next day, I thought about how to approach Tabitha. Somehow, I didn't feel as though calling her would yield the results I wanted. It felt more like a face-to-face kind of conversation. Preferably one where she didn't know we were going to have it.

It would be fantastic if we could speak honestly and directly, straighten out our differences, and agree to keep the peace henceforth.

But that was never going to happen.

I was a firm believer in confronting misunderstandings, but this wasn't that type of situation. Tabitha and her friends were simply the kind of people who felt better about themselves only by putting other people down. No matter how I approached her, she was going to come at me with negativity.

If I stayed calm, though, was there any possibility of getting through to her? Of helping her see how damaging her claims were? Of convincing her to act like a compassionate human being?

It was hard to imagine, but I hoped to be able to switch her from the Nora-and-Emma-are-murderers narrative to something else.

The best plan, as far as I could tell, would be to surprise her with an argument that she didn't have time to anticipate.

I pondered how to make this happen and soon. It was almost closing time. If I could locate her whereabouts, I could take care of this tonight. At least expressing it would help me think more clearly. I didn't know how much longer I could carry around the increasing sense of frustration, which was distracting.

And I had enough to handle, getting ready for Calliope's big night.

Lucy wandered in and flopped down in the chair next to the desk. "Whatcha doing?"

"Trying to find Tabitha."

She wrinkled her nose. "Why?"

I explained my plan. She pulled the chair around next to me and watched as I checked Tabitha's social media feeds.

"Okay, here's a picture of her posing with Melody, posted an hour ago, but I can't tell where they are."

"Are there any hashtags?"

"No."

Lucy squinted at the screen. "What *is* that? It looks like a broken-down house."

The background consisted of gray wooden shingles and part of a weather-beaten window frame.

"Let me look at the people she tagged and see if they shared the location." I clicked around and didn't see any recent postings from them.

"That's the haunted house," a deep voice behind us said. Lucy and I both jumped.

A handsome man with dark-red wavy hair pulled back in a short ponytail apologized for scaring us. He wore a tan flannel shirt—with a puffy blue vest that matched his eyes—over jeans. His face was lightly freckled, and his cheeks were ruddy. The overall vibe was lumberjackian.

Lucy recovered first and pointed to the man. "Emma, this is my friend Ryan Mahoney. Ryan, this is my sister Emma."

"At last we meet," I said. "I've been hearing your name a lot lately."

"Really?" He smiled uncertainly.

"We met your sister," Lucy explained. "And I've been telling Emma about your theater experience."

"Ah," he said. "Well, it's nice to meet you, and sorry again for sneaking up. I wanted to stop by and chat about the lighting plans, make sure I had everything you needed."

"That's so kind." Lucy smiled at him.

"I should have made an appointment first. Don't know what I was thinking. Happened to be nearby and thought I'd check in before you closed up shop for the night."

"It's fine. And it's nice to see you," my sister told him. "It's been a while."

"Things have been really busy at the theater." He told us about the current production, which had a cast that apparently wasn't jelling the way it should, leading to quarrels, prop shenanigans, and walkouts. High drama indeed.

"I've been meaning to see a show there," I said. "Maybe that's the one I should attend, knowing the inside scoop. I'll probably spend the whole time trying to guess which cast member threw out the other's shoes."

"Please be my guest when you do—pick any one and I'll comp your tickets."

"Wow, Luce, you have good taste in friends," I said to her.

He laughed.

"Okay, so what haunted house is this?" Lucy asked him, tapping the screen.

"It used to belong to the Terry family—"

"Are you talking about the abandoned house outside of town, back in the woods?" Lucy asked.

"The very same."

"That's the phrase your sister Claire said when I asked if the Ryan she was talking about was you, by the way. She used those exact words."

Ryan grinned. "My father used to say that."

"Funny how family language sticks," she said.

If I was going to catch Tabitha there, I'd need to hurry, so I tried to steer them back to the matter at hand. "You were saying something about a house?"

"People have been claiming the Terry place was haunted for years," my sister said solemnly.

"And now it's intentional," Ryan said. "Construction crews have been working on it for weeks, reinforcing the inside—"

"But leaving the outside dilapidated, obviously," Lucy said.

"—to make it safe. Some of the theater crew worked on the special effects. It's to raise money for the Silvercrest Foundation for our citizens in need."

"That makes sense," I said. "Tabitha's involved with that organization . . ." I trailed off, not wanting to divulge that Nora and I had pored over her profile page. "Or at least that's what I heard, anyway."

"Want to check it out? I have my truck." I thought Ryan was asking us both, but his eyes were on Lucy.

"Sure," she said. "I haven't been to a haunted house in ages."

"Neither have I. On purpose." I did not like jump scares.

"My sister and I went last week. It's not too terrifying," Ryan said.

"Not *too* terrifying? But still terrifying?" I wanted to get my facts straight.

"Medium terrifying," he allowed.

"She didn't bring Finn, did she?" Lucy's eyes were full of concern. "That would scar him for life."

"No, my mom and dad watched him that night."

"It's so great that they're here in town and Finn can grow up with his grandparents." Lucy made eye contact with me.

I braced myself for the wave of melancholy that followed.

"Shall we?" Ryan asked, unaware of the emotion we were sharing at the thought of our parents not meeting their grandchildren.

His upbeat demeanor helped. I patted my sister's arm, and both of us stood to leave.

Nora came in to retrieve her coat, and Lucy invited her to join us.

"I'd forgotten about the haunted house." My aunt was looking down as she buttoned up.

Puzzled, I asked what she meant. "We hadn't even decided to go until a minute ago."

She wrapped a scarf around her shoulders. "Some of us were asked to work there tonight."

"Who? How?" Lucy asked, as confused as I was.

"Each department on campus was invited to help out as actors one night this month. Tonight is English's turn. I'm not going, though. I don't want to have any more confrontations with Tabitha right now."

Funny, that was the exact goal I had in mind.

* * *

Spotlights aimed into the sky crossed and uncrossed next to the main gate of what had been named, according to a billboard at the end of the driveway, Silvercrest Screamfest. We followed the line of cars until we reached a parking lot, where individuals with flashlights directed us into a spot and told us to follow the Trail of Terror. We found the marker at the trailhead and moved with the stream of people along the path, which had small flickering electric torches on either side, into a dense woods. It twisted and turned so often that I completely lost my sense of direction.

"Wow, this is eerie," Lucy said. She threaded one arm through mine and one through Ryan's.

Finally, the path wrenched us to the left around a huge boulder, and we emerged through the pines in front of an imposing house. Several stories high, it seemed to lean forward, defying gravity—the bell tower on the top looked as though it were minutes away from toppling over on us. The large, rectangular windows were dark, except for random pulses of light. A crowd of ghosts suddenly slid across the front, thanks to a hidden projector, and monstrous faces carved out of wood were illuminated one by one, leering at us from the second floor. Screams could be heard despite the blaring rock music.

"I probably don't need to go inside," I said. "I only want to find Tabitha."

"Oh no," Lucy replied. "We *are* doing this."

"Why, though?" I had no desire to tromp through the house. Having found a body had already scared me enough for the rest of the year, thank you.

"It's an adventure . . . with surprises."

"Right now, I need the opposite of surprises."

"C'mon, Em. Sister time," she insisted, tugging me forward.

"It's kind of fun," Ryan said.

"Kind of? Not *fully* fun?" I asked, as we reached the front porch, where a booth was set up.

Ryan already had his wallet out and was buying tickets from someone in a very realistic-looking werewolf mask. We thanked Ryan as he handed us each a ticket.

After he turned to go inside, I stepped up to the werewolf and raised my voice. "I'm here to see Tabitha Baxter. Is she around back or something?" That would solve the whole we-are-doing-this thing. Hopefully she was in a nice, quiet office sipping Chardonnay, where I could chat with her in private.

He pointed to the front door.

"She's inside there? Are you sure?"

He nodded, the crest of hair above his face waving in the breeze.

Sighing, I turned and went through the red velvet curtain hanging over the front door. Shrieks and thumps came from other parts of the house. Lucy and Ryan were ahead of me, and I took a step to catch up, but the crowd shifted and I lost sight of them.

Then the room went black and the music stopped. An ominous voice came over the speakers, telling us that it was our last chance to leave . . . alive. Laughter followed, and an illuminated arrow appeared, pointing downward. The crowd shuffled forward. Music once again assailed our ears—something thrashy and very Ian-esque. This was what it would be like to be at Hatchet: extremely dark and incredibly loud. Only there we would be drinking and dancing.

"I'd rather be at Hatchet," I muttered.

That was something I'd never expected to hear myself say.

Moments later, we had arrived at a long wall with seven doors. Illuminated arrows once again pointed down above them.

"Make your choice," the voice instructed us. "And choose wisely."

The line of people began to divide into smaller groups in front of the doors. I couldn't see a thing other than the arrows. Maybe if I hung back, Lucy would be waiting for me too so we could reunite. I stepped off to the side and let everyone go past me. When it felt as though the room had emptied most of the way, I called her name.

Silence.

"Lucy!" I shouted as loudly as I could, then drifted toward the farthest door, opening it to see if I could find a shortcut.

Suddenly, I was shoved through it. I flailed my arms around, but whoever had pushed me was gone. The door slammed behind me. I was all alone in the space, and my heart was pounding. I crept forward toward a slit of light that was low to the ground on the other side of the room. When I'd made it about halfway through, a spotlight revealed a rocking chair moving backward and forward by itself. A loud cackle seemed to come from everywhere, audible even over the music. I noted that I was on a walkway, with railings on either side, presumably to keep us on track. When I was once again plunged into darkness, I took a moment to slow my breathing, then aimed myself forward until I was touching a door, which I pushed open. When it closed behind me, I was in another dark room, again with a bar of light on the other side.

Dark rooms were not my favorite thing. I pulled out my cell phone and turned on the flashlight.

"Douse the light," the same voice commanded me.

They were watching us? Creepy.

I walked forward, holding on to the railing. This time, the spotlight showed a pit-and-pendulum arrangement, the blade far too close for comfort—which Calliope would have loved—before I reached the other side. Something silky brushed my head unexpectedly, ratcheting up the discomfort.

The pattern repeated itself several more times in different rooms, spotlighting various unnerving scenes. People in masks began to pop up and screech at random intervals, adding another layer of anxiety, and twice someone grabbed my ankle from below the platform. I shook them off and raced ahead.

Finally, I found myself in a long hallway with strobe lights that only highlighted bursts of movement, so I couldn't see anything clearly, no matter how hard I stared. It was packed—apparently all the rooms emptied out here—and screams came from different directions. After I worked up the nerve to go forward, unseen hands suddenly poked me in the side. By the time I turned around, whoever had done the poking was gone. A few feet later, the same thing happened. More poking occurred as I went along. Although it was unpleasant, I'd just about settled into the rhythm of it when someone whispered into my ear, their breath hot on my neck, "You better watch your back, Emma Starrs."

I whirled around, but whoever it was had disappeared in the crowd.

Stumbling forward, I entered a room of mirrors. Thankfully, it was lit, if dimly. Although I was disoriented and numb with fear, I was able to quickly navigate it, and I was grateful to burst through the door into the backyard. Lucy and Ryan were still nowhere to be seen, so I wandered around among the clumps of people, looking for someone I knew.

"Emma!" said a figure with a pumpkin for a head.

I froze.

"Hold on." Both hands removed the pumpkin to reveal Farley Jennings.

"Farley!" I pitched myself forward, hugging him.

"Er, hello," he said, awkwardly. He gave me a few tentative pats in response to my clinging to him.

"I'm sorry," I said, stepping back. "I know you don't know me very well. I'm just . . . it's all . . . I can't . . ."

He looked into my eyes. "What's going on?"

Two witches came over and removed their masks as well.

"Are you okay?" Katrina asked, peering into my face.

"Let's find you a place to sit down," Bethany added.

Once we'd located a picnic table, I told them what had happened.

"Oh, it was probably Able," Farley said. "He likes to mess with people."

"He's here?"

"They're all here." Katrina craned her neck. "Able and Dodd are dressed up like vampires—which is so on point, because they can drain any committee meeting of life in like two seconds flat."

Bethany giggled. "And Cornelia and Prescott are trolls or something unidentifiable."

"Curious," Farley agreed.

"Don't worry, Emma," Katrina said.

"Maybe she *should* worry, though. Look what happened to Tip." Bethany's eyes widened. "Sorry. I didn't mean to say that out loud."

Katrina and Farley both gave her a look.

"Why don't I go buy us all a beer? Our shift's over," Farley offered. "We've been here all night."

"That's very kind of you, but no thanks," I said. "I need to find Tabitha."

"I saw her heading over there." Katrina pointed to a small building with a patio surrounded by people. "That's the staff headquarters. Want me to walk you over?"

"I've already taken up too much of your time," I said. "And I need a minute to clear my head. But thank you all so much for talking me down. I think I just got freaked out in there."

"It's scary if you go through alone, even if someone isn't threatening you," Farley commiserated. "I tried it earlier to see what it would be like, and I am pretty sure I'll be having nightmares tonight. No shame in being human. Who wants a drink?"

They said good-night and went to the crowded outdoor bar, which was draped in spider webs, perhaps left over from the ceiling decorations inside.

I marched up to the staff headquarters, where I discovered the entire country club clique except for Tabitha sprawled around the patio in folding chairs, drinking beer. I waved at them and knocked on the door, which was opened immediately.

"Emma." Melody faced me. "What a surprise. What do you need?"

"May I please speak to Tabitha alone?"

She gestured in an exaggerated *be my guest* kind of way, as if I were making an unreasonable request, then stormed out past me after I came inside.

The room was a small square with a row of file cabinets, a utilitarian desk, and a landline. Tabitha looked up from the paperwork in front of her and zipped her fleece jacket to her neck, as if to prevent any contact with me. "Yes?"

"You're busy, so I'll make this quick. Please stop walking around telling anyone who will listen that Nora and I are responsible for . . . what happened to Tip."

She leaned back and laced her fingers together. "You want me to stop?"

"Yes. You *know* that we had nothing to do with it."

"I don't, actually. I'm only saying what I believe to be the case."

"It's not the case. And I know that you don't like me, but that doesn't mean you should ruin my aunt's life."

"I shouldn't blame her anymore?"

"Yes. Thank you." Relief surged through my body.

"I should blame you instead? Is that what you're saying?"

"No." I sighed. "Tabitha, just tell the truth."

She lifted her chin. "I will continue to say *whatever* I want to *whoever* I want."

"Whomever," I said automatically.

Her eyes went even colder than usual.

"We're done here." She pointed toward the door.

That hadn't gone quite like I'd imagined.

Chapter Sixteen

By Wednesday, things seemed to be calming down in general. We hadn't had any calls from the police, Jake hadn't come cruising into the store to pelt us with additional questions, and Tabitha hadn't returned with more confusing flowered signs. The haunted-house threat didn't make my throat clench quite the same way in the bright light of day, though it was still worrisome. My family had advised me to be more alert than usual but not let it consume my every thought. None of us liked the fact that the threatener had used my name specifically, but realistically, there wasn't much to be done about it.

"Here you go. On the house today." Diandra Katz set down two Starlit Lattes on the bistro table. She was a wiry woman with a no-nonsense gray bob who had never, to my knowledge, taken a day off since opening Riverside Coffeehouse next door to the bookstore. We'd had a good long chat when Nora and I ordered, during which she'd shaken her head in disapproval when confiding that she'd heard about what Tabitha had done at BOO.

The free drinks were her way of supporting us.

I told her that I would drop off the book she'd mentioned. Also on the house.

We exchanged thanks, and she wiped her hands on her apron, which was a masterpiece, with a study of columbines embroidered across the upper half. She did the embroidery herself, and there was a rack along the side wall with aprons for purchase. Her flower scenes were so gorgeous that between the Etsy shop—run by her wife and business partner, Ariadne—and the coffeehouse traffic, each batch often sold out the same week she added them. Diandra wore them for work, not minding if the coffee grounds or stray jelly from a pastry left a mark, because she would just whip up another.

"If you need anything else, please let me know." She smiled and went back to the counter, where a tired-looking young mother was waiting with a double stroller full of precious but fussy cargo.

I decided to give the steaming latte a minute to cool, then asked Nora how she was doing, considering.

She grimaced. "I have to say, this is a new one for me. I've never been accused of murder before."

The young man in a Silvercrest College sweatshirt at the next table looked up, startled.

"*Accused* of," I said to him. "Not guilty of."

He put his earbuds in and returned his attention to the textbook in front of him.

That was probably better for all of us.

She regarded her drink thoughtfully. "It's giving me all kinds of insight into the psychological effects of false accusations. I'm already coming up with ways to incorporate that into a future book."

"Silver lining—I hadn't even thought of that."

My aunt gave me a meaningful look. "And you can use this experience too, darling. You know that I don't want to meddle or put any pressure on you, but when you're ready, I'd love to introduce you around my writing circles. You should come to some of the mystery conferences this spring as a start."

I blew on my latte. "I would love that, thank you. Would you be willing to read my manuscript after I revise it? I may be joining the critique group that meets at the bookstore."

She laughed. "I thought you'd *never* ask. Didn't you notice me hovering over your bound dissertation copies at the house all summer? I understand how those things go, so I didn't want to pry, but I've been dying to read it."

"You are welcome to read my dissertation whenever you like, but I'm planning some fairly extensive revisions, so you might want to wait."

"I'll wait. I'm glad about the critique group. By the way, do I understand correctly that Jake Hollister is running it? He's extremely talented."

"So I hear." I took a sip of my latte as a distraction and closed my eyes in response. It was restorative on multiple levels.

Nora tilted her head and studied my face. "Did I say something wrong?"

I hastened to assure her that she hadn't done anything. I couldn't quite explain it, but right now, simply hearing Jake's name reignited my irritation with him. So I changed the subject to the committee work.

"It's funny you mention that. I thought it would take ages for the next step to happen. You know, they'd have to hire a new dean who would have to get up to speed, then hem and haw about everything for a while. But the provost gave our proposal to the president, who approved it overnight. The move is happening next week."

I held up my cup and toasted her. "Congratulations!"

She frowned, which wasn't the reaction I had expected.

"What is it?"

"The speed with which this has gotten under way is unprecedented. In all my years at Silvercrest, I've never seen anything like it. It makes me worry a little. I'm not sure why."

"Oh, don't worry. You convinced them, that's all. And it's a good plan."

"Would you like to see the new space? I'm going over to campus now to do some packing and would love to show you around."

"I would, in fact. Lucy wasn't expecting me back today anyway, as I have some errands to run for Calliope's party. But I can do those later."

Nora took a sip of her latte. "I'm delighted that she's taken a shine to you."

"Calliope's taken a shine to me?"

She set down the mug. "You don't think she hands out nicknames all the time, do you, Raindrop?"

"It's *Raven*."

* * *

The elevator doors at the Arts and Humanities building opened with a soft ding, and we stepped out into a bright, airy space with a pair of doors to the left.

"Main office and chair's suite," Nora said.

Straight ahead was a waiting room with sofas and elegant lamps on polished wooden end tables. Puffy white clouds against a bright-blue sky were visible through glass along the far side. Nora veered to the right and down a long hallway of open doors. Each office had a large rectangular window and a wall of built-in bookshelves. Everything was a pristine white.

"Sorry about the paint smell. I'm not sure whose idea it was to add a fresh coat." My aunt shook her head. "It's the exact same color and probably cost a fortune."

"I could see why you wanted to move here." It was nothing like the dark caves the faculty members inhabited now.

"I hope the department likes it." Nora turned abruptly at the end of the hallway and went into a corner office. "The chair has emailed the assignment list, and this one is mine."

It was slightly larger than the other offices and had additional windows.

"It's beautiful," I said, smiling at her. "And you deserve it."

She looked around happily. "I can't wait to move in."

The elevator dinged, and a conversation could be heard. She put her finger to her mouth. I didn't understand why it would matter if we were found here, but I knew she had her reasons.

As the muffled voices grew closer, they became clearer and instantly recognizable.

"So what if we're not supposed to be here yet. What are they going to do, fire us?" Dodd said.

"Wait, lemme check the list. Yep, here's my office. . . ." Able's voice trailed off, and there was a low whistle.

"Quite suitable," Dodd said begrudgingly.

"What am I supposed to do with this big window, stare out of it all day? I have things to do," Able whined.

"You *can* lower the shades. You have a choice."

"That's true."

"And it's clean," Dodd pointed out.

"That's true too."

"Though there's nowhere to hide your whiskey. The shadows in your old office made for excellent camouflage."

"I might even have to thank Nora and her gang of suck-ups," Able snorted.

"Perish the thought. It will go straight to her head."

My aunt rolled her eyes.

Their voices grew louder. "Gotta say, I never really did care if we moved here or not, Dodd."

"Then why did you fight so hard against it?"

"Why not? It's been entertaining. Take every chance to make a ruckus, I always say."

"You *do* say that, Able."

"What about you?"

"The same, I suppose."

There was a long silence.

"It wasn't *only* that, though," Able said haltingly.

"Go on," Dodd encouraged him.

"Tip had plans for this floor. He reached out to me." Able sounded proud. "Asked for my help. Offered a little something."

Nora and I exchanged a glance.

After an extended pause, Dodd spoke. "He reached out to me as well."

"Well, whaddya know about that?" Able chuckled.

"Genuinely surprising," Dodd agreed. "Now which one is mine?"

Nora fluttered her arms, indicating that I should move behind the door. She squeezed in next to me right before they arrived at the office.

"Oh, look at *this* one," Able said, stopping outside. "Nice. Who's in there? Check the list."

All it would take for us to be discovered was either man making eye contact. I held my breath and stared at the hinges, willing them to provide enough cover for us.

Dodd looked at his phone screen. "Nora. Of course."

"Seriously? What *is* it about that b—" Able began.

Dodd continued as if he hadn't said anything. "Mine better be *at least* this good."

They moved down the hallway to the other corner office, where they stopped. I watched through the crack as Dodd poked his head inside. "This'll do."

"*I* don't need a corner office," Able said, though he didn't sound convinced and mumbled under his breath.

"If you do, I'm sure we can come up with a reason to have Nora reassigned. Tomorrow, let's plead your case to the chair."

"Yes! But tonight, let's grab a drink and strategize. On *you*, my friend."

"Nice try. I bought last time, Able, so *you're* buying!"

They laughed themselves all the way to the elevator.

When we heard the doors close, we came out from our hiding spot.

"Did they say that Tip bribed them to vote against the English department move?" I asked.

"That's what I heard too." Nora peered down the hallway, checking to make sure they'd gone.

"And that they're going to try to steal your office?"

"Don't worry . . . they will *not* win *that* battle."

"We should call the police immediately about the bribery," I said firmly as we walked away from her office. "Clear things up. Doesn't this give them a motive?"

"Let me think about it," she said. "I don't know if it does. Why would Able and Dodd kill the person that was giving them something? And what was being given, anyway? We don't know whether it was money or a new position or what."

"Good point. Though does it matter? *Something* was given. And maybe we don't need to figure that part out ourselves. Let the professionals take it from here." I pushed the elevator button.

"Still, we weren't supposed to be on this floor, any of us, yet. All of the professors were *specifically* told that this was off-limits until moving day. Something about insurance. That's one reason I didn't want them to find us here. It would have been awkward."

"It would have be even *more* awkward if they'd discovered us hiding from them behind the door."

"True, but at least this way we didn't have to explain ourselves. Especially since I'm sure they wouldn't have been pleased to know we'd overheard them."

The doors opened, and we took the elevator down to the ground floor.

"They'd probably have used the off-limits rule against us," she continued.

"But they were here too," I protested, "and they were talking about a bribe."

Nora laughed. "With people like that, it doesn't matter what *they* do. It matters what they can accuse *other* people of doing."

"I feel like I should be more shocked to hear that, but I'm not."

"Then you're ready for a career in academia." She gave me a rueful smile. "Anyway, I don't want to get a breaking-and-entering slapped on top of whatever charges may be in the works right now."

"I understand. I wish we'd recorded their conversation, though."

"Who knew it was going to take such a turn?" She put her hand over her chest. "That was legitimately shocking."

We walked out of the building. It was a stunning fall day, with leaves gamboling along the sidewalk. Students were taking full advantage, soaking up the sun on the quad. A Frisbee crashed next to us, and Nora sent it flying back with a flick of her wrist. Her aim was perfect, delivering the disc right to the man who had thrown it. He responded with a respectful salute.

"What do you think Tip wanted to do with the space?" I asked. "Why would he resort to paying professors for it?"

"That's the million-dollar question," she replied.

"A million dollars?"

"Metaphorically speaking." She moved behind me to allow a biker to pass. "Or not."

I twisted my head to address her. "What do you mean?"

She took a few quick steps to catch up again. "In some cases, we're told there's no funding available *anywhere*, but in other cases, it simply appears out of nowhere. That is one of the greatest mysteries of the college budget process."

"Do you think the dean offered a bribe to Prescott and Cornelia as well?" I mused. "They were on the committee too."

Nora stopped abruptly. "Hadn't considered that. You're right. We'll have to ask. But first, let's go over to the dean's office."

"Now?"

"Yes. We can ask his executive assistant some questions. She's lovely." Her eyes sparkled. "You up for it?"

"*So* up for it."

We crossed the quad and entered the Cottingham Administration building, named after the donor whose edifice had enticed all the muckety-mucks away from Arts and Humanities with a better view. One step into the lobby, I could understand the allure. Through the glass wall across from us, the river was rushing by. A pile of boulders created multiple small waterfalls—the cascade flowed against the dark moss like an animated painting. I could have happily sat and observed the sight all day long.

Nora smiled at my response and led me into the elevator. Unlike the one in the Arts and Humanities building, which was perfectly nice as far as elevators went, this one was indisputably luxurious, with marble panels trimmed in gold. Instead of neon, it had the kind of soft lighting that movie stars of a certain age began demanding in their contracts.

"We should take every photo in here from now on."

She laughed. "I agree. We've never looked better."

"This whole building, wow."

"I know. You really can't blame the people who moved here when given the chance. We all probably would have done the same. Though I'm not complaining—my new office is going to be sheer bliss." Nora pointed to the ceiling. "Do you want me to do the talking up there?"

"Please."

"Feel free to jump in if you think of anything, but I do have a bit of a plan, I think."

"Go for it."

When we reached the twelfth floor, the doors slid open silently, and we stepped into yet more opulence. A middle-aged woman with blonde hair scraped back into a bun and pink lipstick that matched her jacket smiled at us. A ceramic tulip pin added a bit of whimsy. The engraved plaque on her desk read *Eve Case, Assistant to the Dean*.

Nora introduced me as her niece and, once again, included the fact that I was a new PhD—all part of her privately stated goal to wedge me into the appropriate circles at Silvercrest so that if any classes became available, they would know who I was. She had also told me that if I did work there as an adjunct, it would be useful when a full-time position became available. I wasn't so sure about that—some schools wanted to bring in fresh faces—but I trusted her inclinations.

"It's a pleasure to meet you, Dr. Starrs," Eve said. I detected a faint southern accent.

"Likewise, and please call me Emma."

She turned to Nora. "Hello, Professor Haven."

"And please call me Nora," my aunt said. "I tell you that every time."

"You do," Eve replied. "But I'm in the habit of addressing the professors formally. Some of them, and I'm not going to name names, *definitely* care about that. And Dean Baxter fell into that category, so it's been our practice here in the office."

Nora smiled at her. "Whatever's easiest for you. Speaking of the dean, I'm so sorry for your loss—I know you've worked with him for ages."

Eve's eyes filled with tears. She opened a drawer and pulled out a tissue, which she used to wipe away the ones that fell. I was struck by the difference between her palpable grief and Tabitha's lack thereof. I reminded myself that just because Tabitha didn't *seem* sad didn't mean she wasn't.

"I was very fond of him," she said. "I know he could be difficult at times. I think all great men can be, though."

"Is there anything I can do for you?" Nora asked.

Eve beamed up at her. "Oh, I'm fine. But thank you for offering. That is so sweet."

"Call me anytime."

"I appreciate that." Eve picked up a page from her desk, then put it down again. "But where *are* my manners? You came all the way over here, and I haven't even asked how I may help *you*!"

"Nothing major—I wanted to make sure that everything was in order for the move," Nora said. "Thank you again for processing the materials so quickly, getting them up the chain."

"Well, I know you've been working on that project forever and a day," Eve said. "It was the *least* I could do."

"It has been a long time—you're right," Nora said with an appreciative laugh. "There was a phase in there where I thought we might miss out."

Eve looked intrigued. "Why?"

"Well, I'm not sure I should say anything." Nora made a show of looking around to be sure no one was listening.

Eve leaned forward, clearly open to any juicy gossip. "Just between us."

"I heard that Tip was talking to some of the professors on the committee off the record . . ."

She waited for Eve to fill in the blanks, but nothing happened.

Nora lowered her voice. "Making arrangements to put someone else in there."

Again, Eve didn't contribute to the conversation but maintained her rapt expression.

"Instead of the English department," Nora said, with a hint of exasperation.

"Oh, I knew about *that*," Eve replied, her face falling. Obviously she'd anticipated something spicier.

"Which department was it?"

Eve put her elbows on the table and rested her chin on one palm. "I'm sorry, I can't think who it was. Ever since the dean passed, my memory has been a bit foggy."

"I understand," Nora said softly. She waited a beat, then went on, watching Eve closely. "I do know that some of the English faculty were involved in discussions about it. Professor Stimson, I think, was one of them."

"Right. He and Professor Holley came over for private meetings."

"Was there any sort of discussion about a . . ." My aunt trailed off.

"Honorarium?" I offered.

"Yes, *thank* you, Emma. Was there an honorarium involved with the project that you were aware of, Eve?"

Eve looked blank. "What do you mean?"

"I mean"—Nora waved her hand around in tiny circles while she thought of the right phrasing—"the possibility of perks, I suppose."

"None that I heard about."

"Well, if you think of anything, will you please let us know? It's important." I didn't mean to blurt that out, but there it was. I'd revealed that we were interested in more than chat. A skilled interrogator I was not.

Eve scrutinized me. "Do you work here at the college?"

"No. But I'm at the bookstore in town." I said it with authority, as if that explained why I was fully qualified to press her for information about professors. I fished a card out of my bag and handed it to her.

"Oh, I *love* Starlit Bookshop," Eve said happily, much to my relief. "That's right—I knew your family owned it, Nora. Sorry. I'm planning to do some holiday shopping there before too long."

"Please do, and I hope you'll join us for Calliope Nightfall's release party on Halloween in the meantime," I said.

"I'll try." Eve started talking about Calliope's last book, and Nora sighed almost imperceptibly.

I didn't dare look at my aunt, since I knew I'd ruined the flow of her investigation.

When Eve stopped gushing, Nora repeated the request to let us know if she thought of anything.

"Sure! And I hope I'll see you at the party," Eve said to me.

"The more, the merrier, so please bring friends. The specific details are on the website," I told her. "But you can call the store anytime if you have questions. Our number is on the card."

"Time to go, Emma," Nora said.

I followed her into the elevator, an apology already spilling from my lips.

Eve called out, "Oh, I remembered something: that Ian person also used to come by too."

I stuck my hand out and stopped the doors, then we hurried back to her desk.

"Are you talking about Ian Gladstone?" I asked.

She brightened. "Yes, exactly."

"How many times did he come by?"

"Wait." She tapped a few keys and pulled up a calendar on her computer. She did a search and turned back to us. "Six times in the past year."

"Do you happen to know what it was about?" Nora asked.

"I can't hear through the door. Unless they're shouting." She laughed, then stopped suddenly. "Although one time they *did*. Something about a tub or a barrel? And there was another whole week devoted to chairs. It didn't make any sense to me."

"Did you see any paperwork go through in either of those situations?" I didn't know exactly what I was looking for, but I sensed there was a trail to be followed.

"Sorry. It was all phone calls and meetings. Maybe emails, but I don't have access to the dean's account."

"Could you get access?" I asked Eve.

Eve shook her head briskly. "Oh no. The school is extremely serious about privacy."

"Now that he's no longer . . . around," I said, "who would have access to his email account?"

"IT, maybe?" Eve shrugged. "Above my pay grade, I'm afraid. Sorry about that. I wish I could be more helpful."

"You have been," I assured her. "Thank you very much for your time. We'll see you later."

At least that sounded professional. Ish.

In the elevator, I apologized to my aunt again.

"Don't worry about it," she said. "I think we did rather well in our interrogation."

"It's interesting that Ian would meet with Tip, don't you think?"

"Yes." Nora pursed her lips as she thought. "Doesn't mean it's related to anything happening with Able and Dodd, though."

"True."

"Do you think they even know each other? It's not like Able and Dodd are part of the Tabitha-and-Ian crowd."

"And Ian wasn't at the dinner party," I said. "Which still makes me suspicious, even if Jake doesn't think it's important."

"I hear you, though maybe let that go for now. If you zero in on him to the exclusion of everyone else, it could prevent you from seeing the bigger picture."

When we reached the ground floor, a new thought perked me up. "How strange is it that we're talking about Ian and Tip? Two of Tabitha's *husbands*. Why wouldn't she be part of that? Did she even know they were meeting? I have so many questions."

"Do you think we might need to start worrying for her safety?" Nora asked. "The husbands could have been planning something reprehensible."

I pondered this. "Not the way Ian looked at her in the pictures."

"Probably not," she agreed.

"Unless . . ." I paused, working out a new angle.

"Unless what?"

"Unless there's something he wants more than he wants Tabitha."

Chapter Seventeen

On the sidewalk outside, Nora and I regrouped.

"Should we talk to Dodd and Able about this? Do you think they'll actually tell us anything?" I asked.

"Maybe not, but their body language might reveal something."

"Good point."

"We're not going to mention that we overheard them on the top floor, right?" She repositioned the bag on her shoulder as we headed toward the Arts and Humanities building.

"Right. You said that might create other problems. But how do we ease into the fact that we know something was going on? We can't tell them we overheard them. We can't tell them we asked Eve about them behind their backs. What can we say?"

Nora mulled this over. "Maybe that we heard there were side conversations with the dean during the committee work and that was of concern?"

"The old 'rumor has it' approach?"

She made a face. "It's not my typical style. I do prefer to be more direct. But in this case, perhaps the vaguer, the better."

"Aren't they going to wonder why I'm involved in the conversation? I don't work here."

"They saw you at the restaurant meeting, though, so it might not seem wholly unexpected. If you feel uncomfortable, you could stand in the hallway within hearing distance while I speak to each of them alone."

"Um . . . not a chance."

She laughed. "I didn't think so."

"What about IT? Do you have any connections there who could check into Tip's emails?"

"Hack into, you mean?"

"I didn't say *hack*, Nora. I said *check*."

"Tomato, tomahto. And no, unfortunately. I think something like that would be difficult for anyone who isn't a hack—a *checker*. Eve is correct that they're serious about privacy around here. You should see what you have to go through just to get a campus email account in the first place. And if you forget your password, heaven help you."

"Aren't there brilliant students who could do it in a heartbeat?" I gestured toward the busy quad.

"Probably students *and* professors. But the problem is that I don't know who they are. It's not like we could send out an all-campus email asking for the hackers to identify themselves."

"In the movies, there's always someone who knows someone in these kinds of situations."

"Too bad we aren't living in a movie."

I held the door for Nora, then followed her inside and down the hall to the English department. As we approached, the atmosphere seemed increasingly electric. I wondered if she sensed it too. It felt as though we were getting closer to discovering something important.

A few minutes later, however, our hopes were dashed. Neither professor was in his office. It was as if we'd been racing across the waves in a sailboat, finish line in sight, and the wind vanished.

As we stood there dejectedly, Prescott and Cornelia drifted past and greeted us. My aunt's eyes lit up, and she angled her head toward their backs. "Let's talk to *them*," she said in a low voice.

"I'm game." It would be a shame to waste all the interrogation energy we'd roused up.

The couple went into Cornelia's office, which was large but extremely cluttered. Dolls were sitting along the window ledges and bookshelves, with more in a row on her desk in front of her. She must be an avid collector.

Nora rapped on the door. Prescott, in the same suit he'd been wearing the other night, was leaning against the wall; he didn't say anything. Cornelia, on the other hand, proclaimed her happiness at seeing me again and welcomed us both into her office. She was wearing a ruffled apron over a gingham dress and very much resembled a doll herself. The similarity was intensified when she inquired how she could help us; her voice was soft and high, like Felicity's.

"I won't take up too much of your time," Nora said. "But I wonder if you could help me with something. I have two quick questions."

"Sure," Cornelia replied warmly. "Please come in." She waved us over to her massive oak desk.

The farther into the office we moved, the creepier the dolls became. Some of their eyes didn't even have irises, only empty white spaces.

"First, does it look like we might have any classes available for adjuncts this spring? As you know, my niece here has the appropriate credentials and has moved to Silvercrest permanently. She'd be a wonderful colleague, though I do recognize I am a bit biased in that regard."

Awkward.

Especially with all the blank stares that the dolls were giving me.

Cornelia removed a sheet from a notepad and picked up a pen.

"You have to apply," Prescott said brusquely. "On the human resources website."

"I was writing that down for her," Cornelia told him. There was something in her voice that I didn't expect, a tone telling him to back off. He did, which I also didn't expect, but he crossed his arms and resumed glowering at us.

After she had carefully—and slowly—added the information, she held the paper out over her desk, next to a baby doll with painted-on eyebrows that turned its expression practically demonic. I had a flashback to the unnerving doll in the lost-and-found box all those years ago and swallowed hard.

She shook it gently, so I took a step forward and accepted the note, which had an image of flowers bursting from a metal watering can in the corner. It was completely on-brand for Cornelia.

"Once you go through the formal application process, then I can contact you for an interview and discussion about potential teaching." She gave me a quick smile.

I thanked her.

"When there's an opening," Prescott mumbled.

"Fabulous, thank you," Nora said. "And now that you've settled that, I wanted to make sure we were on track for the move."

"As far as I know," Cornelia replied.

Prescott's lips tightened. Cornelia's eyes darted in his direction and away again, as if she expected him to say something. If there was lingering animosity, I wouldn't be surprised, given that they'd split their votes on the moving issue.

"I appreciate your supporting the proposal. I think it will be a positive change for the department." My aunt smiled at her.

"I hope so. It certainly is a lovely space."

"It is." Nora paused, then asked if she could close the office door.

Cornelia approved her request, and the door was closed. Prescott appeared much more interested than he had before.

When my aunt returned to her spot, she lowered her voice. "It's come to my attention that there may have been some . . . complications . . . during the committee work."

Prescott looked over the top of his glasses, paying close attention.

"What do you mean by 'complications'?" Cornelia asked.

"Some . . . outside interference, perhaps."

"Say what you mean, Nora," Prescott snapped. "No need to cloak it in mystery. Tell us. What happened?"

"I'm afraid I'm not at liberty to offer particulars," she said, "but I've been given the impression that someone may have been attempting to tamper with the voting process."

Cornelia sucked in her breath.

"Do you mean that the last vote shouldn't count? I couldn't agree more. The way you all took the opportunity to charge forward was despicable." Prescott shook his finger at my aunt for good measure.

"I don't understand," the department chair said. "Do you want us to undo the most recent vote?"

"No," Nora said quickly, realizing that her strategy might be backfiring. "I mean there may have been interference long before that."

"Before that? Seriously? Then what are you complaining about?" Prescott demanded. "You got your way. You won. Take the win, Nora."

"Pres—" Cornelia said, pushing both of her palms lower in the air to indicate that he should calm down.

"Don't shush me, Cornelia. I am outraged!" He stalked over to the door and flung it open.

We were all silent after he left. If I'd thought it was awkward in the office before, that was nothing compared to this.

"I'm sorry," Nora said.

"No, *I'm* sorry," Cornelia replied. "It's not you. He's angry with me for not voting his way, which he considered to be unsupportive of his needs. But I had to do what was best for the greatest number of people. I am the department chair, after all. It's my job."

"That was very brave of you," my aunt replied.

"Perhaps, but I'll be paying for it a long time."

Nora startled. "Certainly not in any dangerous way—"

"No, not like that. He needs to get himself through the sulking phase. It may take a while, but he always comes around." Cornelia gave her a reassuring smile.

I looked around the room, not wanting to intrude on their apologies. Then I hastily returned my attention to Cornelia and Nora because the dolls made my skin crawl.

"Emma, I see you admiring my dolls," Cornelia said. "Please choose one to take with you. I love to give them away to people who recognize their beauty."

Oh no.

"I couldn't possibly," I said. Her smile faltered just enough that I saw any chance at a future teaching career at Silvercrest hanging in the balance. "I mean, they're all so . . . it would be too hard to choose."

"Don't worry, I have *many* more at home."

I imagined the Abernathy house teeming with dolls staring from every possible angle and shuddered. Then I tried to cover that up by murmuring something about the pervasive chill in the autumn air, which Nora picked up on and repeated, mercifully, despite the blatant non sequitur.

Cornelia didn't seem to notice. "Please do pick one. It gives me joy to find a new home for my dolls. Also, whenever someone takes one, I get to go on the hunt again to replace my stock. It's a win-win."

Maybe not so much for the recipient.

I moved hesitantly toward the window ledge. Cornelia leaped up from her chair and came around the desk to stand next to me. She began to introduce me to every doll down the row, telling me its name and whether it had come from a garage sale, online auction, or flea market. To forestall learning the provenance of every single one, I reached out and grabbed a nearby black cat propped against the window as if it were surveying the campus. When I turned it around, I jolted. Her oversized gemstone eyes seemed to stare into my very soul.

Cornelia clapped her hands. "Ooh, Ghost Kitty is very special."

"Ghost—" I looked down at the thing in my hands with trepidation.

"Kitty, yes. She came from a secondhand shop in London. The owners said that they had no memory of anyone bringing her in. Isn't that strange? No donation, no paperwork, no explanation whatsoever. She simply appeared on the shelves one day as if she'd materialized—hence her name."

"If she's special, please keep her," I said, holding the cat out and hoping my tone didn't come across as the plea that it actually was.

Cornelia waggled her head. "No. She's obviously chosen you. How lucky you are!"

Nora, behind her, was blatantly biting back a smile.

Cornelia instructed me to take good care of my new companion and insisted that I offer updates about her in the future.

"Be careful," she said, as we were leaving.

With Ghost Kitty.

Chapter Eighteen

"What is the current status of the life-sized pit-and-pendulum display?" Calliope inquired two days later. She had taken to dropping by the store regularly as the date of her launch grew closer. She had also changed her mind about every detail of the party, often only to change it back again a few hours or days later. I was trying to accomplish everything she wanted, but at this point, I didn't want to undo a single thing.

I had a flashback to the dark rooms at Screamfest and shivered.

Calliope put a stuffed raven back into the box and patted its head. "I reached out to some of my theater friends to see if any of them are willing to play the victim. And happily, one of them probably has access to enough rat props as well."

"Wait, what? You want *rats* in the—"

"They're very important!" A muscle twitched in her cheek.

"There isn't room for a pit. And there will *not* be rats involved in any way at the party," I said firmly. Lucy would have a fit if I manifested all of what Calliope was describing. I had to draw the line somewhere.

The author fiddled with her necklaces—she had a chunky onyx pendant as well as smaller assorted crystals on multiple cords—as she processed this.

I forged ahead. "I think we'll be fine without that. What we have already put together is going to be spectacular."

Once she had untangled the jewelry to her satisfaction, she raised her head. "I don't think we're *quite* there yet."

I sent up a prayer to the universe that whatever request came out of her mouth next would be small and easy to accommodate.

"Let's turn this into a costume party!" She patted her hands together lightly, applauding her own idea.

I was able to keep my voice calm, but inside I was shrieking. "The launch is happening so soon, though—"

"*And* make it clear that we are doing this invitation-only." Calliope began to pace back and forth. "Everyone *must* wear a costume or they will be denied entrance."

"But we've already been publicizing it *without* saying anything about invitations or costumes."

"Where?"

"The website, the store newsletter, and flyers around town."

She applauded again. "Perfect. You can update them with an addendum."

"An addendum that *un*-invites the general public? I strongly suggest that we do *not* do that. We want to keep everything positive and bring in the highest number of readers." For the sake of both Calliope and the bookstore.

"Perhaps you're right about the invitations." She tapped her chin. "But I *insist* upon costumes."

"Won't it be too late for people to get a hold of costumes?"

"They can make something from whatever they have around the house." She swirled her hand around. "It will be a chance for them to be creative. Everyone needs more creativity in their lives."

Not *forced* creativity.

Calliope threw her hands up into the air. "They could use scarves or sheets and just . . . add a hat. I don't think I'm asking too much, do you?"

I did, but I kept that thought to myself, pointing out instead that giving anyone a reason to stay home—for example, not wanting to deal with the hassle of producing a costume—would mean fewer sales. The boxes of books we had ordered were stacked to the ceiling in the stock room. We wanted to sell every last one, not ship them back.

She laughed softly. "Oh no. They won't stay home. My launch parties are always standing room only. People in this town are *very* interested in my work. And this *must* be my greatest launch yet!"

"Are you sure this is what you want? People don't usually have to dress up in order to attend a reading."

"*This* time, they do."

I could see that there was no going back now.

"To clarify, you don't mean that they have to wear a costume that has something to do with Poe, do you?" As soon as I heard the words come out of my mouth, I winced. Why would I even *put* that idea into her head?

Calliope looked up at the ceiling, considering my question. I'd never been so relieved to see someone's mouth form the word *no.*

"I'd like to see what they come up with on their own. Halloween provides a meaningful opportunity for people to present themselves in a way that is not always available to them, as you are aware."

"Yes. Good. Great."

When I agreed so readily, she frowned. I half-expected her to change her mind again, to be contrary. But instead she patted my hand, the little bells on her bracelets jangling. "I believe in you, Raven. I know you can make this happen."

She picked up the black plushie bird and looked deeply into its glass eyes. "This little guy wants to come home with me."

I ushered her over to the front before she plundered any more of the decorations.

"I'll be checking in with you later," she said.

Of course she would be.

Calliope floated outside, hugging her new friend.

Sighing, I closed the door behind her.

"Given her affinity for that stuffed bird, I have a feeling that Calliope would love Ghost Kitty," Lucy said from behind the register. "If you feel like gifting her something else."

"I'm afraid that Cornelia will ask me to send her a selfie in the future, though, and I won't be able to do that. Or she'll see the doll at Calliope's house and know what I did."

Lucy lifted her shoulders. "Or she might be delighted that Ghost Kitty went to live with such a renowned author."

"Chances are that Calliope probably already has some dolls from Cornelia's collection, don't you think?"

"But she doesn't have Ghost Kitty," my sister said.

"Could we stop talking about Ghost Kitty, please?" I shot a glance over to the front window, where I'd shoved the doll after returning from campus. She'd blended in surprisingly well with the existing display. "I don't want her to get mad."

"You don't want her to get *mad*?" Lucy was struggling to keep a straight face.

"The last thing Cornelia said was 'be careful.' I don't know if she was issuing a warning about the doll being fragile or something much more ominous. So maybe let's not laugh at Ghost Kitty?"

"I'm not laughing," she said, laughing.

Which made me laugh too.

Uneasily.

"Moving on," I said, "I have to get started on the new costume requirement."

"At least it will be fun to see people dressed up." Bless my sister for trying to come up with a positive spin.

"We'd better get started on ours," I said, "as if we don't already have enough to do."

"Hang in there," Lucy said, as I passed her to go into the office. I signed on to the store's website and updated the event post with large, bold letters: *COSTUME REQUIRED FOR ATTENDANCE*. Then I sent a newsflash to our mailing list, informing them of the situation. Next, I printed out the same line on a piece of paper and taped it to the poster in the display window. Finally, I copy-and-pasted the line over and over again on a document and printed out enough copies of the addendum to tape to the flyers we'd plastered all over town. After cutting the page into strips, I left in a hurry, trying to remember all the places where we'd distributed them the first time.

After I'd updated them—at least the ones I could find—I stopped by Riverview Vintage, a nearby consignment store owned by a friend of mine, Marlowe Markson. I preferred to try to cobble costumes together from secondhand pieces rather than buy a packaged set, if possible. It was one of my favorite stores—and not only when I needed a costume—full of carefully curated clothing and accessories. I often emerged with unexpected treasures, from jewelry made by local artisans to one-of-a-kind jackets from earlier eras.

A chime rang out softly when I walked through the doors. It was a large space filled with a dizzying array of styles. The racks had been arranged to allow maximum ease of movement, not only on the floor but on the wall as well. The accessories were artistically displayed on shelves, like a gallery installation. I couldn't imagine how difficult it was to keep them in such precise order, but Marlowe and her staff were on top of it.

"Em! What a nice surprise." Marlowe hung whatever she was carrying on a rack and came toward me. Her long jacket, nipped in at the waist, and pencil skirt were paired with lace-up ankle boots. She had pulled her dark hair back into a chignon and added bright-red lipstick and winged eyeliner.

"How are you?" I asked. "Fantastic outfit, as usual."

"You're sweet, as usual. Thank you. And things have been excellent. The university theater department sourced so many costumes and props for their production that my whole 1950s section was cleaned out! Had to repurpose the area." She pointed to the rack where she stored special items from midcentury, which now held a collection of capes and witch hats.

"Well, get ready for another influx, because Calliope Nightfall decreed that anyone attending her launch party next weekend must wear a costume in order to be granted entry."

"Bring it on." She laughed. "We've overstocked for Halloween anyway, so I'd be glad for it. If anyone asks for a recommendation, please send them here."

"I always do."

"And I love you for it," she said, blowing me a kiss. "Is there anything special I can help you with today, or are you in a browsing mood?"

"I need a costume."

"I have a wide variety of witchy gear over there, as you saw," she said. "Feeling Maleficent?"

I laughed. "Um . . ."

"Give me a minute." She zipped around the store, confidently pulling items together from various places and putting them on an empty rack near the register. I wandered over to the accessories wall, where I spotted a square black messenger bag—not too large, not too small—that would come in handy if I decided to join West Side Writers and needed to carry pages around.

Who was I kidding? I'd decided to join the second Jake mentioned that he was writing thrillers and detecting at the same time. But for some reason, I kept going back and forth about officially admitting it.

I pulled the bag down and inspected it carefully. It looked brand new. No marks or peculiar smells. The flap had a silver buckle closure that wasn't tarnished. The more I looked at it, the more I loved it. It felt somehow like a confirmation that it was the right time to commit to my novel.

"Ready for you," Marlowe called from the other side of the store. When I turned around, bag in hand, my mouth fell open. She had arranged several choices for me, with accessories.

"First we have a . . . hmm." She stared at the sky-blue silk dress and white faux-fur stole while she searched for the right title. "A fancy lady."

"Ooh," I said. "That *is* fancy." Marlowe presented some long white gloves and a navy-blue hat with a veil. The ensemble was very similar to what Tabitha had worn to the murder mystery dinner, though. Pass.

"Next, it's . . . the western woman." The leather jacket and long skirt looked like something I'd seen a sharpshooter wear in an old photo. Cowboy boots and a wide-brimmed felt hat rested on the counter next to it.

Marlowe took one look at my face. "Never mind."

"It's nice!" I protested. "I'm just trying to imagine myself in it."

"No. Not for you. That's okay. You know I love providing options." She slid the first two outfits to the end of the rack to reveal the third item, a black silk sheath dress with a beaded duster jacket. It was indescribably beautiful. "This one is . . . a glamorous sleuth. It even has pockets for your pistol and magnifying glass."

"Sold."

She laughed. "Don't you want to try it on?"

"No. I want to buy it, please. The beading is exquisite."

"It's your size, so it should work. If it doesn't, you can always return it."

"Even if it doesn't fit, I want to have it in my closet and be able to look at it once in a while."

Marlowe smiled and handed me a small velvet purse and matching headband.

"Perfection," I told her.

"Everything here has already been dry-cleaned and is ready to go, so you should be able to wear it without any further ado."

"You are the best, my friend. Thank you so much. And may I say yet again that you are superb at styling?"

"That's very kind of you."

I added the messenger bag to the pile.

She frowned. "That doesn't really go with the rest, I'm sorry to inform you."

"No, that's for everyday." I told her about the critique group opportunity, and she approved.

"You should join us too!" I exclaimed. Marlowe wrote fiction as well. We'd traded drafts for years. Her work in progress was a collection of short stories about a brilliant African American private investigator who tracked down criminals in a city much like Denver. Marlowe had always said it was the way she envisioned her life would be if she hadn't inherited the vintage store.

"Let me think about it," she said. "I haven't had time to write much lately. It's been so busy here. I'd love to beta read for you, though, anytime."

"Thank you, and likewise. I hope that you'll keep working on your book."

"I'm not giving up. I'm taking a break. But shouldn't you become a member of the writing group before you start inviting other people?"

"Perhaps," I said. "I do tend to get ahead of myself. But I know they'd love to have you. Who wouldn't? You're fabulous."

"I'll think about it. Thanks, Em."

While she was ringing everything up, I told her about Tabitha and Tip. She said she knew, regardless of the rumors, that Nora and I were innocent.

"I wouldn't believe anything *she* said, anyway." Marlowe hadn't forgotten how Tabitha and her friends had hassled us in school when we were just sitting there, reading. It had really seemed to bother them that books made us so happy. But in murder mysteries, Marlowe and I found solace from some of the injustices of life, and our fondness for the genre had only increased from there.

"Between us, Nora and I are trying to figure out what happened on our own," I confided.

That caught her attention. She gave me a thoughtful look. "So you're an *actual* detective now? Like the ones in our books?"

"Very funny. No. We're trying to gather information."

"I think you mean you're gathering *clues*." She winked.

After swiping my credit card, I accepted multiple bags from Marlowe.

"Speaking of Nora, I'm going to have a hard time keeping this outfit away from her."

"You're going to have to keep a secret. Like any sleuth worth her salt."

Chapter Nineteen

I bent the skeleton's arm into yet another position and took a step back to evaluate. It looked as though it were waving hello.

I was waving back when my cell phone chimed.

"Hi, Emma, it's Vivi. I know it's *extremely* last minute, especially for a Saturday, but is there any chance you might be free tonight? I have a small staffing issue that I'm trying to solve and wondered if you might be interested."

"How can I help?" I was surprised by the request, but I was available. Max and Bella were working the bookstore, and I didn't have any plans other than popping some corn and watching a movie.

"I would need you to be a floater—sign people in, then serve punch, run trays, that kind of thing. But I was thinking that if you brought business cards, I could introduce you to some attendees who regularly throw their own events and are always looking for wonderful planners and interesting locations, both of which Starlit Bookshop offers. This is a pretty big party, so it could work out for both of us."

"Oh, I so appreciate that. Thank you. What should I wear?"

She gave me the particulars and the address where I'd need to show up. I went downstairs to the office to fetch a stack of our business cards, allowing myself to daydream about connecting with the kind of client who would generate so much business that we'd never have to worry about our budget again. A whale, as they say in corporate circles—elusive but highly sought.

Though in landlocked Colorado, a whale of any kind seemed downright unimaginable.

* * *

The phone app directed me to the address Vivi had given me, which turned out to be the Silvercrest Country Club. It was surrounded by a towering brick wall that culminated in a monogrammed iron gate with *SCC* in elaborate cursive, surrounded by ornate scrollwork.

I gave my name to the sentry—or whatever you called him—out front, who checked my name off the list and waved me through. The driveway circled around a fountain that was lit up from below, highlighting the multiple urns that merrily spilled water from one level to the next.

Instead of heading for the clump of valets in yellow vests, who brought to mind a hive of buzzing bees, I turned right into the parking lot, where I sat gripping the steering wheel and observing the long rectangular building with three stories. Ivy twined up the right side, holding on for dear life to the brick wall. Red shutters matched the double front doors, and hanging lamps illuminated the pair of stone lions staring coolly ahead on either side of the stairs.

I had never been inside, but I'd sneaked onto the golf course and tennis courts with friends a few times in high school, so I'd seen the outside of the club from the back, where an oversized patio with round iron tables and more marble urns filled with flowering shrubs could be found.

The Silvercrest Country Club didn't pretend to be anything other than what it was, an exclusive place for people who could afford the exorbitant fees. Members were sponsored by other people who hand-selected them for membership. Needless to say, it left a good portion of us out.

Which was, after all, its purpose.

Many a business deal had been struck behind those walls, a situation that offered a particular challenge to those who couldn't afford access. The town of Silvercrest had been petitioned again and again by small business owners and other interested parties trying to force the club to revise its guidelines and fees for membership, but as of yet, no one had been successful. The answer had always been that it was a private club, with a right to determine its own procedures.

I was curious to go inside, but it was daunting. After a lifetime of exclusion, it felt like I would be crossing some sort of boundary that I wasn't sure I wanted to cross. As I wrestled with the unexpectedly complicated emotion, a van pulled up next to me. Once I caught sight of Vivi's flower logo, I shoved my confusion back down to wherever it usually resided and climbed out of the car. Vivi flashed me a smile as she opened the back doors of her van and began handing things to her team, who seemed to be heading toward us from every direction.

"Thanks so much for coming," she said. She ducked into the van and removed a white jacket with silver piping, which she handed to me. "Ready?"

"Ready." I pulled the jacket on, then followed her out of the parking lot.

Once we reached the sidewalk, she handed me a bag and a clipboard. "Would you mind doing check-in? Place the name tags from the bag on the table in alphabetical rows. When people arrive, find the guest's name on the list, check it off, and point to their name tag if they can't locate it themselves. If someone shows up who isn't on the list, call me."

"Got it. What's this event?"

"It's a party to welcome the latest class of country club members. Usually events here don't have name tags because people know each other, but it's done at these gatherings to help the newbies."

She led me around the side to the staff entrance, through the already busy kitchen, and down a hallway to a door that opened onto the lobby.

The walls were papered in a muted gray-and-cream pattern. A tapestry with another monogram in the same cursive as the gates outside took up much of the back wall. Small half-circle tables along the sides held tasteful flower arrangements, and an oversized crystal chandelier hung from the center of the room, demanding attention while providing soft illumination. The atmosphere was one of hushed luxury.

Vivi hurried up a short flight of thickly carpeted stairs to a landing where a skirted table had been set up and pointed to the tufted chair behind it. "This is your station. Call me if you need anything, okay?" She pushed her long braid over her shoulder and disappeared through the door we'd used before. When closed, it blended seamlessly into the wall, becoming invisible—I wondered how many of the members had ever noticed it.

I finished alphabetizing everything in orderly rows moments before the guests began arriving. Wave after wave of couples in elegant gowns and suits picked up their name tags, murmuring polite thanks.

Until someone drawled, "Oh look, it's Emma Starrs!"

I looked up to see Melody, Felicity, Ainsley, and Tabitha standing before me, in surprisingly demure dresses of varying shades accented with wide silver ribbons at the waist. Their husbands were lined up behind them, all in black tuxes—though Tabitha was alone. She seemed more a merry than a grieving widow, laughing it up with her squad.

I greeted them and waved my hand over the remaining name tags on the table. The men quickly applied theirs and moved down the hallway, but the women lingered.

"Name tags?" Ainsley yawned.

"It's like we're at a high school reunion or something," Felicity giggled.

"Those will ruin the effect of our dresses," Tabitha sighed.

"But it's for a good cause," Melody reminded her.

Tabitha peeled off the backing of her name tag and stuck it to her chest. "Yes, I know, but sometimes I can't believe the number of *sacrifices* we make in order to be *welcoming*. We really need to make a formal complaint about this."

I waited for her to laugh, to indicate that she was making a joke, but none was forthcoming.

"Have a nice night," I said.

One side of her mouth curled up in scorn. "Oh, we will. Have fun *working* at your little table. Too bad you won't be joining us."

The group drifted away. I could hear someone repeat "little table," followed by laughter.

Whatever.

I checked everyone else in without incident, remaining long after dinner had been served to accommodate latecomers, of which there were quite a few. Eventually, Vivi texted and asked me to move into the dining room to be available in case I was needed. I packed up the clipboard and leftover tags and went through the hallway back to the kitchen, where I set down her bag on the cart the caterers were using for equipment, along with the batch of business cards I'd brought along and didn't want to lug around. One of the servers headed out through the swinging doors with an empty tray to clear tables, and I followed him into the cavernous room.

Windows along the far wall of the dining room looked out onto the patio with cozy flickering firepits and, beyond that, the perfectly manicured green. Some of the guests were outside, some were still at their tables, and some were dancing to bland music provided by a sedate band on a riser behind them. It was thoroughly dignified, if a bit lackluster. The diamonds on the women added sparkles here and there.

I made my way through the room and found an unobtrusive spot by the interior side doors opposite the windows. Watching the dancers, I was amused by the antics of the younger guests, several of whom were obviously not familiar with the more formal dances effortlessly performed by the longtime members.

The doors beside me opened, and Tabitha's friends and their husbands walked in.

"That was worth it," Bruce said. "I haven't climbed into that fountain in years."

"It *was* getting boring in here," Ainsley replied, though she was always bored, so her take was unsurprising.

"Do you think we can use the fountain picture—?" Clive asked Bruce.

"Not if we are missing people," Aston interjected.

"Where *is* Tabitha?" Felicity asked. "She's been gone forever."

"You know how she gets," Melody replied lightly. "She probably found someone to chat up for a committee project or something."

I took a few steps toward them, slowly moving sideways. I thought I was being pretty stealthy until Melody, who was closest to me, whirled around.

"What do you want, Emma? And why are you sliding along the wall like a *crab*?"

My face flushed. "I wanted to ask if we could speak privately."

She patted her hair while she considered my request, then shook her head slightly. "Anything you want to say, you can say to all of us."

"I wanted to talk to you about Ian Gladstone—"

"Why?" Melody sounded suspicious.

"Because of what happened to Tip. I wanted to know if Ian—"

"Ian!" Felicity squeaked happily.

"Yes," I said, confused about why she was repeating his name.

She pointed at something behind me.

Ian walked in from the patio with his arm around Tabitha. She was glowing, laughing prettily at whatever he was saying. He spun her slightly to face him, and they slid onto the crowded floor. They began to dance—stepping, twirling, and dipping with confidence. Their moves became more energetic with every lap, and others soon stopped their own dancing to watch them. The couple's movements seemed perfectly choreographed. When the band switched songs, Ian and Tabitha took center stage. The floor full of people cleared the way for them to perform a gorgeous tango.

"Well, don't they look divine," Melody breathed.

Ainsley and Felicity both had tilted their heads to admire all the gorgeousness. Even the husbands had stopped talking to watch.

"I don't know why they ever broke up," Melody declared. "They were made for each other."

"She got tired of him," Ainsley said, without looking away from the spectacle.

"She fell in love with Tip," Felicity added dreamily.

"It could be said that our Tabsies has a short attention span," Bruce boomed, then chuckled. The other men joined in.

Suddenly, the lights went out.

The band faltered on for a few notes, then stopped.

I put my arms out in front of me and turned around, groping for the switch I'd seen on the wall. I didn't know why I felt compelled to flip it, as I knew that it would likely do nothing, but I had an overwhelming urge to try. When I had made contact with the wall, something smashed into my side, twisting me around and knocking me to the floor. I landed hard on my back and, for an excruciating moment, couldn't catch my breath. Then I was taking great, ragged gulps of air as adrenaline spiked through my body. I pulled myself to a sitting position until I felt steady and climbed up gingerly, using the wall for support, thankful that no one had stepped on me. Around the room, cell phone flashlights began to twinkle, one by one. I had just tapped my own screen when the overhead lights came back on.

I turned my head to study the group, trying to discern which of them had shoved me, but they were all looking forward, blinking rapidly as their eyes adjusted. Nary a one was rubbing their hands in villainous glee, which would have been helpful in identifying the guilty party.

Moving quickly, I repositioned myself so that I was facing them, like a teacher at the chalkboard. "Did you see someone come through here?" I chose my words carefully, thinking it might be better not to accuse them all outright.

"Through the doors?" Melody asked. "No. We would have heard it. Why?"

I gestured to the floor beside them. "Because someone pushed me—"

"Pushed you? Like, down to the ground?" Her perfectly plucked eyebrows rose, but the surprise didn't seem to reach her eyes.

"Are you okay, Emma?" Felicity asked, putting her hands out as if to steady me from afar. Aston gave me a look of concern.

"Yes, thanks."

Melody and Tabitha—when had she come over here?—were whispering, and the other husbands were clapping Ian on the back and saying hearty things to him, as if he'd scored a touchdown. Bruce was also waving a napkin that had something swirly scribbled on it, Clive was trying to grab it away from him, and Aston was good-naturedly shaking his head. Ian was chortling along with them, though his eyes were fixed firmly on Tabitha.

Ainsley, meanwhile, could not have looked more uninterested if she'd tried.

My right shoulder blade began to throb, so I decided to abandon the unproductive conversation in favor of a soothing bag of ice.

No one seemed to mind—or even notice—when I said good-night.

* * *

Vivi caught up to me in the kitchen, where I was leaning back with the ice between me and the cinder-block wall. "I'm sorry, Emma, I haven't had a chance to introduce you to anyone. Should we make a round?"

I put my hand down behind my back to catch the bag as it dropped when I took a step forward.

Vivi stared at the ice. "What happened to you? Are you okay?"

"Someone shoved me to the floor when the lights went off."

She clutched the towel she was holding so hard that it was crushed into a ball. "Who? And why would they do that?"

"Pretty sure it was one of the people I've known since high school. It was probably a little reminder to stay in my lane, remember my place, or whatever else it is they think their bullying tactics express."

"All it really expresses is that they are unkind. Can I do anything, Emma?"

"No, thanks. The ice helped."

She folded the towel and dropped it on the nearby cart. "I'm going to ask you to fill out a form later, since it happened on the job."

"There's no need for that," I said.

"Oh, it's happening. I record every incident. But do you want me to introduce you around first? A large percentage of the guests here have been my clients in the past, and it might lead to some new gigs."

I hesitated, not sure I was feeling up to anything other than going home. But then an image of Lucy in the bookstore popped into my mind. I'd said I would do everything I could, so I needed to honor that promise. I went over to retrieve the business cards I'd stashed on the cart. I took them out of the plastic baggie and divided the pile into two stacks, which I slid into the pockets on either side of the white jacket so they'd be easy to reach.

When I returned, she pointed toward my arm. "You have a little something on your sleeve."

I knew she was taking a chance on recommending me, and I didn't want to embarrass her. I brushed at the spot, and luckily, whatever it was disappeared. Then I smoothed my ponytail and straightened my shoulders. "Ready."

She nodded in satisfaction. "Follow me."

We went through the swinging doors, and she aimed for a clump of people near the silver coffee dispenser. For the next half hour, we worked through the entire room—meeting person after person, talking about literary event services, throwing in a good word for the bookstore, and giving out cards. Vivi's blend of charm and dazzling smile was compelling; without exception, people began smiling back immediately after she approached them.

We covered a great deal of ground and developed a rhythm.

Smile, meet, pitch. Smile, meet, pitch.

It seemed to be going very well—until Tabitha came up to us at the end. She shook the napkin that Bruce had been waving around to emphasize her point. I knew it was the same napkin because it sported the same spiral squiggle. Didn't seem like a particularly funny thing to me, though the guys had been laughing it up. Must be an inside joke. Or maybe everything had the potential to turn into a joke for them, like the jousting that had broken out at the Baxters' party.

I focused on what Tabitha was saying and caught the final comment, which was that she thought it was *super* tacky how we were spamming the guests.

"No worries. We're done now," Vivi said, aiming her smile in Tabitha's direction.

Tabitha was clearly confused by Vivi's refusal to take the bait. Her mouth flopped open and closed a few times before she settled on an attempted smirk, then flounced away.

It was the best moment of the night.

Chapter Twenty

The next day, I found an open parking spot next to Vivi's store and considered myself lucky—the lot was full of vehicles, not only in the designated spaces but also crammed every which way along the edges. After locking my car, I hurried around the corner to the front door, which had *Silver Blossom Catering* stenciled on the frosted glass.

A bell tinkled merrily as I stepped inside and was immersed in the aroma of baking bread and something more complex with a medley of spices. Behind the metal counter, Vivi's team was cooking. They moved gracefully, as if in a well-rehearsed ballet, among the industrial appliances and plumes of steam.

When Vivi had reminded me to fill out her accident form, I was glad to have the opportunity to visit, as I hoped to sneak in a few questions about the murder mystery party her staff had worked. I hadn't mentioned that part to her, so I was feeling a little undercover-agent-y, which was oddly delightful.

"Thanks for coming," Vivi said, drying her hands on a white towel as she approached me. Her face was flushed, and wisps of dark hair escaped her braid. "It won't take long to fill out the paperwork."

"I don't need any workers' compensation," I said, "just so you know. I'm feeling much better today."

"I'm glad you're better, and I appreciate your coming by." Vivi led me back to an office no larger than a closet that held a desk, computer, filing cabinet, and phone. A milk crate boasted an array of clipboards.

"Sorry that it's kind of cramped," she said over her shoulder. "I'm looking for a new space."

"No problem," I said. "I was marveling at how precise every movement seemed to be in the kitchen."

Vivi laughed. "We've had to develop a choreography over time."

After I sat down in the folding chair, she placed a sheet of paper and a pen in front of me. "Fill out as much as you can, and I'll add the company information. I'll be back in a flash."

Quickly, I went to work. When I reached the box that asked for a description of the incident, I had to think for a moment. What should I say? Probably not *shoved by persons unknown for reasons unknown after the lights went out.* I decided to go with something less weird and wrote *accidental fall.* If the bureaucrats wanted to know more, they could ask.

I left the form on the desk and edged out of the office. Vivi was up at the counter speaking with a customer, so I took the opportunity to meander into the kitchen.

The man from Tabitha's party with the handlebar moustache looked up from chopping asparagus and smiled. "Hey, I know you."

"Emma Starrs of Starlit Bookshop," I said, blushing halfway through at the realization that I was making myself sound like some sort of medieval knight. I might just as well have said *Sir Emma of Silvercrest.*

"Chad," he said, waving his knife. "Hope you're doing better. Last time I saw you . . ." He trailed off, wincing.

We'd been performing CPR on Tip. I didn't want to verbally fill in that blank either, so I resorted to a quick nod.

"Shame," he said. "Seemed like a nice guy."

"He did."

"That was the worst gig I've ever been part of." He resumed his work. "Not only because of what happened to him but because of his wife. What a piece of work."

"What do you mean?" I perched on a stool near the wall.

"She was yelling at us from the second we arrived. Everything we did was wrong. You saw me setting the table, right? It was the fourth time I'd tried. She rejected the napkin shapes, then she didn't like how the wineglasses looked with the silverware, then after I'd driven back here once to get new ones, she made me come back again for different plates."

That unfortunately tracked with the Tabitha I knew.

"How frustrating."

He agreed. "I couldn't wait for that night to end."

"You didn't happen to see anything suspicious, did you?"

Chad tilted the cutting board to slide the asparagus into a pan.

"It's kind of hard to say, given that it was a murder mystery, so everyone was supposed to be under suspicion, right?" He chuckled.

"That's true."

"People were dressed up and acting like someone else the whole time." Chad added some olive oil and a pinch of salt and pepper. After he tossed the asparagus, he slid the pan under the broiler. "But I don't know how they normally behave. Were they being their true selves?"

It felt like things were getting a little philosophical.

"I guess I mean, did you see anyone . . . I don't know . . . lurking about?"

"Lurking about?" He grinned.

"Separated from the group? Off by themselves?"

He stepped over to the sink and washed his hands, frowning at the lather as he thought. After he'd dried off, he shook his head.

"Okay."

"I have an idea." The kitchen was humming with activity, but when he clapped twice, it was as if he'd pressed a pause button. "Hey, all, this is Emma Starrs from Starlit Bookshop."

Greetings came from different corners of the room.

"Remember the Baxter party?" he went on.

"Murder night?" asked one man, as he skillfully flipped the contents of a pan.

"Murder *mystery* night," Chad corrected him. "Sorry," he said to me before continuing. "Anyone see anything suspicious?"

A young woman with a nose ring who was holding a cantaloupe raised it over her short dark hair. "There was the argument out back with the blonde lady."

"Which blonde lady?" I asked.

"One of Ms. Baxter's friends."

That didn't narrow it down, since they all intentionally had the same hair shade, something I'd never really understood. Did they *want* to look exactly like Tabitha? Or did she insist that they go for Brittle Blonde Number Nine or whatever as a sign of loyalty? And why did they dress alike too? Someday I was going to get to the bottom of that whole thing.

"Do you remember her name?" I asked.

She tossed the cantaloupe up and down a few times as she thought. "Annie? Amy, maybe?"

"Ainsley?"

"Yes, that was it. I was wiping down the shelves of the patio bar when they came outside. I stayed crouched down so that I didn't embarrass them, because they were arguing."

"What about?"

"I don't know, but at the end she called her husband a bore, and he said something in return in a really nasty tone, then she slapped him across the face."

"What happened next?"

She shrugged. "They went back inside like nothing was out of the ordinary. That was all I saw."

"Was this before or after dinner?"

"Right after," she said decisively.

"Were they the only ones on the patio?"

"Yes."

"Anybody else?" Chad inquired. There was an extended silence, then everyone went back to what they were doing before. "I guess that's that," he said.

I thanked him and went over to the woman who had told us the story. Even though Chad had already done so, I introduced myself again. This time I said only my first and last name, though. Lesson learned.

"I'm Alana," she said in return. She wiped her forehead with the back of her wrist. It was extremely warm in here, but she didn't seem to mind.

Meanwhile, I felt like a baked potato inside a foil wrap.

"Did you tell the police what you saw?"

"No. I left early to pick up my son, so I wasn't even there when Mr. Baxter passed away."

"If you think of anything else, would you please call me?" I gave her a business card. "And the police would probably want to hear your story."

She tucked the card into a pocket. "Nice to meet you, Emma. I hope they catch whoever did it."

"Same on both counts," I said.

When she turned to wash the cantaloupe in the sink, I thanked her again and joined Vivi at the counter. She was staring out the front window and jumped a little when I came up next to her.

"Are you okay?" I asked.

"Yes," she said. "I'm trying to figure out how we're going to store everything she asked for. We've grown faster than I expected."

"Because you're amazing," I said.

She smiled. "That's very kind."

"Just being honest."

"You are welcome here *any*time," she said with a laugh.

"I wanted to thank you for letting me help out last night and for introducing me to all of those potential clients."

"I hope you hear from them before too long."

"Me too."

She pulled out a bottle of cleaner and sprayed it on the counter. "How did Calliope like the menu?"

"She loved it. That's the one thing she hasn't made a single change to. Like I said, you're amazing."

Vivi wiped the surface in circular motions with a towel until she reached the end. "Has she been changing her mind about a lot of things?"

"Let's just say that she has new ideas. Extremely often."

She gave me a sympathetic look. "Hang in there."

"I will. And if I can ever do anything for you, say the word. I owe you."

"Pshaw," Vivi said. "We're business owners helping each other. It all balances out in the end."

"Do you mind if I ask you a question about the Baxter party?"

She took my sudden change of topic in stride. "Ask away."

"Did you notice anything strange there?"

"In what way?"

"I don't know. Something or someone out of place. A snippet of conversation that caught your attention. Whatever you saw or heard."

Vivi rearranged the wildflowers in a vase next to the register. "The only thing that might fall into that category was the rather heated discussion that Tip and Tabitha were having when we arrived. I went up to the back door, they were in the hallway near the kitchen, and I could hear them through an open window. It seemed like an eternity deciding whether or not to ring the bell. I didn't want to embarrass them. She told him that he was lucky to have her, and he said *he* could say the same about *her* and that in fact people already did behind her back."

"Then what happened?"

"One of the guys walking up behind me dropped a pot and it made a crash, which ended that conversation. Tabitha opened the door, all sweetness and light, and I pretended I hadn't heard anything."

"Did you tell the police?"

"I was so tired at the end of that night that now I can barely remember what I told them. But I'm sure I did." She bit her lip. "I probably did."

"Maybe you could tell them now, make sure they are aware."

"Good idea." She tilted her head. "Oh, and thanks again for taking care of the form. Sorry you had to come all the way over here."

"No problem. It was lovely to see your shop."

After we'd said good-bye and I'd aimed my car toward home, I turned the new pieces of information over in my mind.

The fact that Ainsley was once again bored was no surprise, but the argument—and especially the slap—were. As was the altercation between Tabitha and Tip. Could either of the women have been involved in his murder?

I gripped the steering wheel harder. Was that why Tabitha was trying so hard to pin it on us?

Chapter Twenty-One

Monday was surprisingly busy at the bookstore. It was late afternoon before I had time to update Lucy on my little fact-finding mission at Silver Blossom Catering. Nora walked in halfway through with pumpkin-flavored treats from Riverside Coffeehouse that Diandra had sent over, so I went through the story a second time, adding as many specific details as I could remember.

"Ooh," my sister breathed. "Both of them were arguing with their husbands? That seems significant."

"Depends what they were fighting about." Nora handed us each a cup of coffee.

"Sounded like relationship issues, both of them." I took a bite of warm scone and a sip of the latte and let the sweet and spicy flavors mingle together. Heavenly.

"And the question is: are those issues related somehow to the crime?" Nora asked.

Just then, a clump of people came pouring into the store. They were all dressed in black shirts and pants—and some wore hats or scarves. Without a word, they arranged themselves in front of us and posed in dramatic ways, all twisted limbs and frozen expressions, forming a woven circle with their arms.

"What is happening right now?" Lucy asked.

The group silently reformed themselves into a different position, one that resembled an enormous bird, wings outstretched.

"Can we help you?" Nora spoke in their general direction.

"It's a performance," I said. "A tableau?"

"Hmm." Nora continued to observe them. "I think you're right."

Lucy moved up next to me. "Explain, please?"

"A tableau vivant is a living picture, where people act out a scene or concept."

"We prefer to call this one a *Poebleau*," one figure said, breaking from the group.

"A Poe blow?" Lucy mused.

"Our version of a tableau evoking moments from the brilliant stories of Edgar Allan Poe. The first was a rendering of his famous maelstrom; the second I hope you recognized as—"

"The raven," I said.

"Bravo. And we have much, much more to offer." He swept a top hat from his brown hair and bowed. "Tanner Shock, director. We're a small group of performers based in Colorado who travel around the country and share the gift of our vision in an attempt to raise money for the preservation of art and culture."

"What are you called?" Nora asked him.

"We are Troupe Tableaux. We focus especially on American authors, and we heard about your upcoming event with Calliope Nightfall, who is one of our particular favorites. Since there is a Poe theme, we came to offer our services, should you be interested in adding us to the lineup."

"How did you hear about it?" I asked.

"She reached out to some of her theater friends—I believe there was a pendulum scene involved—and, you know, word got around."

"How much do you charge?"

He produced a sheet from somewhere with a flourish. "Our services."

"I'll ask her," I said. "Is there a place where she can view your work in action?"

Tanner tapped the bottom of the page. "That's the link to our channel, where she can stream videos of our many performances."

"What do you have in mind?" I asked. "So that I can present it to her when we chat."

"We could perform inside, outside, or anywhere you like. We can hold a single pose for five minutes; then we'd need to segue into another one. Muscle fatigue, you know. So we'd need to know how many positions she'd like us to come up with. But we can rotate through them continuously for up to a half hour."

"Great," I said. "We'll be in touch if Calliope is interested."

He snapped his fingers, and the rest of the players filed out behind him.

"That was unexpected," Nora said.

"Why didn't they email you?" Lucy asked.

"Maybe they thought the effect would be more appealing if they showed us what they were capable of," I said, dialing Calliope.

It was a short conversation. Once I described what had happened, she thought about it for ten seconds, then expressed her belief that it would be distracting for her fans.

I asked her to please at least look at the videos and get back to us, suggesting that they could provide an intriguing layer of activity outside as the guests arrived. She asked me to make sure that her guests would be intrigued enough that no additional layering was required.

Well, that had boomeranged.

* * *

The glass stars hanging from the ceiling and the orange lights festooning the railings glowed softly. The skeletons circling the second level offered an eerie sense of camaraderie. Black birds swayed slowly above, and a heartbeat sound seemed to come from everywhere all at once. Then a blast of light blinded me. I blinked and put up a hand against it.

"Still too much," I called down. "I can't even keep my eyes open, much less read a book from here."

"On it," Ryan said, switching off the spotlight. "Let me try something else."

"Don't worry—we'll get it right," Lucy added reassuringly.

Ryan bent down to pick something up. "We have three days to experiment, yes? I can bring some other options over if we can't sort it out today."

Only three days. The thought sent a chill through my soul.

"Thank you, Ryan. Sorry that this has been such a nuisance." I shut my eyelids to recalibrate my vision, taking the opportunity to breathe deeply a few times. Afterward, I pulled out my cell phone and turned off the heartbeat, which was giving me a headache. Calliope's reading was nearly upon us, and the pressure was mounting.

When I opened my eyes and looked down at Lucy and Ryan, she was handing him a shade. He smiled and took it from her. She smiled back shyly and watched him attach the covering to the light as if it were the most fascinating thing she'd ever seen. Was it my imagination, or was there a little spark between them?

Ryan wiped his hands on his flannel shirt and asked if I was ready to try it again.

"Yes." I moved my sunglasses from the top of my head down, covering my eyes as a precaution.

When the light came this time, I carefully lifted the glasses and was relieved to discover that not only could I keep my eyes open but also I could see things on the second floor.

"Much better. You must have reduced that a lot."

"Quite a bit," Ryan said. "Can you read?"

I picked up a book from the podium, opened it, and read a few lines. It was one of my childhood favorites, *Anne of Green Gables*. My mother had introduced us to L. M. Montgomery's books early on—we'd fallen in love with them, like so many other readers. Of course, we had our very own feline Anne Shirley, who was currently stalking something on top of one of the bookcases. I hoped it was a dust mouse, not an actual one. As I watched, she pounced and meowed triumphantly.

Lucy slid the ladder along the rail so that she was parallel with the cat's position, then climbed halfway up and peered across the shelves. "It's a ribbon," she said, with relief. "Maybe from the gift wrapping I did yesterday."

"How did it get up there?"

"Annie probably dragged it over earlier and forgot, then rediscovered it." Lucy began to descend.

"That's a great ladder," Ryan said.

"Want to try?" My sister hopped off and waved for Ryan to come over. Interesting. No one outside the family was typically allowed to use it.

He'd climbed up to the top when a ferocious screech cut through the quiet, followed by another guitar riff and a thumping bass.

My sister and I looked at each other in alarm.

"What is that? I almost fell off the ladder," Ryan yelled, scrambling back down again.

I shouted, "It's our new neighbor, Ian. He's opening a club where they play live music."

Ryan grimaced. "That's awful. And I can't imagine that it will work very well for a bookstore."

"It's devastating," Lucy yelled in agreement.

"What are you going to do?" He stared at the far wall.

I pointed next door. "Talk to him. Want to come?" Although I didn't relish confronting him alone, someone had to do it.

They shook their heads.

Guess I was going in solo.

* * *

Ian was hammering nails into a half wall. That, combined with the pounding bass, was more than I could stand. I hurried up to him and waved my hands. He paused, set down the hammer, and removed a nail from his mouth.

I put my hands over my ears until he turned down the music.

"Ian," I said. "We need to talk."

"What's up, doll?"

I ignored the doll part for now. "The music isn't going to work. We have a bookstore next door."

"What's wrong with a little music to soothe the soul?"

I couldn't help myself—I laughed.

He blinked. "What's so funny?"

"*That* soothes your soul?"

"Yes. I find all music to be soothing."

"Do you happen to have any harp music? Or anything in the lullaby category?"

He laughed. "No. Gonna be rockin' all day long."

"Well, whatever kind of music is played, it needs to be *much* quieter. And preferably not coming through our wall at all."

"What are you talking about?"

I sighed. "Could you please turn your music back on at the same volume as before and follow me?"

He did as I asked. When we were inside Starlit Bookshop, the guitar wailing and the drums pounding, he stood in the middle of the store facing his own property.

Rather than apologizing, however, he snapped his fingers and started swaying back and forth.

"Do you see the problem?" I shouted.

He bobbed his head to the beat.

"I have to yell in order to converse," I yelled.

Lucy and Ryan watched from the back of the store.

Ian grinned at me, adding a few dance moves to his performance. I stared at his feet; his white sneakers, covered with blue-inked spirals, moved confidently and quickly. The man could dance, I had to admit.

I walked outside, waving at him to follow me. The music was still loud on the sidewalk, but at least I didn't feel like I had to scream in order to be heard.

"This isn't working."

He made a sad face, but the grin sneaked its way back.

"It's unbearable, Ian."

"Maybe you need to develop better taste in music," he said. At my glare, he stopped dancing and put both hands up as if he were surrendering. "Okay, okay. I can turn it down."

"But even if you do turn it down to an agreed-upon level today, what's going to happen when there are bands in there?"

He hopped a little bit in anticipation of the bands.

"There has to be a way for us to coexist, Ian. I think that additional soundproofing would go a long way toward fixing this situation."

Ian stroked his chin as he thought. "I mean, that might be something. But since we're only soundproofing to make *you* happy, I think you should pay for it."

I stared at him. "All of it? That's not fair."

"You're the one who wants it—"

"Pretty sure there are regulations about sound," I said, but he ignored me.

"I already have a bid. Let me find it in my files and get back to you. Though if you decide *not* to go forward with that expense—and it is a hefty expense, I can promise you that—you might try to think about it this way: you and your customers are getting free music, selected by someone with impressive expertise." He jerked a thumb toward himself. "Why don't you add *that* to your advertising?"

He danced back into his place.

I was speechless.

* * *

I channeled my fury into action, sweeping the porch and setting up the new outdoor furniture we'd invested in—thanks to Tabitha's substantial paycheck. At first, I'd worried about spending any of the money, but Lucy had thought it was worth the expense because it would pay us back over time, and she'd negotiated a great deal from a friend of hers who ran a furniture store. I unrolled the magenta, yellow, and black outdoor rug and arranged the wrought-iron sofa, love seats, chairs, and tables in a pleasing way. Then I unwrapped the solid all-weather cushions and tied them on, adding a few cheerful suzani pillows as accents. I hung solar lanterns from nails and, as a finishing touch, strung lights along the ceiling. By the time I was done, my muscles were screaming along with the guitar next door.

I dragged the wrapping materials to the garbage cans and stuffed them in. When I was replacing the lid, Lucy emerged from the bookstore and did a double take, then applauded.

"Em, this looks amazing! Why didn't you ask me to help you?"

I shrugged. "I wanted to surprise you, and I had some extra energy to burn off."

She wandered around the space, taking everything in. "It's beautiful. I could live out here."

I sat down and patted the cushion next to me. She kept turning her head to take in the objects surrounding her, then came over and joined me on the rocker love seat.

"I can't get over it. What a transformation. Thank you so much. I don't know why we didn't do this years ago."

"I'm glad you like it."

"Let's sit here for a bit and enjoy."

We did just that, rocking slowly. Between the gentle back-and-forth motion and the familiar burbles of the river, I could feel the anger that had fueled my decorating cyclone slipping away.

Lucy angled her head toward Ian's. He had switched over to something without guitar solos, but an annoyingly repetitive drumbeat was still rat-a-tatting through the wall. "We are going to have to do something about that. Any ideas?"

"Not yet," I said, "but did I mention that he was at the country club event? Dancing with Tabitha, even."

"Really? I thought they were divorced."

"They are, but they looked quite cozy. And they're talented, I have to admit. At one point, everyone on the floor stopped dancing and watched them go."

"They were good?"

"Competition-level good."

My sister thought about this. "Do you think it means anything, their acting like a couple?"

"Clearly they still get along. I don't know if means anything more than that, but if they *are* back together again, it could suggest that he may have been involved somehow in Tip's murder."

"Well, you probably shouldn't go stomping into his place by yourself anymore, Em."

"Stomping in?"

"When you get mad, you sort of stomp—didn't you know that?"

I laughed. "No, I don't."

"Well, you walk harder than usual," she contended.

"I don't think so, Luce."

"That's not my main point anyway. What I'm trying to say is that if he *is* a murderer, I don't want you alone with him."

"I don't want you alone with him either."

We hooked pinkies to seal our vow.

Chapter Twenty-Two

"You're going to join us, right?" Jake asked me on Friday night, as he stopped at the register with the other West Side Writers in tow.

I set the book I'd pulled for a customer on the hold shelf. Jake's self-assurance still irritated me. Some people—myself excluded—had found it attractive in high school. He'd had influence as a star of the soccer team and editor of the school paper and never seemed to doubt that he had the right to decide things.

Must be nice.

"Not sure if you received the email, but we're here to meet. We usually only do it one Friday a month, but we called another meeting this week since we didn't have a chance to finish our discussion last time. You know, after the intrusion." He pointed toward Ian's bar. "Quiet over there now, though."

"It is quiet," I said. "Thankfully. We had another little incident yesterday, though."

"Well, maybe he finally took your complaint seriously," Jake said.

"Doubtful. But I shouldn't attend tonight. I'm really busy, I didn't get the email, and I don't have any feedback prepared." I stopped short of blurting out that the dog ate my homework.

Alyssa beamed at me. "*Please* come sit with us. We want you to join our group permanently."

Tevo nodded. "It works much better with an even number of people, in general. Then we can do two chapters each time. You know, switch off."

With all three of them looking expectantly at me, it was extremely hard to say no. After all, I had a manuscript that needed feedback.

I smiled at them. "I'll be there in a minute."

"Yay! You're a West Side Writer now!" Alyssa applauded softly.

"Welcome to the team," Tevo said enthusiastically.

"Yes, welcome to the team." Jake's grin suggested that he thought he'd won an argument.

We'd see about that.

* * *

By closing time, we'd worked our way through a chapter of Alyssa's fantasy novel, in which there was a great hunt going on for a mythical beast that would decide the kingdom's fate. We'd had a lively discussion about the possibilities for magic that could be used by the princess hunting him—in disguise, because she was a royal—as well as the potential limits of a curse placed on her family centuries ago that was hindering her ability to track the animal.

Jake was in the middle of pontificating about why my idea of a curse reversal scene wouldn't work with the pacing Alyssa had established. I had opened my mouth to defend my suggestion when my aunt walked up to the table.

"Sorry to interrupt, but I'm getting ready to lock up," she said. "Do you need anything before I go?"

Lucy had a date with Ryan—about which she was beyond excited—and both Max and Bella were attending a Halloween party on campus. Nora had agreed to work with me, as we tried to have at least two people at night whenever possible for safety purposes. She didn't work here often but was willing to step in when necessary.

I looked around the store, which was empty except for the five of us. "I think we're good. Thank you, Nora."

"I do have a quick question about the register report first, though. Do you mind taking a look?"

"Not at all."

We went over to the counter, where she picked up the tape that tallied the day's transactions.

As she handed it to me, a scream shredded the silence.

We stared at each other, then I faced the wall next to Ian's bar. "What on earth—"

There was a second scream, louder than before. And it sounded very much like my sister.

I turned and ran for the door, saying over my shoulder to my new team, "Please call the police and keep an eye on things, okay?"

I wrenched the door to Hatchet open and entered with Nora close on my heels. All the lights were on, and the place appeared as it had in the daylight: a construction site, with clear plastic sheets drifting in the air currents. I hurried through the space, turning my head from side to side, searching for any sign of my sister and calling out her name. When I came around the half wall that Ian had been working on before, I gasped.

There were two bodies on the floor. A plastic sheet was covering their upper halves, so I could only see their legs.

I recognized Ian's sneakers right away.

The second pair of legs ended in stilettos. Or at least one foot did. The other was bare.

Could it be Tabitha?

Their stillness was palpable; my stomach twisted violently.

Nora came around the wall and gasped too. Jake followed her.

"What are you doing here?" I asked, confused.

He ignored me.

"Freeze!" a voice said from the back door.

The room was suddenly swarming with police moving everywhere. It was terrifying.

"Don't move," Jake instructed us.

Nora and I didn't move.

"Put your hands up!" came the order, and we complied.

Some officers surrounded, then separated, us.

Some went over to the bodies.

We were quickly moved far away from the legs.

"How did you get here so *fast*?" I asked the officer escorting me to the side wall. He was shorter than I was but had muscles for days.

"Someone on the riverwalk called in some screams."

That must have been the first pair we heard too.

He peppered me with questions, barely seeming to listen to the answer I gave before asking me another.

"I have to find my sister," I said desperately, over and over again.

The questions continued. After fifteen minutes, my phone rang. I begged him to let me answer.

"Show me the screen," he said gruffly.

I pulled the phone out of my pocket and teared up when I saw Lucy's name.

"It's her," I told him. "It's my sister."

He nodded.

When I pressed the button, Lucy's voice came spilling out. "Where *are* you? I came into the store and no one's here and there are police cars outside. Are you okay?"

I was so relieved, I almost sank to my knees. "Nora and I are next door, but please stay there for now. I'll explain everything later."

"I will."

"There should be two people from the writing group watching the store for us."

"They're not here. Maybe they went outside to see what was going on?"

Way to go, team.

* * *

After I'd given my statement, Jake came up and asked how I was doing as he handed me a bottled water. I took a long drink, said I was doing as well as could be expected, and thanked him.

"I told my colleagues I was here with you," he said, his eyes locked on what was happening across the room with the victims.

"Well, you *were* here with me."

He smiled. "No, I meant they know you didn't murder Ian and Ainsley."

"Ainsley Fowler? Are you sure it's not Tabitha Baxter?"

"It's hard to tell, because her face is—" He stopped and redirected himself. "That's what the license in her purse says. We're going to confirm, obviously. Why did you think it was Tabitha?"

"We saw her coming in here alone the other night, remember? When we were outside the bookstore?"

"That's right." He snapped his fingers.

"What happened to them?"

"Someone hit them with a hammer," he said grimly. "Over and over."

I flashed back to the image of Ian hammering nails into the half wall and flinched. "What was Ainsley doing here?"

"She didn't say."

I stared at Jake. "That's not funny. Not at all."

"I'm sorry. Humor gets kind of dark sometimes in my line of work. It's a survival mechanism."

The way he was looking at his shoes when he admitted that hurt my heart. I imagined he'd seen some horrible things. "That makes sense. And I don't know why I asked you what she was doing here as if you'd know."

"It caught you by surprise. I understand." He held my gaze. "Why don't you seem as surprised that the other victim is Ian?"

"He owns this place."

"Ah."

"And I recognized his sneakers. When he was dancing yesterday, it drew my eyes to them. The way his foot was turned, I could see one of the shapes he'd drawn on both toes."

"Did you say he was *dancing*?"

"He was blasting the music like he did the other day when you were with me, so I asked him to accompany me to the bookstore. I wanted him to experience how the noise came in through the wall, because I thought he would understand and turn it down. But when he heard it, he didn't even care. He started dancing."

Something moved behind Jake's eyes. "Then what happened?"

"I brought up the soundproofing issue. He told me that if I wanted it installed, I was going to have to pay for it myself."

"Wow."

"Right? I mean, that takes some nerve. I couldn't believe it."

He took a step closer and lowered his voice. "I get that you're angry, and understandably so, but you might want to be careful about how you tell that story."

"What do you mean?"

"Let's just say that it's a good thing you were with me tonight. Otherwise, someone could make the case that you are a pretty good suspect."

"Me? I am definitely *not* a good suspect."

He started ticking things off on his fingers. "You knew both of the victims, by your own admission. And you argued with one of them the day before he died."

"By my own admission?" I could hear my volume rising, but I didn't care. "Why is it a crime to *know* someone? Everyone in this town knows everyone else!"

"That's not really true."

"Okay, it's a generalization, but you know what I mean. If it makes someone a good suspect simply to know the victims, then why aren't you talking to other relevant people?"

He blinked rapidly. "We talk to everyone who may be relevant. That's *literally* what we do."

"Well, I have some feelings about who—"

"Forgive me, Emma, but this is not a game. You and your aunt write mysteries, so it may seem natural to you to want to play Nancy Drew. But in the real world, there are procedures that must be followed. Cases are not run by emotions. They're not run by intuition. It would really be better if you let us do our job."

I counted to ten to calm myself down as he ran a hand through his hair. It looked exactly the same afterward as it had before. He probably never had to look in a mirror to maintain his perfection.

Perfection? I shook my head. That must be the shock talking. I refocused on the words coming out of his mouth.

". . . and please be sure to tell Nora as well that I'm basically your alibi."

"We need *alibis*?" My voice went up a little more than I'd meant, into squeak territory.

He shrugged. "I did already vouch for you and your whereabouts. And if it comes to it, Alyssa and Tevo also will confirm it."

His air of self-importance aside, I was grateful and said so.

Still, the fact that I seemed in *any* way suspicious was disconcerting, especially since Nora and I kept being accused of Tip's death.

My aunt walked up and wrapped her arms around herself, shivering. "Can we go? I could use a drink."

"You may," he said. "Want a ride home?"

"No," I said. "We still have to talk to Lucy and lock up the store for the night. And speaking of Alyssa and Tevo, they took off."

"Is that a problem?"

"I asked you all to *stay* there."

He looked blank.

"Over my shoulder. When I was running out of the store."

"Yeah, I don't think anyone heard you."

"But wouldn't it be *obvious* that someone should stay? They knew we were gone. We'd had that whole conversation about closing. And yet they left the cat in charge of the store."

He rubbed his chin. "I don't know. Would *you* sit there like a bull's-eye in a store after you heard multiple screams nearby?"

Oh.

"Actually, I don't know why I asked you that, Starrs. You're clearly the kind of person who goes running into the exact place where multiple screams have been heard."

"I thought it was my *sister*. I wouldn't go running in for just anyone." That didn't sound right when I heard it aloud, because obviously humans should help other humans. I tried again. "I mean, I *would* go running in if someone was in distress. As long as it seemed safe to do so."

Jake studied my face.

"Though *not* if it was one of those too-stupid-to-live situations. Like if I were completely outnumbered. Or if everyone had weapons and I wasn't, uh, packing."

"That's a lot of conditions," he said, one side of his mouth quirking up.

"That's right. It *is*." I didn't even know what I meant by that—but I was compelled to respond to his smugness.

Jake turned to Nora. "I was telling Starrs here that I have explained to my colleagues that the three of us were at the bookstore and came into this space together."

My aunt smiled pleasantly at Jake. She appeared to be waiting for the punch line.

"So they know you aren't the killers," Jake clarified.

"Oh, thank goodness," Nora said, putting her hand up to her chest. "That's all we need, someone *else* thinking that Emma and I are criminals."

I made one of those slice-across-the-neck gestures so that she would stop talking about us being criminals, which I immediately regretted, because it seemed like something that an actual criminal would do.

"What?" she said to me.

"What?" Jake said to her.

Nora flapped her hand at the detective. "You've heard the rumors. We talked to you about that already."

"Ah. For a minute there, I thought you meant maybe there were *other* people accusing you of murder."

Nora laughed uncomfortably. "Well—"

"We should go," I said to my aunt.

We thanked Jake again and walked back to the bookstore, where an anxious Lucy was waiting. After we had filled her in and answered a thousand questions, I asked about her date.

"It was lovely," she said, her face aglow. "We're going out again tomorrow. And Ryan said he'd be available Sunday to lend a hand so you don't have to worry about the sound and lights during the party. His theater is closed for Halloween, so he's available."

"Thank you. He is pretty handy to have around."

"He is," she said dreamily. "He is undeniably handy."

I hadn't seen her this smitten in a very long time. She blushed every time she mentioned his name.

"Happy for you, darling," Nora said, smiling at her.

I echoed Nora.

Sometimes the best thing you can do is keep your mind focused on positive things.

Even if minutes ago you walked out of a crime scene.

Chapter Twenty-Three

"Oh my goodness, these all taste amazing," I said to Vivi, who had stopped by the bookstore Saturday morning with samples for the party. We were sitting in the office at the shabby—shabby *chic*, Lucy insisted—farmhouse table that served various functions, from hosting meetings to providing project space to offering a quiet lunch spot.

At the moment, it held a veritable feast of desserts.

It was a relief to be absorbed, however momentarily, by something other than what we'd seen last night. Today was filled with party tasks—and on top of that, I'd promised to help Nora pack up her office. This was probably going to be the most relaxing part of the day, so I tried to be fully in the moment, focusing on the delicious treats.

I took another bite to deepen my mindfulness.

Also because: yum.

"So you're happy with everything?" Vivi asked, her pen hovering over the list of items she would provide for Calliope's reading-slash-costume-party.

"Absolutely," I said.

Lucy, whose mouth was full, nodded emphatically in agreement.

Vivi smiled. "That's a relief, since they're all packed up and ready to go for tomorrow. What time do you want my crew to be here?"

I set down my fork. "The event starts at six, so how about five?"

"You got it. They'll bring everything, including folding tables for the buffet." She made a note on the page in front of her, then folded and tucked it into her crisp white jacket.

Not for the first time, I admired her logo, a stylized flower, embroidered in silver thread on the pocket. "You really are a dream, Vivi. Thank you."

She inclined her head slightly. "My pleasure. How's the event planning going?"

"The first event ended with a murder and the second is shaping up to be extremely weird. Not a great track record so far," I admitted.

"The good news is that you were booked again right away." She twirled the pen through her fingers. "Literary events are a very specific focus. Have you thought about widening the scope?"

"I am willing to branch out, to an extent, but mostly I'm hoping that offering more book-centric events will not only engage existing customers but also draw a substantial community of new readers and writers our way."

She considered this. "I bet it will. One thing I know is that when you love what you do, it makes everything better. I started out in sales, which made me feel like I was dead inside. But when I went to culinary school, the joy came back. And my company has grown so much in the past few years that we're already bursting at the seams. Anyway, I look forward to working with you as much as possible in the future."

"Oh, I feel the same way." I smiled at her.

"If I can arrange it, I may sneak out of the other party and swing by on Sunday—I'd love to hear Calliope read."

"Please do. I don't know what to expect, exactly, given her personality."

"Expect the unexpected, I think," Vivi said.

* * *

I drove north to Silvercrest College, listening to Bach. If I'd had more time, I'd have walked, but right now, quick trips around town were necessary. Plus, they offered a much-needed calming oasis. Whenever I wasn't in my car, things were frenzied.

Most of the items on my to-do list had been completed, which was helpful, since Nora had asked me to assist with the move to the department's new offices. However, the remaining necessary duties were weighing on me. I resolved to put them out of my mind for now and focus on the present.

After parking in the lot, which was half full of cars, I went inside and made my way down the hallway. There were many people in various stages of packing, and I had to tread carefully. Individuals in red shirts with a Silvercrest College Facilities Management logo stamped on the back were everywhere: stacking, lifting, and transporting boxes up to the new floor.

When I reached Nora's almost-empty office, she was seated at her desk, sorting through a pile of papers. "So lovely to see you, but I was about to text you to let you know that I'm ahead of schedule. All that remains to be packed is this bookshelf. I've been squirreling things away all week into boxes, and I guess I accomplished more than I'd realized."

"I'm glad to help with the last bit." I went over to her metal shelves. "Is there a particular method you'd like me to use?"

"No. Go ahead and shove them into anything available."

I started pulling books down and stacking them inside the banker's box next to me. When I was done with that, I filled another. And another. Before long, the shelves were empty.

"How are you this morning, darling?" She sounded concerned.

"Sad and confused. Even though I wasn't friends with Ian or Ainsley, it's shocking and terrible. How about you?"

"That covers it for me as well." She threw one pile of the pages into the recycling bin and stuck the rest into a nearby box.

"It seems awful to confess this now, Nora, but after our conversation with Eve, I was starting to think that Ian might have been one of the best suspects."

"He may have been. Perhaps his death has something to do with Tip. If he did harm him, there could be revenge involved. Or Ian was being silenced because he knew something. If he was mixed up with the wrong people, who knows what could happen. But I have to say that I'm sorry that you've been through so much, Emma. First finding Tip, now the others. Such tragedies have an impact on the psyche."

"Thank you, but you were there too," I reminded her. My aunt always seemed so strong, but I was worried about the effect on her as well. "And I'm sorry you're going through all of this."

"Much appreciated, darling. I do want to say that it's important to acknowledge your feelings, whatever they may be. Don't be so stoic that you repress emotions."

"I'll keep that in mind."

She picked up a permanent marker and wrote *HAVEN* on the boxes, along with her new office number, and taped them shut. "That's the last of it. Shall we take a stroll through the department and offer our help?"

I followed her out and around the corner to Bethany's office, which was also nearly empty.

"You're done," Nora said approvingly. "Fast."

Bethany stretched her arms over her head. "But now I have to go tackle Dodd's office. I finished Able's yesterday." She lowered her voice. "It was unbelievably gross. I don't think anyone has cleaned it for centuries. I hope Dodd's goes faster."

Nora glanced at me. Against my better judgment, I nodded.

"Would you like some help?" Nora asked her. "Emma and I are available."

Her shoulders sagged in relief. "Yes. I would very much appreciate that. It was all well and good to offer to pack up their offices in my minute of bravado, but my back is on fire right now. Let me go ask the main office to unlock it. Meet you there."

Nora led me farther down the hall to a closed door with an engraved plaque that read *Professor Dodd Stimson*. I leaned against the wall, fighting an antsy feeling inside. Now that Nora was all set, what I really wanted to do was knock off the final items on my list and take a lavender bath. We'd been going at full speed for so long that my body was starting to ache.

"Raven!" Calliope's raspy voice pulled me out of my thoughts. She had poked her head out of her office next door. "What are you doing here? Shouldn't you be working on my party?"

My thoughts exactly.

"Hi, Calliope," I said. "Everything's under control."

Mostly.

She came out and looked at the closed door quizzically. "Are you here to see Dodd?" Electrical cords were hanging around her neck, and she held a keyboard in one hand.

"No," I said. "I'm helping Bethany and Nora box up his office."

"Whyever for? The rest of us are packing on our own." Her eyebrows were pulled together in displeasure. "And we *all* have much better things to do."

"Bethany offered to do it, as encouragement," Nora said. "During the last committee meeting."

Calliope snorted. "Encouragement? Seems like Dodd is getting"—she added air quotes around the next word—"*encouraged* from all directions."

"What do you mean?" I asked.

"Tip Baxter was in and out of there urging him to do something. I didn't catch exactly what was being said, but I could hear the tone of his voice through the walls."

"How would you describe the tone?" I pressed Calliope.

"Pleading."

"Interesting," Nora murmured.

"As you know, it's uncommon to see the dean of Arts and Humanities on the working floor so often. It was never before five PM, so other people may not have noticed, but the night is my prime writing time, so I'm here a lot with my door closed, *creating*." She waved the keyboard around in a circle. "Thus, I noticed."

Nora and I exchanged glances.

"Rest in peace, Tip," Calliope added, bowing her head.

We followed suit.

Then I addressed her. "Did you hear *any* words at all?"

Calliope brushed her bangs out of her eyes. "Something about internet profiles."

"Are either of them on social media?" Nora asked. "That would be surprising."

My aunt didn't mention that we'd already researched Tip online, for which I was grateful. I pulled out my phone and did new searches with variations of both of their names. Dodd's didn't come up outside work-related posts and directory listings. Tip's appeared more often, in society columns with Tabitha's and in school-related pages, as we'd seen before. But neither man had a public profile on the usual sites, or at least I couldn't find one if they did.

"Could they have been planning to promote something online?" I asked.

"*I* certainly wouldn't know," Calliope said. "Creating means I'm in the dimension of the imagination, entirely unaware of what's going on around me. I only happened to catch those sounds because I was done for the night."

"I get that." Nora smiled at her.

"More importantly"—Calliope focused her attention on me—"are we ready for my party?"

"We are ready," I assured her.

"I can't *wait* to see my costume."

"Your costume?"

"Yes, my Annabel Lee costume. You did procure it for me, right? I'm *sure* I texted you about it."

I looked down at my phone again and scrolled through every text from Calliope. It took a while because there had been a lot of them. Like Tabitha, she was a most prolific sharer of thoughts. Finally, I lifted my head and met her eyes. "I'm sorry, there's nothing here. I had no idea that you wanted me to help you with your costume."

She exhaled sharply, then crossed her arms over her chest. Each word that followed was delivered through gritted teeth. "Not help. *Provide*."

"Calliope," I said softly, "it's the day before Halloween. I don't know what will be available at the last minute. I'd be glad to find something for you, but I can't promise that it will be exactly what you're thinking."

She didn't reply.

"What *are* you thinking, by the way?"

"Well, Raven, what would Annabel Lee wear?" She tapped her temple, suggesting that I should ponder the question more deeply.

"I—I don't know."

Another deep sigh. "If you don't know, I can't bother explaining."

Actually, the correct answer was *no one knows*. Was there a line in the poem about what Annabel Lee was wearing this season? No, there was not.

But I didn't say that.

Calliope wrung her hands dramatically. "I suppose it doesn't have to be Annabel Lee, though that is a crushing blow indeed. But whatever I wear must be the color of midnight, and it must be large enough to fit." She gestured above her head. "As you can see, I am amply blessed in both height and strength. I myself am larger than life because nothing one iota smaller would be able to contain this much creative energy. And this glorious event requires a glorious costume. It must draw all eyes to me and express the theme without saying a word. In short, it must be *perfect*."

"Is there a particular size you want me to—"

"Goddess!" The word was a thunderclap.

I didn't know if she was summoning the goddess or articulating an answer to my question, but my aunt was making shooing motions behind Calliope's back. I'd been excused.

One last-minute perfect costume coming up.

* * *

I drove as fast as I could to Riverview Vintage and parked out front. So much for my Calming Oasis Commute plans.

When I went inside, Marlowe took one look at my face and towed me through the curtain of beads that marked off the stock room, into a far corner where no one could see us. She asked what was wrong, and I explained about Calliope's surprise costume demand.

"Is that all? No worries. I have you covered," she said. "What size?"

"Um, she might have said goddess-sized?"

Marlowe did a double take. "Meaning?"

"I'm not sure, exactly. That's the word that was used, though."

Marlowe nodded. "I've seen Calliope. She cuts an imposing figure. But it's hard to tell what's going on underneath sometimes. What type of silhouette, do you think?"

"She said she wanted to dress like Annabel Lee from the poem, whatever that means. Usually she wears layers upon layers and lots of necklaces. Oh, and it has to be, and this is a direct quote, 'the color of midnight.' "

"Annabel Lee. Black layers. Got it." Marlowe looked up at the ceiling, thinking. Today she was wearing a dark corset underneath a matching tailored jacket with trousers. Her nails were painted a seasonally appropriate bright orange.

"Yoo-hoo, is anyone *here*?" we heard Tabitha Baxter sing out.

"I can't deal with her today, not on top of everything else." I put my face in my hands and groaned.

"I'll handle it." Marlowe patted my shoulder and told me to wait a minute while she maneuvered Tabitha away. My directions were to then slip into one of the dressing rooms, where she would bring me options for Calliope's costume.

Marlowe went through the bead curtain onto the sales floor and greeted Tabitha, who sounded as though she were on the verge of hysteria over a Marie Antoinette costume that wasn't located where it had been last time. I peeked around the doorframe as Marlowe soothed her and led her to the front.

When the coast had been cleared, I scurried over to the first of four vertical cubes that served as dressing rooms and sat on the little wrought-iron bench inside. Each was painted a different pastel color with flower embellishments. I'd claimed my favorite: yellow with a daisy theme. Pulling my legs up, I rested my back against the side wall.

"Shhh, don't say anything until we're inside," I heard. Two people—I could tell from their legs underneath the divider—went into the purple-with-lilacs cube. After the clatter of hangers being thrust onto the wall rack subsided, I recognized their voices.

"Is this okay?" Felicity asked, her pitch even higher than usual.

"Yes, but talk fast," Melody replied in her distinctive drawl.

"I mean, it's really sad about Ainsley, so I feel kind of awful repeating this—"

"Talk *faster*," Melody urged.

"Ainsley was having an affair with Ian. *Don't* repeat that."

There was a huge gasp from Melody. "I would *never*. But why didn't she tell us?"

"Maybe she was ashamed," Felicity said primly. "About cheating."

"How did you find out?"

"My husband's a lawyer," Felicity reminded her. "He hears things."

"Well, Ainsley's husband does—or did—ignore her, it's true."

"That doesn't make it right," Felicity said. "It's still cheating."

"And here Tabitha was worried that Ainsley was having an affair with *Tip*." Melody sounded like she was talking out of the corner of her mouth. "And let's be honest, they did flirt quite a bit. *Don't* repeat that."

"I would *never*."

"But Ian? I can't believe it. Does Tabitha know? She would—"

Felicity giggled. "She would probably be madder about Ainsley hooking up with Ian. He's a thousand times hotter."

"So true. Tabitha *loved* shoving all that handsome right in our faces."

They both giggled.

"Stop," Felicity said. "We shouldn't be laughing."

"You're right," Melody said. "We shouldn't."

That set them off again.

"What are you two going on about?" Tabitha's voice snaked over the partition.

"These clothes," Melody said quickly. "So revolting, they're comical. I don't even want this fabric touching my body. Hold on. We're coming out."

There was furious whispering back and forth in the cube next to me, but I couldn't make out any words.

The door swung open and the two women exited.

"They don't have anything I want here." I could practically hear Tabitha smirking. "That Marie Antoinette costume was the only one I could imagine wearing. The rest of the choices are unsuitable for someone of my station."

"We didn't find anything either. No worries. We don't have to go to that reading," Felicity said soothingly. "Forget about costumes. Let's go get some drinks instead."

I sat up straighter. They were thinking about attending Calliope's reading? Why? Tabitha hated books.

"It's going to be awful," Melody said.

Is not, I thought indignantly.

"And so very boring, I'm certain. But I want to get a look at the space in action. If we're going to expand, let's see what we're working with." Tabitha laughed.

"Wait, we're still going through with a business?" Melody asked. "Now that Ian's gone—"

"And Ainsley," Felicity added.

"—*and* Ainsley," Melody repeated. "I thought we'd be leaving Hatchet behind."

"Why would we do that?" Tabitha asked. "Ian did a super job negotiating that lease for us."

"He did," Melody said slowly, "but Ian was the only one who loved live bands. It's not like the rest of us were into it."

"Hey! Speak for yourself. I enjoy rocking out from time to time," Felicity chirped. "It would have been fun to run it with Ian."

"I only wanted to invest in it as a tax write-off," Melody continued.

"If you'd all listened to Tip from the start," Tabitha said angrily, "maybe we wouldn't be in this predicament. You knew that he wanted to create a supper club, something exclusive and upscale. We would have had a lovely place at our disposal, away from the riffraff, for whatever we wanted. But all of you had to agree with Ian that it should serve a different crowd, and *now* look what's happened."

"Silvercrest *is* a college town," Felicity pointed out. "Ian might have been onto something."

"That may be the case, but the point is that now we don't have either of those two things," Melody said. "No supper club *and* no bar. We only have a mostly empty building that looks like an industrial warehouse. No furniture, no decor, nothing."

"That's true," Felicity said. "We need a plan."

Melody continued complaining. "Starting all over again is going to be too expensive."

"Money, schmoney. I can take care of that," Tabitha scoffed. "Though—"

"Why would we keep going? Do you really want to wrangle a bunch of drunk college students every night?" Melody's voice was rising.

"Would you hush for a second? I'm trying to tell you something important. We're going in a new direction," Tabitha said, her voice one degree louder than Melody's. "And please remember that it isn't my fault we're in this predicament."

"It kind of is," Melody said. "Maybe if you didn't try to force your two husbands to work together, none of this would have happened."

"Ian was my *ex*-husband," Tabitha said. "And I fail to see how bringing them together for a project was a mistake."

"Well, they're both dead now, aren't they?" Melody snapped.

There were multiple gasps.

Including mine. I clapped my hand over my mouth.

"How dare you, Melody?" Tabitha fumed. "After all that my husband did for you? Bruce wouldn't even have a company if it weren't for Tip's investments. He would have been horrified to hear you talk like that."

After a long silence, Melody apologized profusely.

"You know what? I need *not* to talk to you for a while," Tabitha said evenly. "Go stand by the front, Melody."

Heels tapped away from the dressing room as her banished friend headed for a time-out.

Felicity said, "It won't be the same without Ian to run it anyway. Maybe we should forget about the whole thing."

"Oh no," Tabitha replied. "I've had a brilliant idea. Listen carefully: we're going to turn it into a bookstore."

Chapter Twenty-Four

"She said she was going to turn Hatchet into a bookstore!" I paced back and forth in front of Lucy and Nora. "Can she do that?"

"I think she can," Nora said softly. "If she puts her mind to it. She has the money, especially now that she's inherited everything from Tip, most likely. They didn't have any children."

"People won't shop there," Lucy said. "They'll be loyal to us." She gestured at the shelves beside her.

Nora shrugged.

I turned to face them. "It sounded like her plan was to not only turn Hatchet into a bookstore and compete with us but also to *absorb* our store into hers eventually. She said that's why she was coming to the party tomorrow, to check out 'the space in action.' "

"Why would she think that our space was available?" Lucy asked. "Who knows our business?"

Nora made a sound of annoyance. "Clive Fowler is the manager of Silvercrest National Bank."

"That's right." My sister whistled. "He knows exactly how much we have in our account. But we're not renting—thank goodness Mom and Dad bought this place—so they can't take the store away unless we default on the mortgage."

"Maybe that's what they're counting on," I said. "They think we'll have to sell the building when we run out of money."

"I can keep paying for the mortgage," Nora said briskly. "So don't worry about that."

"And I'll try to get more events lined up," I said. "I've already added the information to the website, but I could widen the scope into Denver. Do some cold calls, follow leads, that sort of thing."

"That would be great," Lucy said. "But we still have to bring in enough to keep the business part alive. Tabitha's payment will get us through the holidays. After that, we could see an upturn, couldn't we?" Her voice was wistful.

Nora and I stayed silent. No one could make a promise like that.

"No matter what, Clive Fowler shouldn't be revealing our financial situation to anyone," my aunt said angrily. "Isn't that against the law?"

"It's outrageous," I agreed. "And why would Tabitha want to open a bookstore? She doesn't even like books!"

"It is *absurd*," Lucy said.

We all vented for a while.

Lucy put her palm up. "Maybe it's not about books at all. Maybe it's about you two. No offense."

"None taken," I said. "You may be right."

"She did accuse us of being involved in her husband's murder," Nora said thoughtfully.

"More than once," I added.

"In public," she said.

"Ooh, she makes me *so* mad." Lucy clenched her fists and shook them.

The sentiment was unanimously shared.

"Well, we're not going down without a fight," I said. "Let's think about it and make some kind of plan. And while we're at it, let's figure out a way to get the committee members talking. Speaking of money, I am still wondering why the dean bribed some of them to keep the top floor empty."

"What?" Lucy's mouth fell open.

My aunt filled her in on what we'd discovered.

"It's strange, right?" I said. "But Nora may have to execute a stealth plan herself, because I have no business being on campus all the time."

"Oh, but they're all coming to Calliope's reading," Nora said. "Although there are many things we do not manage to accomplish as a department, one thing we *do* seem to have a grasp on is showing up to each other's professional development activities."

"How nice," I said. "Good to support each other."

"It's not so much nice. It's more that the administration has made it clear that showing up for your departmental colleagues is expected. Silvercrest College culture is supposed to appear to be supportive to the outside world. And make no mistake, it *is* noticed if you don't attend and *will* be held against you in the future."

Lucy giggled. "Do they know they have to wear a costume or she won't let them in?"

Nora laughed. "Now that you mention it, I suspect that's why Calliope is requiring one in the first place, to force the entire department to dress up. She does like her little jokes."

"What do they think about her?" Lucy asked. "She's such a character."

"She's fearless, so of course many of them are intimidated by her."

Having run to the costume store at the last minute in a panic because she'd ordered me to, I could relate to that.

"Speaking of Calliope, I need to check her costume," I said.

"Aren't you the one who bought it?" Lucy asked, confused.

"I was in such a state after overhearing Tabitha's evil plan that I agreed to the first thing Marlowe brought back, without really looking at it."

I walked over to the shelf where I'd hung the garment bag and unzipped it. Everything inside was black, as Calliope had requested. On the first hanger was a long, flowing dress in a stretchy material. The second held a floor-length chiffon vest in the same length. The third had an overlay that looked as if it had been woven out of a web, the fourth held a pair of glittering wings, and the attached bag revealed a dark crystal tiara that looked like something a wicked queen in a fairy tale would wear.

I stared at it, speechless.

"Is it supposed to be a spider?" Nora asked.

"Or a fairy?" my sister suggested.

"A butterfly?" I guessed.

"A princess?" my aunt replied.

"A sprite?" Lucy tried.

"More importantly, does that add up to Annabel Lee to you?" I asked.

We studied the items for a few moments in silence.

Finally Lucy whispered, "I think it's kind of gorgeous."

"It's either supremely fantastic or completely ridiculous," Nora said. "Hard to tell."

I couldn't even imagine Calliope's response.

* * *

When I texted Calliope to tell her that I had her costume, she asked me to bring it over immediately.

All the way there, I tried to visualize a scenario in which I could drop it off on her front porch and drive away. Could I say I'd received an important call? Had an appointment? Was running out of gas?

I pulled up to the address she'd given me. Tall hedges surrounded the property, making it difficult to see anything except the decorative iron gate and a bit of roof at the top. It was the type of place that all the neighborhood kids probably dared each other to go to.

I climbed out of the car and walked through the gate. Her two-story house was painted dark purple, with black shutters, and it was fully decorated with smiling ghosts, witches, vampires, and mummies—as well as a healthy supply of bats and cats—hanging everywhere. A row of twinkling orange lights stretched across the front, adding a cheerful shine.

Once you got past the gate, it was adorable.

I walked up the steps and rang the doorbell. The button was inside the mouth of a skull. I half expected a dirge to play, but it was a simple two-note tone. The door swung open slightly and Calliope's face appeared in the crack. When she saw it was me, she pulled it open and invited me inside. Her outfit—a dark dress with an orange shawl—matched the decor.

"Your decorations are terrific," I said, after we'd exchanged greetings.

She looked confused.

"For Halloween?" I gestured above me, where the feet of a witch were dangling.

"Oh, I haven't had a chance to put mine up yet," she said. "I was going to do that tonight. But you've heard good things about my holiday decorations, have you? I'm not surprised. The neighbors simply rave about my festive beautifications."

I made a noncommittal sound—there was no appropriate response if the existing monster exhibition was business as usual—and stepped into the foyer, where an aromatic cinnamon cloud surrounded me.

"Smells wonderful," I murmured.

"I'm baking apple pies," she said. "Come into the kitchen."

I followed her down the hallway, passing a parlor with acanthus fan wallpaper and flickering sconces, then a dining room dominated by a heavy claw-footed table with a large candelabrum at the center.

"By the way," she said over her shoulder, "I'm thinking coffins. Lots of coffins. What say you?"

"It would be a mood," I agreed. "But I'm sorry, it's too late to add those, Calliope."

She sighed.

The kitchen had a black-cat theme: cat clock, cat towels, and cat teapot. An actual black cat was curled up in a window seat attached to the sliding glass door.

Calliope pulled on padded mitts—with more cats—and carefully removed a pie from the oven, which she placed on a metal rack next to an identical pie.

"Would you like some?"

"No, thank you," I said. "I just wanted to drop off your costume."

She set the mitts on the counter and took the garment bag from me. "Stay here while I try it on," she commanded.

"I really need to go—"

But she was already gone, having disappeared down the hall and through a doorway.

The moment of truth had arrived.

I perched on the edge of a bench next to the kitchen table, trying to come up with a plan B for when she rejected the costume.

Calliope made a sound of surprise. “What the—”

My heart sank.

I heard rustling, then more sounds that I couldn’t identify.

The cat in the box meowed, sounding disappointed.

“Sorry,” I said over my shoulder.

I hoped she didn’t cancel the event. We needed to sell books now more than ever.

Calliope burst through the doorway and came toward me.

I prepared to apologize.

“This is *perfect*,” she said, her eyes glowing. “Look at me!”

Somehow it all worked together to create a breathtaking artistic vision. The different textures combined into a shimmering and mysterious splendor. The wings added gossamer whimsy, and the tiara was fierce, not at all ridiculous.

“You look amazing.”

She bowed her head.

“Do you need anything else?” I asked.

“Shall I drop by for a run-through?”

“I don’t think that’s necessary. We’ve already calibrated the lights and microphone.”

“But *I* haven’t calibrated anything. I would like to set up some crystals on the podium to direct the flow of positive energy.”

Of course she would.

“You can come by now—we close soon, though,” I said. “Would you like to ride with me?”

“No, I’ll bring my own car, thank you.”

As I walked to the front, she called after me. “Raven, I knew I did the right thing hiring you. Even if you didn’t manifest any coffins.”

“Please tell your friends,” I said.

“Coffins *aside*,” she added.

* * *

Back at Starlit Bookshop, I rang up a few customers while Lucy chatted with Ryan, who had arrived to pick her up for dinner.

I signaled to her between shoppers and finally caught her eye as the last customer walked out the front door.

“What’s up?” When she came to the register, her tea rose perfume floated over too. She was pulling out all the stops, using her favorite scent. It was the same one my mother wore.

I explained about Calliope’s imminent arrival and asked if she and Ryan could show Calliope the light effects and stick around for a few minutes in case she had any questions.

“Yes, of course. By the way, when you said you were going to do special events, I never dreamed of something this big. Everyone in town is coming, seems like.”

A wave of dizziness hit me. “Everyone?”

“That’s the word from my book club chat. And those folks are seriously plugged into the town current, as you know.” She smiled brightly. “I bet after this, you’ll have tons of people wanting to hire you to do events.”

“Maybe, if it goes well,” I said. “I can’t mess this up.”

My sister touched my arm softly. “Please don’t put any more pressure on yourself. It’s going to be great, Em. Better than anything I could ever have imagined.”

“It’s gotten away from me,” I said. “Readings aren’t usually this—”

"Because authors aren't usually *this*!" Calliope laughed, gesturing toward herself as she approached us. She had changed back into her black maxi dress and shawl. "People are drawn to my aura. I can't help it."

Lucy shot me a look.

"Romance, did you see my costume? Very otherworldly fabulous, no?"

"I did," Lucy confirmed. "It's spectacular."

Calliope did one of her head bows, and Lucy went off to help Ryan in the back of the store.

"Where did you find that on such short notice, by the way?" Calliope asked me, adjusting her shawl.

"Riverview Vintage."

"Oh, I should have known. Marlowe Markson is *magnificent*."

"Agree a thousand percent," I said, registering a flicker of happiness within at Calliope's praise of my dear friend.

"I'll have to gift her something special," she mused.

Maybe Marlowe would be getting a nickname from Calliope too, like the rest of us.

I waved to Ryan, who dimmed the star pendants, turned up the twinkle ropes, then added the spotlight. When that was done, I surreptitiously added the heartbeat effect.

Calliope turned around slowly, taking it all in.

I held my breath.

When she'd made a complete circle, she clapped her hands. "Exactly as I'd envisioned it. Brava. I'll go set up my crystals now." She hoisted her enormous bag onto her shoulder and climbed the stairs. I thanked Ryan and Lucy and sent them off to dinner.

After Calliope had organized her crystal placement to her liking and descended again, she handed me a small package. "For you. Please open it."

It was a silver disc, suspended from a black cord, with a woman's silhouette inside a series of increasingly larger circles.

"Arachne, the weaver. To enhance your creative energies." Calliope smiled. "I know it's hard to prioritize your writing when other things press in. But don't give up. Honor your purpose. Spin your stories."

"Thank you," I said softly, moved by her act of kindness.

"Put it on," she urged me.

I slipped the cord over my head. The pendant seemed to buzz with energy.

Or maybe Calliope was rubbing off on me.

* * *

Back at home, I was sitting in the long-anticipated bath, breathing in the lavender essential oil scent and trying to relax.

When I'd agreed to organize Calliope's launch, I'd thought it would be a typical bookstore event with the author doing a brief reading and taking questions, followed by a book signing. No skeletons or ravens or twinkle lights.

This had snowballed out of control fast.

Now that it had basically turned into a costume party and rumor had it the whole town was coming, I was worried about how many people would show up. Did we have enough room? There was some overflow on the newly set up porch, anyway.

Too bad we weren't charging for admission, though perhaps it was something to consider for future events with large-draw potential. But at least it wasn't costing us anything. Calliope was paying for the catering and her costume, so if we sold all of her books and then some, the stress would have been worth it.

Even if Tabitha and her friends were coming. I'd been so distracted by everything that needed doing, I hadn't been obsessing about what they'd said as much as I typically would.

Maybe that was a blessing.

I told myself to let go of everything for the moment so that I could relax. After another deep and cleansing breath, I leaned back against the edge of the tub and closed my eyes. The warm water was soothing, and I felt my muscles begin to loosen.

Then I had a thought that made me shoot straight up, sloshing the water over the side.

I needed to call the police.

Chapter Twenty-Five

After dressing in jeans and a faded Silvercrest Art Festival sweatshirt, I pulled out the business card Detective Trujillo had given me.

Before dialing, I paused and wondered if I should call Jake instead.

Then again, he had all but patted me on the head and told me to go play nicely outside when I'd tried to offer him a theory before.

So forget *that.*

I punched in the numbers, hovering uneasily between wanting the detective to answer and not wanting him to answer. I had a feeling that it was going to be a difficult conversation.

"Trujillo." He picked up on the first ring.

"Hello, Detective. It's Emma Starrs."

There was no response.

"From the—"

"I know who you are."

"Sorry to bother you, sir. You said I should call you if I thought of anything else, so—"

"What do you have for me?" He sounded annoyed, so I sped past the rest of my preamble.

"I wanted to give you some information. Did you know that Ian Gladstone wasn't the sole owner of Hatchet?"

"Hatchet?"

"Oh, that's what Ian was going to name his bar. I forgot he hadn't put a sign up yet."

"And?"

"There were several investors, including Tip Baxter."

There was a long silence.

"I thought that might be useful to know, since both men were, you know, murdered. Oh, and Ainsley Fowler too, of course."

"What makes you think Ian and Ainsley were murdered?" An edge crept into his voice.

"I mean, I'm *assuming* they didn't hit themselves with a hammer."

"How do you know about the hammer?" he fired back.

Oops. I didn't want to get Jake in trouble for telling me about the hammer if he wasn't supposed to have mentioned it. For all I knew, Detective Trujillo was his boss.

"I was there that night. In the building." That was technically true. Maybe I hadn't exactly seen the weapon with my own eyes, but I'd been in the vicinity of it. I *could* have seen it.

"Why were you in the building?"

His suspicious tone jump-started the realization that now it didn't seem to be so much about Jake getting in trouble as it was about me looking like the murderer. Again. The next bit wasn't going to help that perception either.

"I . . . I was the one who found them. With my aunt." Putting Nora and myself at the crime scene was definitely not the best way to counter the accusations Tabitha had been throwing around town. A bead of sweat rolled down my back.

The silence this time was even longer.

"You found the victims." I couldn't tell if he was surprised. Had he not read the report? Or was he messing with me?

"Nora and I did. Well, and Detective Hollister followed us."

"That's your second such discovery this month."

"There was a scream next door. I thought it was my sister," I protested.

"Very unusual to come across a single victim in anyone's lifetime, much less three, wouldn't you say?"

"I didn't mean to," I whispered.

"What was that?"

I cleared my throat. "I didn't *mean* to find anyone. It just . . . happened."

"Mm-hmm."

"But what I called to tell you was that there were multiple owners of the bar. Since it appears that some of them have been attacked. In case you didn't know about the investors. Which maybe you did."

"Thank you for calling," he said, in a tone now verging on iced. "But I would ask that you leave the rest of this investigation to us."

"You're welcome," I said faintly.

"And Ms. Starrs, I will also ask that you try *not* to find any more bodies."

That was a bizarre thing to say.

"I didn't *try* to find any in the first place," I said.

"You have to admit, it looks a little unusual."

"I agree, but I don't know how to prevent myself from finding something that I didn't set out to find, especially if I don't know that there's something to be found before finding it."

He made a sound I couldn't categorize, a sort of harrumph and snort mixed together.

Was he laughing at me? My face warmed.

"I'm only trying to help," I said stiffly.

"Well, please stop helping. The next time I see you, I hope it's because you're *innocently out taking a walk*."

He hung up.

Innocently out taking a walk? As I stared at the phone screen, the front door opened.

"Hello, darlings? Anyone home?" Nora's voice called up the stairs. "Come join me in the kitchen."

I did as she said, plunking down at the round wooden table.

"Tea?" she asked, turning on the stove.

"Yes, please." I wanted to get to bed in order to be fully rested for the big day tomorrow, but if I went up now, I knew I'd lie there rehashing the day's conversations in my head and wishing I'd had better comebacks.

"Chamomile?"

I agreed. When the kettle boiled, she came over with two steaming mugs. Then she went back for the tea bags, spoons, a plate of cookies, and a jar of honey. We prepared our drinks in companionable silence.

"Are you ready for tomorrow? Anything you need from me?" my aunt asked, after taking a sip.

"Calliope was happy about the setup, so that's good."

"What did she think about her costume? I'm afraid to ask."

"She was thrilled."

My aunt smiled. "I'm so glad."

"All put together, the effect is extraordinary. And it suits her."

"I can imagine. How are you feeling?"

"Strange. Exhausted but oddly elated, like I've *almost* completed a quest. I'll be holding my breath until it's over, of course, but I'm as ready as I'll ever be." I nibbled on a butter cookie.

"Congratulations, darling."

"How about you? Did you have a good evening?"

"Yes, in fact." Nora picked up a cookie and dipped it into her tea. "My new office is organized, so next week I can walk right in and start working. I'm starting a new book, so the timing is perfect. I bet I'm more productive than I've ever been, with that view to inspire me."

"Oh! I wanted to help you set it up," I said. "I'm sorry."

"It's not your job, Emma. No worries. I had a delightful time deciding where to put everything. The built-in bookshelves are a thing of beauty, I must say." She took a small bite, then set the cookie down.

"Did you run into any of your colleagues?"

"Not a single one."

"I can't stop thinking about the whole Tip-bribing-Dodd-and-Able situation. What do you think that's about? And they may not be the only one who received something in exchange for blocking the vote."

"I don't know, darling."

"How can we find out? What would Agatha Christie do?"

We sipped our tea.

"I suppose we could ask them directly, like we were planning to do before," she said.

"Yes! Corner them, extract a confession, and turn them in to the authorities."

"*That* seems a bit extreme, darling. Have you been watching those television shows about—"

"I'm serious."

"But the reason for the bribe is very likely something political. Not criminal. It probably has to do with an academic matter. Or some attempt to gain power."

"But Tip is dead!"

She tapped her lip thoughtfully.

"So it's not only the bribe," I continued. "It's the *murder* of the person who was bribing them too."

"Which may or may not be connected." Nora held her teacup in both hands and looked out the window.

"Right." I went over to the little alcove desk that served as a catchall and retrieved a legal pad and a pen. "Let's make a new list of people who might have been involved in Tip's murder. Maybe we should press them all a bit more at the party. What we've done so far hasn't led us to any conclusions."

I was working hard to ignore the fact that both detectives had told me to stay out of the case. My rebellious streak was alive and well.

"Obviously, add his wife," Nora said, "at the top."

"Should I go ahead and write down anyone who was there that night?"

"Oh yes. That speeds things up a bit."

I added the names of all the dinner party guests.

Nora looked at the list. "You don't have me down."

"But *you* didn't do it."

"If there's one thing we should have learned from our love affair with mystery novels, it's the need to be thorough."

I laughed and added her name. "Moving on . . . I don't think the caterers have any stake in this issue, do you? Especially Vivi."

"Probably true. It's doubtful that the caterers are involved in this."

"Which would make them excellent suspects, if this were a book."

She nodded gravely. "That is also true. It's very confusing, isn't it?"

"Reserve the right to expand the list later," I said. "But I can only focus on so many people at once right now."

"Understood."

"Now we need motives."

"Hmm." She waved the cookie around. "The entire committee was angry with him, as we've discussed before."

"Surely that's not reason enough for someone to want to kill him."

Nora shrugged. "Committee work can be intense."

"So you think we should question the whole committee?"

"Yes, though we already spoke to Prescott and Cornelia with no luck, so perhaps we don't need to bother them." She took a sip of tea.

"I don't know. There may be value in touching base with them again. But all signs point to the space you were arguing over, and that's also where the bribe comes in. Tip wanted Dodd and Able to block the vote. Maybe someone on your side was tired of waiting and thought that disposing of Tip would hurry things along."

She looked shocked. "I can't imagine any of the colleagues on my side hurting anyone."

"But you would say that people on your side were passionate about this subject, right? Could it have been a—"

"Crime of passion?" Nora interjected excitedly.

"Not what I was going to say, but sure, that works. Which means that we need to speak to *all* the committee members, not only the ones we think most likely to be—"

"Malicious beasts?"

"Again, not what I was going to say, but sure. Do you want to talk to Katrina, Bethany, and Farley, and I'll talk to Prescott, Cornelia, Able, and Dodd?"

My aunt blinked twice. "I can't help but feel as though you are getting the short end of the straw with the latter two there. And we haven't even discussed Tabitha and her friends yet. They may be harder to crack. Professors like to hear themselves talk, so that's to our benefit."

"I would submit that Tabitha *loves* to hear herself talk."

"That would be helpful. But the more I think about it, darling, the more I think we need to draw a line between committee members and non–committee members. How about I'll take the Silvercrest faculty and you question the others. That seems like more of a natural division."

"I'll do my best, though I don't know if I'll be able to get *any* of Tabitha's friends to speak to me. I have been trying." I ate the rest of my cookie.

"I have faith in you, Emma."

"I have faith in you too. Remember to turn on your phone recorder before you speak to them . . . wait, is that legal?"

"It is in Colorado, as long as you're part of the conversation yourself and you agree to record."

"How do you know that?"

She smiled. "Research for my books."

"Should we come up with a cover story? Something that lets us ask them without being overt about it?"

"I don't know. Wouldn't it be valuable to see how they react when we catch them off guard with a direct question?"

"Excellent point." I drank some tea. "For the professors, what if we asked them how they felt about the move, for starters? It's general but could lead into the heart of the matter, which is, 'Did you kill Tip?' Though now that I say it aloud, I don't know how to phrase it."

"Well, 'Did you kill Tip?' is *not* going to garner any affirmative responses," my aunt said.

"But as you suggested, it's going to cause some sort of reaction, and that's what we need to watch. Like we did in Cornelia's office."

"Indeed."

"I'm honestly not sure if this is the best plan, though—to march up to people and start firing questions."

Nora began to clear the table. "It *is* a plan, in any case. We have to start somewhere. How exciting! Now, what are you wearing tomorrow?"

"A fancy dress and long beaded jacket combination that Marlowe called 'glamorous sleuth.' Phryne Fisher–esque. How about you?"

"Trench coat and fedora. It's my go-to costume," she said.

I laughed. "They'll see us and our investigative intentions coming a mile away."

"No one has ever proved definitively that subtlety is a virtue, darling."

Chapter Twenty-Six

On Halloween night, the bookstore began to fill up shortly before the start of the event. In paraded Silvercrest residents in all manner of costumes, from a simple bedsheet toga to a pair of unicorns with cotton-candy manes. They made their way to the caterer's tables in the back and partook of the delicacies.

Nora was accomplishing her tasks in record time. She had immediately cornered Prescott and Cornelia—who were dressed as Hamlet and Ophelia—then moved on to Katrina, Bethany, and Farley, all of whom were clad completely in white with wings and halos. Were they were attempting to send a message about their angelic natures, or had those been the only options left at the store? I imagined there had been quite a run on costumes after Calliope's decree made its way through town.

I still hadn't spoken to a single person on my list yet.

Calliope was already on the second floor, barely visible behind one of the skeletons. She wanted to have a bird's-eye view early on but make a grand entrance when it was time for her reading. I was perched on the spiral staircase searching the crowd for my targets, but the costumes made it harder to identify people. Hadn't factored that in when we were cooking up our plan.

Marlowe slipped inside and waved at me. She looked marvelous in a mod minidress and go-go boots. Eve Case was behind her, dressed as a ladybug. I waved to them both.

"How much longer?" Ryan asked from the bottom of the stairs, splendidly done up in a waistcoat, trousers, and riding boots. My sister was wearing a white muslin gown and teal silk pelisse she had designed herself years ago and saved for a special occasion. Her love of romance novels had been sparked early on by Jane Austen—and she'd developed a particular fondness for *Emma*, which had led to an impassioned teenage proposal that we sisters switch names. My mother had gently declined.

"Miss Woodhouse and Mr. Knightley, I presume?"

They performed a curtsy and a bow, respectively.

"You both look incredible." I smiled at them.

"You too," my sister said. "Very sparkly."

The costume had been a perfect choice, thanks to Marlowe. It fit as though it had been made for me and actually did make me feel kind of sparkly, now that Lucy mentioned it. The pockets were even coming in handy for storing items temporarily as I ran hither and yon taking care of party business.

I thanked my sister and checked my watch. "Calliope is supposed to start in twenty minutes. I'm going to do a loop, then I'll meet you back here in ten."

"Sounds good," Ryan said.

My phone pinged with a text from Calliope. *Where is the heartbeat? It should be unsettling the audience now, then silenced to showcase my reading.*

On it, I texted back, then started playing the sound clip.

As the heartbeat filled the room, the crowd paused to listen.

"It's so pretty!" With the momentary halt in conversation, Felicity's squeak caught my attention. She, Tabitha, and Melody were standing near the front door like a trio of princesses. They were wearing gorgeous ball gowns in the same cut—but varying shades, as was their signature style—and appeared to be dripping in diamonds. I didn't think those *were* actually costumes—probably something they'd worn to a club function once upon a time, accessorized with actual jewels.

Likewise, Bruce Crenshaw, Clive Fowler, and Aston Edwards were in suits. Dressing up as businessmen when you were businessmen didn't qualify as wearing a costume in my book either, but since I planned to interrogate them later, it would work against my purposes to kick them out. Plus, I knew Nora had plans to challenge Clive's decision to share our store bank account balance with those who wanted to buy it out from under us. It was important to pick my battles.

I was surprised to see Clive here, but perhaps he was one of those people who would rather be out drinking away his sorrows. Or maybe his friends had talked him into coming so that he wouldn't be alone. Considering that Clive's wife had met her maker right next door, however, it was odd how relaxed he seemed. Then again, he and Ainsley had never appeared to be a loving couple. Tabitha and Tip had come across as genuinely affectionate—I'd give her that.

The men moved as a unit toward the back, having presumably spotted where the drinks were coming from. The women, however, stayed put. They were craning their necks around, examining every corner of the store. Even if I hadn't known what they were up to, measuring it for their future take-over, I would have considered the looks on their faces to be hungry.

The thought that they were planning to steal our store out from under us was unbearable.

I turned on the phone record function, put it in my pocket, walked up to the women, and reached down deep for a gracious tone. It took all of my power not to shriek, *You'll never get your hands on our bookstore!*

"Good evening," I said.

"Good evening," they responded in unison.

"This is *so* pretty," Felicity said again. "We should hire you to do our—"

"Shut up, Felicity," Melody said. "We don't hire *murderers*."

So *that* was going to be on the recording. Great.

It was time to set some boundaries. "You're welcome to come inside, and I hope you enjoy yourselves. However, there will be no more accusations. We all know that Nora and I didn't have anything to do with Tip's passing. This is *our* store. If you come to this event, you must be respectful."

Felicity, standing slightly behind the other two, mouthed, *Sorry*.

I smiled at her, then addressed Tabitha. "May I speak with you privately, please?"

She sniffed. "Anything you have to say to me, you can say in front of my dearest friends." Everyone in that group said the same thing each time I tried to request an audience. They obviously felt that their strength was in numbers.

"Your call. Could you follow me outside, please? It will only take a minute."

"The drinks are in the back, right?" she asked.

I nodded.

"Okay then, but only because I want one of those *divine* cocktails." Tabitha pointed to a nearby glass.

When we passed Ryan, he tapped his wrist, and I held up one finger. I had to get this over with.

I led the women past the catering tables and onto the porch. The crowd had not spilled out here yet—probably because no one knew it had been set up as a place to sit.

"So pretty." Felicity's refrain of the day was followed by "Ow!" as if someone had elbowed her.

I turned to face them. "Are you sure you want me to do this in front of other people, Tabitha?"

"Whatever," she said, while pointedly examining her nails. She could not have looked more bored if she'd tried. Meanwhile, my heart was pounding louder than the heartbeat soundtrack inside. I didn't want to mess this up.

I watched Tabitha closely. "Who do you think killed Tip?"

Suddenly, her boredom dissipated. She appeared, if I had to put a word on it, wary.

"You already know who *I* think did it. You and Nora."

"No. We didn't, I promise. But I'm trying to find out who did."

"Why?"

"*Because* you keep accusing us of it," I admitted tersely. "I don't have any other choice."

There was an alertness to her that I had rarely seen before: she was listening to me.

I pushed ahead. "Was there anyone who had threatened Tip? Argued with him?"

"Nora—"

"Tabitha. Stop saying my aunt's name. *Tell the truth.* I'm trying to *help* you figure out what happened to your husband."

She remained silent.

Felicity and Melody were watching Tabitha, fascinated. They seemed to be holding their breath.

Almost as if they knew something and were waiting to see if she said it.

"Someone at the college, then? *Not* Nora," I said preemptively.

"I don't care much for his assistant, Eve," Tabitha said decisively.

"The woman dressed like a ladybug?" Felicity asked happily.

Melody rolled her eyes.

"She always seemed to be calling and emailing and reminding him to do things," Tabitha said.

"Wasn't that her job?" I couldn't help myself.

She lifted her slim shoulders the tiniest bit. It was the least amount of effort put into a shrug that I'd ever seen.

I decided to steer her. "Anyone from English, perhaps?"

"Not to my knowledge," Tabitha said. "Aside from Nor—"

"Thank you," I interjected firmly, before she could finish saying my aunt's name yet again. I wasn't getting anywhere, so I veered. "I'm so sorry about Ian and Ainsley too."

The women blinked.

"But I'm wondering something . . . do you think that Ian might have been the one who killed Tip because he wanted *you* all to himself?"

Eyes widened all around. If I'd been standing on their front porches, three doors would have slammed in my face simultaneously.

"What do you mean?" Tabitha asked through clenched teeth.

"I mean that I saw you going into the building next door to meet Ian one night. Alone."

Felicity gasped. "*You* were having an affair with Ian?"

Melody shushed her.

"Also, I've been told that you and Tip fought the night of your party, when the caterers first arrived. So if you're about to say that it wasn't about Ian, perhaps you could tell us why you and your husband were arguing."

Tabitha's mouth tightened, and she started waving her hands around as if trying to grasp words, any words. The two women, one on either side, turned to face her, and the triangle burst into conversation. I heard only bits and pieces, but the word *key* emerged clearly.

Ryan came outside, frantically waving at me.

"Hold that thought. We're about to begin. I'll come find you later," I said to the group, then ran into the store.

"Not if I see you first." Tabitha's voice carried, as she intended.

Inside the store, I turned and peeked through the window. Tabitha, Felicity, and Melody were arguing.

Looked like there was trouble in princess paradise.

* * *

Ryan signaled for me to turn off the heartbeat effect. Then he dimmed the lights further, which quieted the crowd, and switched on the spotlight.

I took the small cordless microphone that Ryan held out and read the prepared introduction Calliope had provided.

"Thank you for joining us on this very special occasion with award-winning author and Silvercrest College professor Calliope Nightfall. Dr. Nightfall has won critical acclaim, numerous accolades, and legions of fans with her previous books. Tonight, you will be hearing from her long-anticipated collection of short stories, *The Kingdom of Annabel Lee*. This is the first time she has read her newest work anywhere. Please turn off your phones so as not to interrupt the experience. And now, let the magic begin."

I put the microphone in my empty pocket so I wouldn't lose it and sent out a wish to the universe that whatever came next would, in fact, be magical.

Calliope stepped out from behind the skeleton and took her place at the podium, her head held high. Her glittering layers did indeed make her look like a goddess.

The audience began to clap and whistle.

She leaned toward the microphone. "Happy Halloween to one and all. You look exquisite in your costumes, and I am honored that you've chosen to spend some time with me and my work this evening. First, I'll be reading from a short story called 'Sky Battle.' "

Calliope began reading an excerpt that involved an epic clash between the character of Annabel Lee and the angels who were trying to take her to heaven. She was described as a sort of superhero figure, holding her own with the attacking celestial beings through bravado, trickery, and combat skills. There was an entire passage describing the armor that Annabel Lee wore, which went full-on steampunk. Calliope had just reached the part where Annabel Lee adjusted her goggles before fixing a crucial gear when she stopped abruptly and looked expectantly at the crowd, who burst into applause.

Although we had enough books to build a house with, I hadn't had a single moment to skim her work ahead of time. Calliope's exuberant writing style wasn't at all what I had expected—I would have guessed something darker and slower—but the audience loved it, and I was swept up in their enthusiasm.

She dipped her head in acknowledgment and flipped forward several pages to the next story, the title of which was "Annabel Lee at Laser Canyon." As she led us into another fantastic skirmish, my mind started to wander. Why had the women outside been talking about a key? Did they mean it was a clue to something? Were they trying to figure out what had happened to Tip too? Were we all sleuthing individually? Would it be better if we joined forces? After falling into a daydream in which Tabitha and I were fighting over a magnifying glass, I snapped out of it when the audience began applauding again.

"You can find those and similar stories in the book," Calliope said. "And now, I'm ready to take your questions."

Hands shot up all around the room.

She responded to queries for a half hour, and I was tremendously impressed. Calliope repeated each question before answering it, like a professional, knowing that not everyone in the room might have heard it the first time. Her answers were interspersed with entertaining anecdotes. She had this covered.

"The question was: where do I get my ideas? For this book, I was deeply inspired by the character of Annabel Lee." She launched into the possession theory she'd told me at the restaurant.

Which prompted the biggest applause of all, surprisingly.

"And that seems like a good place to end," she said.

That was my signal. When the clapping had finally subsided, I used the microphone again to tell the audience that we had Calliope's books available for purchase. I explained that the process would be to pay for their selections, then join the line next to the register that led over to where Calliope was available to sign their copies. I also invited them to enjoy the food and drink. Then I thanked them for coming.

I took a deep breath. We were almost done. Ryan shut off the spotlight and brought up the regular lights, but I asked him to leave everything else as it was for now. You never knew with Calliope what might pop into her head; we could find ourselves in a spontaneous second-reading situation. He did as I asked and went to find Lucy. I shoved the microphone back into my pocket and waited to escort Calliope to her new location.

"You were *wonderful*," I said, when the triumphant author descended.

"Thank you, Raven. I hope they liked it."

"They loved it. Follow me, please." We moved across the floor as quickly as we could, though she was stopped and congratulated every few steps. Finally, I ushered her over to the table where she'd be signing. Max was waiting there to flap the books and assist her with whatever she needed. I took a few photos of her to use on the website and told her to have fun.

She smiled graciously.

Lucy and Bella were working checkout. The line was long and only getting longer. I hoped we sold out of the stock we'd ordered.

"Excuse me—Emma, right? We met at the country club. Oh, and the memorial service. Anyway, have you seen Felicity?" I turned to see Aston Edwards smiling beside me.

We met at the *club*? More like we met in *eighth-grade English class*, but whatever. It wasn't important enough to bother correcting him.

But *club* stuck in my mind as he smoothed his tie, which drew my attention to the design: gold triangular spirals against a deep-blue background.

I gestured toward it. "That's a striking pattern."

He followed my gaze. "It's the logo for Bruce's company. It represents the tornado power of digital marketing. Cool, right?"

Suddenly the pieces fell into place.

"I think your wife is outside. I'll show you," I said, realizing it would be my last chance to ask the group questions. Now I knew exactly what to focus on, though. I motioned for him to follow me.

When we passed the office, Max came out with a handful of pens and headed for Calliope's table. I swerved over to shut the door behind him. With so many people in the store, you couldn't be too careful.

As I reached for the handle, I heard what sounded like a scream. Was Calliope acting out something from her book? I paused and glanced around, but everyone else seemed to be unaware.

"Everything okay?" Aston asked uneasily, clearly trying to interpret my expression.

I put my hand out again, and there was another scream, even louder. This time, it seemed to emanate from the far wall.

Two screams from Ian's place. Just like last time.

Anne Shirley raced by, tail puffed, and dove underneath the desk.

My body went on high alert. "Do you have the key for the building next door, Aston?"

"Yes, but how did you know about—"

"There's no time for questions," I said. "Come with me." I waved to get Lucy's attention and pointed toward Ian's. I couldn't tell if she saw me—she turned back to a customer and smiled at them, holding out a receipt—but I couldn't squander another second.

I pushed my way through the crowd, apologizing every few feet, and flew out to the riverwalk.

"Get your key ready," I said to Aston over my shoulder, but when I hurried up to the back door of Ian's and turned the knob, it was unlocked.

I raced down the short hallway, my shoes clattering on the floor. When I turned the corner, Felicity was on her knees, going through the bottom drawer of a filing cabinet. Light streaming through the window illuminated her blonde hair. She had never looked more angelic.

"Hello," she said quietly. "What are you doing here?"

I scanned the area but couldn't see much of anything, as the plastic sheeting prevented a clear view of the rest of the floor. Underneath the farthest one, however, a woman's foot was sticking out.

"Go check over there," I told Aston. He ignored me and went straight to Felicity, asking what she was doing.

Felicity's eyelids closed halfway. She rose to greet him with a smile, keeping one arm behind her back. When he got close, she hit him with a metal bar, and he went down hard.

"None of your business," she yelled at his inert body.

"Where are Tabitha and Melody?" I asked her as she took a step toward me.

"They're sleeping. Sleeping beauties. And it's your lucky day, Emma! I'm going to make you a sleeping beauty too." She spun the metal bar like a baton, as if she were a contestant in a pageant.

My heart thrummed. I looked around wildly for a weapon to defend myself. There was a pile of lumber to my right, but it was a few steps away. I tried to calculate whether I could reach it before she reached me, but math, never my strong suit, failed me. When I put my hands in my pocket to pull out my keys, which I figured I could use to jab her if she came within reach, my fingertips touched the microphone.

I slid the button on the side up.

"Take your hands out of your pockets where I can see them," she demanded as she crept forward again.

I stretched my hands out in front of me as I took a step backward. "Let's talk, Felicity."

She laughed. "What do you want to talk about?"

"The murders. I think I understand what's been going on. But I want to hear *your* side of things. Tell me."

That stopped her. She spun the bar again expertly, looking thoughtfully at it.

"No one ever cares what I think," she said softly.

"I do. I care very much."

She spun the bar a few more times, then spoke. "It's all about *Tabitha*. Did you ever notice that? She was the prom queen. She was the head cheerleader. She called the shots. She made the decisions. She had everything, you know? But why? What made her better than me?"

"Nothing," I said.

"I'll admit that I was jealous when she was married to Ian. I mean, hello, he's *to die for*, am I right? Super sexy. And he was always unpredictable, which was quite the thrill for once. Aston is nice and all, but he is such a *bore*. When Tabitha and Ian broke up and he started writing me love letters, I couldn't believe it." Felicity pointed to herself. "He picked *me*."

I made a noncommittal sound.

She looked back at the filing cabinet. "In fact, I was trying to find the ones I wrote to him. Ian liked to pull them out and read them to me after we . . . you know . . ." She blushed.

Egads.

"The police probably took everything already," I said. "Did they say anything to you about them?"

"No. My letters were typed and not signed, so there's no way for them to know I was the one who wrote them." Felicity lifted her chin. "We were going to run this place together. I was planning to leave Aston and marry Ian. But we needed Hatchet to be a success so that we could get out from under the thumb of the rest of them."

"So you don't believe he wanted to get back together with Tabitha?"

She smirked. "No. Your theory is *way* off base."

"You honestly don't think he killed Tip? Because that theory does provide a very clear motive."

"I do not."

"How do you know for sure?" I pressed.

"Because *I* killed him." Felicity laughed. "Tip was so drunk that he didn't even put up a fight. It was like smothering a teddy bear."

I fought to keep my voice steady. "Why did you do it?"

"Tip was pulling out of the deal because he wanted to have it all his way or no way at all. Ian needed the money to stay in place."

Behind her, Aston began to stir. It took some effort not to watch; I didn't want Felicity to realize he was awake.

I forced myself to keep focused on her face, nodding to encourage her to keep talking. "So you did it to help Ian achieve his dream."

"Yes. You understand, right? I wanted to protect him."

"I see." I softened my voice. "It must have hurt all the more, then, when you caught him with Ainsley?"

"*Exactly*. Thank you, Emma. Why didn't we ever become better friends? You *get* me."

I shuddered inwardly.

Tears began to roll down her face. "They betrayed me. They had to be punished."

Out of the other corner of my eye, I saw Tabitha creeping around the plastic.

"Anyway, it feels so good to get that off my chest. Thank you for listening." She gave me a stunning smile. "I'm so sorry that I knocked you down at the country club, but you raised that whole Ian theory in front of everyone, and I saw red. Had to protect my man, you know? Will you forgive me?"

I managed to dip my chin. Anything to keep her talking.

"Thank you. That means a lot to me." She put a hand over her chest and patted it a few times. "And I'm also sorry that I have to kill you now, because I think we could have been *really* good friends."

Before I knew what was happening, she rushed at me, metal bar in striking position. When she brought it down hard, I somehow caught the bar, though it felt as if both hands were broken in half, the deep ache so severe that I couldn't speak.

Felicity's lovely face was distorted, a mask slipping to reveal the monster underneath. She shrieked and yanked the bar away.

Aston and Tabitha came lurching toward us like zombies—holding their heads, limping, and calling her name. Felicity whirled around to face them, lifting the bar again and aiming for Tabitha.

From behind her, I grabbed the bar and held on as tight as I could while Felicity tried to pull it down in front of her. The white-hot pain radiated from my palms to my forearms.

"Now you know. She *cheated* on you," Tabitha screamed at Aston, who pushed up his glasses and swallowed anxiously. "With my husband!"

"*Ex*-husband," Felicity said, as she struggled to swing. "He loved me!"

"He was only using you," Tabitha snarled. "He belonged to me."

"Are you sure? Because I caught him with Ainsley—" Felicity spit back.

I finally won purchase on the bar and tore it out of Felicity's hands, which sent me staggering backward. Losing the bar didn't faze Felicity, who ran toward Tabitha anyway, her hands curled into claws.

"You sociopath!" Tabitha yelled, throwing her arms up in front of her. "I hate you!"

"I wish I had killed *you* first!" Felicity yelled back, hurling herself at Tabitha. They thrashed around on the floor while Aston tried to separate them.

I was overcome by déjà vu as the police came swarming in as they had when we'd found Ian and Ainsley.

I dropped the bar. The metallic clank reverberated around the room, and everyone looked at me.

Detective Trujillo didn't look happy to see me.

It was probably too late to act like I was innocently out taking a walk.

Chapter Twenty-Seven

"At least it didn't snow last night," Nora said. "It almost always snows on Halloween."

"I can't believe she tried to kill them all. How are they doing, Emma?" Lucy asked. We were on the wraparound porch, facing the mountains, lined up in the rocking chairs that had been here longer than any of us.

"The officers said that concussions are likely, but otherwise they should be fine. I'll check in with Jake later to see if he has any updates."

"*I* can't believe you had the presence of mind to turn on the microphone," Nora said.

I shifted the bag of ice on my aching palms. "What happened in the store when the voices started coming through the speakers?"

She laughed. "People looked around, trying to figure out what was going on. At first, I think some of them thought it was a bonus performance. It would be in keeping with Calliope's reputation, anyway."

Lucy picked up the story. "Then they all started buzzing amongst themselves, and some of them called the police."

"Oh no," I exclaimed, gripped by a horrible thought, "poor Calliope. She must be devastated that her signing was ruined. I'll call and apologize."

"I don't think you need to." Lucy grinned. "She said it was the most memorable launch party she'd ever had. She even snuck over into the club and poked her head inside at one point to watch them process the scene. She was chased away by an officer, which she said was a thrill that she would make full use of in her next writing project."

"I still don't fully understand what happened," Nora said. "Even though I heard it through the speakers, I was too shocked to take in every detail. Plus, Lucy and I were busy running around the store, looking in every nook and cranny trying to find you. Next time you're being threatened, state your exact location, please."

I laughed. "I'll try to remember that. I did point next door to let Lucy know before I left, but I guess you didn't see me."

"I didn't see anything," she said. "I'm so sorry. That line was out of control."

"It was chaotic. Don't worry about it," I assured her. "But hooray for sales!"

"Would you mind walking us through everything?" Nora asked me. "I know we've talked about various pieces of the picture, but I'd like to hear exactly how they fit together."

"Sure. We all know that Tabitha, Melody, Felicity, and Ainsley—and their husbands, aside from Tip—have been best friends since high school. Tip may have been new to the gang, but the others accepted him and even offered business opportunities."

"In a legal, aboveboard kind of way?" Lucy asked.

"Unknown," I said. "But somewhere along the line, two things happened: first, Tabitha convinced them all to invest in Ian's bar idea, and second, Bruce Crenshaw pressured Tip to create an institute at the college."

"Those seem like very different things," Nora said. "How are they connected? And how did you know?"

"They are. The spiral triangle design on Aston's tie at the reading, especially after he told me that it was Bruce's new logo, triggered the realization that the tornado power chant the husbands did at the memorial service and the spiral doodles on Ian's shoes were related." I paused. "It sounds weird when I say it out loud like that."

"We are going to need you to spell that out more, darling," Nora said.

"Question." Lucy raised her hand. "Wasn't Ian Tabitha's *ex*-husband? Why would they invest in his bar?"

"He'd been part of that same group for a long time. It was Tabitha's one amicable divorce, so he continued to hang around long after she'd married Tip. I don't think he and Tip were best friends, but the other husbands were close to Ian."

"Interesting," Lucy said.

"I helped her research that part," Nora said proudly.

"The original idea was to build an upscale supper club, something that made Tip happy. He was glad to invest the majority of the money to have a new place where he could hang out with his pals. Then the plan morphed into a live-band venue, which Tip did not like. It was the opposite of what he had envisioned. He held several meetings with Ian in an attempt to change his mind, which his assistant, Eve, confirmed to us, but Ian wouldn't budge—"

"So when Eve said they argued about 'a tub,' it was about the club!" Nora hit the arm of her chair.

"Exactly. Also, when Calliope thought Tip and Dodd were discussing internet profiles, which we interpreted as social media profiles, it was really about digital marketing."

"Brava," Nora said.

"How did you figure this out?" Lucy asked.

"Oh, a combination of research, interviews, and good old-fashioned eavesdropping," I said, blushing at the thought of being trapped in the dressing room at Marlowe's.

"Carry on," Nora urged.

"Tip was a relative newcomer to the group, whereas they'd all been friends for ages. Everyone went forward with the bar idea despite Tip's reservations, but apparently he was threatening to pull his funding. That made one person in particular very angry: Felicity."

"Why?" Lucy asked.

"She was in love with Ian. It took me a while to realize why she'd demonstrated such shock at the idea of Tabitha having an affair with Ian. It wasn't about cheating—it was that Felicity had been having an affair with him, so she'd probably listened to his dreams about owning a club for years. She said Ian had promised to marry her after the club became successful. Tip was standing in the way, so she killed him."

My sister shook her head. "Even though it was her best friend's husband?"

"I didn't get the sense that said best friend was all that crazy about Tip in the first place, did you?" Nora asked.

"I don't know if Felicity thought about that or was even capable of thinking about that," I said. "Tabitha did call her a sociopath. In any case, she went on to kill Ian and Ainsley when she discovered them together."

"He was having an affair with Ainsley too?" Lucy covered her mouth.

"According to Felicity."

"Was Tabitha having an affair with Ian?" She leaned forward.

"Not sure about that," I said.

"So he was possibly juggling three women at once, all of whom are investing in his proposal? That takes some nerve."

"All of the women *and* their husbands were investing," I said.

"That smells like a con," Nora said. "Have you spoken to Jake about all of this?"

"I asked him to confirm what I've told you. He didn't want to do it, but I argued that it wasn't like he was giving out any information since *we'd* put things together *ourselves*. By which I mean all of you."

"*Mostly* you, though," Lucy said.

"So that's part one. Explain part two, please?" Nora smiled at me.

"Right, sorry. Remember that Bruce is the CEO of Flashtown Digital, and he wanted to donate a heap of money to Silvercrest College in exchange for housing a digital marketing institute. He thought it would be a good look—as well as a way to ensure a steady stream of qualified interns and new hires trained the way he wanted—so he was pressuring Tip to make it happen. Bruce even *told* us about the institute at the memorial service, but it didn't seem connected to anything then."

"Don't beat yourself up for missing that, Em," Lucy said. "I certainly didn't catch it."

"It was a small part of a complex picture," my aunt added.

"That makes me feel better. Anyway, Tip wasn't getting traction with the administration fast enough, but he wanted to ensure that the top floor of the Arts and Humanities building—"

"—was *reserved* for the new institute," Nora broke in. "That's why he didn't want anyone moving in. Got it. And that's why he allowed his wife's friends to come to the dinner party for committee members, which I did actually think was strange. But although we didn't know it yet, some of those people were deeply involved in the committee's business."

"Precisely. Bruce was there as a reminder—or even a threat—to the committee members who were doing his bidding already by blocking the vote, though he looked like simply another member of Tip and Tabitha's circle to us."

"Would the college have even gone for it? Wouldn't there be conflicts of interest galore with that structure?" Lucy asked.

"*Especially* since Tip had invested heavily in Flashtown Digital," I said. "I heard Tabitha remind Melody of that fact when I went to pick up Calliope's costume. The business dealings among the group overlapped more and more as time went on—we can see that for ourselves."

"It would be a conflict of interest," Nora said. "But it would have been tempting to Tip, I'm sure. Perhaps the school lawyers were trying to find a way to unravel the problematic threads and Tip needed time for that as well. What I want to know is, what *exactly* are Dodd and Able getting out of all of this?"

"That's the one thing I did wheedle out of Jake. Remember when Eve mentioned the professors negotiating with Tip about chairs? Well, it wasn't about chairs; it was about *seats*. Dodd and

Able were promised seats on the advisory board of the institute, which came with a nice chunk of Flashtown shares."

She smiled. "So they *were* getting paid."

"Ultimately, they would have been. Though the deal never went through, so there wasn't a payday. Are you going to report them to the college?"

"Oh, that's been taken care of," she said. "Bethany couldn't wait to file a grievance when I told her what we'd overheard about a potential bribery situation . . . though you'll be glad to hear that I left out the hiding-behind-the-door part."

"The hiding? I think you left that out of the version you told *me* too," Lucy said.

"Minor detail," I said. "Not worth mentioning."

Nora went on. "The ethics hearing is scheduled for next week. Even if Dodd and Able hadn't reaped the reward of their scheme yet, they may be taking an unplanned early retirement."

"That seems fair," Lucy said.

"Too bad we didn't capture Felicity's confession on your cell phone," Nora added.

"Oh, but we did capture it," I said. "I forgot to turn off the recording function after I spoke to Tabitha, Melody, and Felicity the first time at the party. *Everything* is on there. The police have it already."

"I hope they enjoy Calliope's reading," Lucy said.

We all smiled at that thought.

Chapter Twenty-Eight

On Wednesday, I repositioned the bowl of decorative gourds that I'd placed in the window display next to a row of sunflowers. We were going with a fall garden theme. Although it had already snowed and more was on the way, thanks to the higher elevation and powerful sun, we'd had a long stretch of warm days. Plus, after all that had happened lately, we were in the mood for something life affirming.

Lucy handed me the wooden board she'd found under the porch and repurposed as an art piece, with the word *gratitude* beautifully rendered in the center with black ink.

"Lovely," I said, smiling at her. "It's perfect, thank you."

She'd begun to branch out from her sketches—calligraphy was a new passion. Ryan had taken her to a workshop and she'd come home glowing from both the art and the company. The two of them had seen each other nearly every day since their first date. Lucy, with her romantic tendencies, did have a history of falling hard and fast, but unlike some of her previous suitors, Ryan seemed to be in the same place. When you looked at them, you could almost see cartoon hearts floating in the air around them.

Nora and I wholeheartedly approved.

I leaned the board against the planter box we'd used to display our November spotlight books. We'd decided to leave Calliope's book in the mix. Her reading had brought in so many people, it was the least we could do. We'd sold every single book that night and quickly ordered more; turned out that everyone had wanted tangible proof that yes, they'd been in attendance The Night A Murderer Was Caught, and yes, they'd heard the shocking details over the microphone. Calliope had been delighted and had promised to send more business our way. Ever since the party, we'd seen an increase in shoppers as well.

"We're going to look from outside," I called to Bella. She smiled in acknowledgment and went back to ringing up a book sale.

Lucy and I stood on the sidewalk, arm in arm, evaluating the display.

"Looks great," Lucy said.

"Your sign is the perfect finishing touch."

She leaned her head against mine.

I had a sensation that everything was as it was supposed to be. I hoped that we could keep the store open. My sister was so happy here.

And I was too.

"Starrs!" Jake's voice shattered the idyllic moment. I looked up to see him walking toward us, in a Silvercrest College tee and jeans.

"I know you don't like the guy, but you have to admit, he's gorgeous," Lucy said. "For the record."

Then Anne Shirley jumped into the display and knocked down the gratitude sign.

"I'll go take care of the cat," Lucy said. "Let you two have a little chat."

"No, please don't leave me—"

"Morning, everyone." Jake jogged the last few yards.

She stayed where she was and greeted him warmly.

He ran a hand through his hair and plunged right in. "I wanted to give you an update, in case you missed the news this morning. Felicity has confessed and is awaiting trial."

"You don't think she can get out of it, do you?" Lucy asked him.

"Why would you say that?"

She shrugged. "People with money around here . . . you know."

"Ah. Well, everyone in the bookstore heard her over the speakers, so that's a whole lot of witnesses. I don't think there's much wiggle room."

A white van pulled up, and Vivi Yang climbed out. She wore a long purple tunic over jeans and held a large circular key ring.

"Hi, everyone," she said. "I'm here to pick up the party equipment."

We greeted her, and she joined us on the sidewalk.

"Thanks so much again for doing the food," I said. "You got a lot of raves."

"That's great to hear, and I have some news. Unless you're in the middle of something . . ."

"Do you want me to leave?" Jake had a strange energy, as if he wanted to say more. I didn't know why he wouldn't just say it. Then again, I'd always found his behavior to be confusing and irritating.

Most of the time, at least.

Well, part of the time, anyway.

Occasionally, I sort of enjoyed his company.

"Not if you don't want to," Vivi said with a laugh. "Okay, here it is. Guess who is going to be your new neighbor?" She pointed at the place previously known as Hatchet, then at herself.

Lucy and I cheered and applauded.

"Congratulations," Jake said.

Vivi bounced lightly on her feet. "Our leasing office knew I was looking for a larger space, so when Tabitha Baxter and Melody Crenshaw broke their lease, they reached out to me."

"That's fantastic," I said. "Welcome to the neighborhood!"

"The space is bit bigger than we need," Vivi continued, "so I was wondering if you wanted to use part of it for your bookstore events? The walls move around, so we will be separating public space from preparation space."

"That's so generous," I said.

"I'm not sure we can afford—" Lucy began.

Vivi held up a finger. "As long as you agree to hire *us* to do the catering for those events, I'd be glad to let Starlit Bookshop use it for free. Works out for both of us."

Lucy and I thanked her enthusiastically.

"And you have won a very deep discount at Starlit Bookshop," Lucy told her.

Vivi laughed. "Thank *you*."

"Oh! This also means that Tabitha won't be putting a bookstore there!" I exclaimed. Lucy and I engaged in another round of cheering and applauding.

"She wanted to open another bookstore right next door?" Vivi asked. "How awful that would have been."

"It was worse than that. She was going to take over our bookstore eventually. Or at least that was her plan."

"Why would she think it was even available?"

"Money's been tight," Lucy said quietly. "Certain people are aware."

"I see."

"And I'm glad that you're the one moving in! Do you need any help?" I asked Vivi. "We're here, if so."

"First, we need to clean the place out. We want to hire professional cleaners since there are . . . special circumstances."

"I can put you in touch with some crime scene cleaners right away," Jake said.

Lucy shivered. "Are you worried about ghosts, Vivi?"

"We're going to have the place smudged and blessed too." She said it matter-of-factly.

"That should cover it," Jake said.

"Anyone want to come inside with me?" Vivi jangled the keys.

Lucy raised her hand. "I do. I want to see how you're going to set it up."

"Me too," I said.

As I followed them, Jake scooted up next to me. "May I say something, please?"

"Yes." I watched my sister and friend go forward, hoping that he kept this short.

He looked into my eyes. "I feel like we got off on the wrong foot."

"Now? Or in school?"

"Maybe both times."

I nodded.

"In any case, I'm happy you joined West Side Writers, and I look forward to working with you."

"I'm not sure I'm going to stay in the group," I said.

"Why not?"

"Honestly? You were always much harder on my pieces than on anyone else's in school, and it was humiliating to have my pages torn apart. I don't know if that's productive for me as a writer at this point."

Jake blinked. "The only reason I gave you so much feedback was because your work was exceptionally *good.* I thought you wanted serious critiques so that you could send out your writing. I was trying to be helpful because I *admired* your stuff so much."

"Somehow that didn't come across."

He took a deep breath. "I'm sorry, Emma." It wasn't an elaborate apology, but it was sincere. I felt the years of frustration that I'd carried begin to fall away. Funny how one corrected perception could change your entire perspective.

"I'm sorry too," I said.

"For what?"

"Everything." A blanket apology seemed best.

"So . . . can we be friends now?" His hopeful expression made me laugh. His green eyes seemed extra vivid, as if he'd had them professionally brightened.

"We can give it a try."

He shoved his hands into his pockets and squinted up at the sky. "Maybe we could get a coffee later on. Catch up properly."

"Sure," I said, realizing that for the first time in a long time, I felt lighter.

We made plans to meet at Riverside Coffeehouse at eight.

As Jake walked down the street, he was whistling.

Interesting turn of events.

* * *

Later, we were about to close up the store when the door opened and Tabitha marched in. Paisley, whose head was visible above the side of the large leather tote, was wearing a brown bow today, matching her owner's long wool coat.

"Chilly," Tabitha said, shivering.

Paisley barked in agreement.

She walked slowly toward the register, a bright smile fixed on her face.

"How can I help you today?" Whenever I'd imagined running into her, I'd thought it would be difficult to stay calm, knowing that she had plotted to steal our beloved store out from under us. Yet now that she was standing in front of me, I felt a strange sense of pity. She must be unhappy herself to want to spend all of her time trying to make other people unhappy.

Tabitha set the tote down on the counter and withdrew a Starlit Bookshop paper bag, then pulled out the red hardcover Poe book she'd bought the day she had hired me.

"I have a return." There was steel in her voice. She was practically daring me to refuse her request. "Since Tip *obviously* didn't get a chance to read this."

I stared at the book, then at her, then at the book again.

Lucy came up beside me and held out her hand. "Hello, Tabitha. May I see the receipt, please? We have a return window of thirty days." I swallowed a smile at my sister's boundary setting.

"Oh, I don't have a *receipt*," Tabitha said, as if such a thing could hardly be expected. "You know me, though. And it's been around thirty days, anyway. Give or take."

Lucy and I looked at each other. She was waiting for me to call it.

"Okay," I said. I reminded myself for the millionth time that Tabitha had lost people she cared about. We could be gracious about a return.

She smiled victoriously and handed over her credit card so that Lucy could process the transaction.

"I'm so glad," Lucy said, "that we're able to do this for you."

Something about the way she said it implied that there was more to come.

"Me too," Tabitha said, with a shade less confidence than she normally possessed.

"No." Lucy shook her head. "I mean, I'm glad that you're *alive* and *can* come into the store asking for a refund."

"Oh, because of the whole Felicity thing." Tabitha made a flourish with both hands and smiled. "Yes. Here I am indeed."

"Because of *Emma*." Lucy focused on the register keys as she said it.

"What?" Tabitha and I said in unison.

That was the only time we'd ever said anything in unison.

"Emma saved your life, Tabitha. By holding on to the rod even though her hands were practically broken."

Tabitha shifted her eyes to me. "I don't know anything about that."

"Show her your hands, Em," my sister commanded.

I held them out so that Tabitha could see the purple, green, and yellow bruising.

She gasped. "That's hideous."

"And painful," Lucy informed her.

"I'm fine," I said.

"Well, I suppose I owe you a thank-you," Tabitha said. "And in return for saving my life, if you *say* that's what happened, what would you like me to do? I don't want to be indebted to anyone. That's not my style."

"Would you be willing to recommend Starlit Bookshop—"

"And events!" Lucy interjected.

"—to your contacts? You know so many people in town, it would be helpful."

Tabitha chewed her lip. "Will do. And I acknowledge that I was a tad bit hard on you—incorrectly, as it turns out—but I may have some projects in the works myself, so if you could not say anything negative about *me* during your future professional conversations with my contacts, I'd be grateful. Do you agree with my terms?"

"These projects—they don't involve bookstores, right?" I watched her closely for any signs of trickery.

"No bookstores."

"Then . . . I agree," I said, for better or for worse.

Lucy handed back her credit card, and Tabitha tucked it into her bag.

"It's been real. See you around," she said, then tapped out of the store.

"Now we sit back and hope that her connections pay off," Lucy said. "Though did you notice that she didn't really thank you?"

"What do you mean?"

"She said, 'I owe you a thank-you,' but she didn't actually *say* 'thank you.' "

I laughed. "That's as close as she'll ever get where I'm concerned. Honestly, I'm surprised that she even went that far."

Lucy laughed too, then snapped her fingers. "Oh! I almost forgot. There were ten voice mails this morning. I'll give you a sneak peek: your Halloween event was such a smash, now everyone wants to hire you."

I walked over to the door and flipped the sign around. Starlit Bookshop might be closed for the night, but it would be open for as long as we could swing it. "Looks like we're just getting started."

Acknowledgments

Heartfelt thanks to the wonderful Terri Bischoff, Melissa Rechter, Madeline Rathle, Rebecca Nelson, Matt Martz, and the rest of the brilliant Crooked Lane Books team; to my fantastic agent Lesley Sabga, the terrific Nicole Resciniti, and the Seymour Agency; to the very talented copy editor Rachel Keith and marvelous cover artist Joe Burleson; to the incredibly generous booksellers who answered my questions: Wendy Withers and Danean Wisely at Books Are Awesome, Uriel Perez at BookPeople, Joanne Sinchuk at Murder on the Beach Mystery Bookstore, Tara Furey at Old Firehouse Books, Jen Cheng at Old Town Books, Devin Abraham at Once Upon a Crime, and Mikaley Osley at Tattered Cover Bookstore; to the lovely friends, family, readers, bloggers, writers, and colleagues who have been so kind and supportive throughout this journey; to my fabulous Chicks on the Case—Ellen Byron, Jennifer Chow, Becky Clark, Marla Cooper, Vickie Fee, Kellye Garrett, Leslie Karst, Lisa Q. Mathews, and Kathleen Valenti—and Sisters in Crime siblings; and to my gifted critique partner/kindred spirit Ann Perramond and cherished advisers Wendy Crichton, Dorothy Guerrera, and William Guerrera. With deepest gratitude to my beloved Kenneth, Griffin, and Sawyer Kuhn for everything, every day; you are beyond amazing.